Calling
All Services

Tara Ford

Pen Press

First published in Great Britain by Pen Press

All paper used in the printing of this book has been made from wood grown in managed, sustainable forests.

ISBN13: 978-1-78003-655-7

Printed and bound in the UK
Pen Press is an imprint of
Indepenpress Publishing Limited
25 Eastern Place
Brighton
BN2 1GJ

A catalogue record of this book is available from the British Library

Cover design by Jacqueline Abromeit

For two of the most important people in my world,
my Mum and my Dad

Acknowledgements

Thank you to my wonderful husband and children for putting up with me while I was writing this book; I will now try to be a wife and mum again. I won't insist that you give me opinions on each and every chapter (although you've read those chapters six times or more), while forsaking dinner, packed lunches, *Britain's Got Talent*, football, friends, clean and ironed clothes to wear, a tidy home and a normal life.

I would also like to thank my sister Jane for enduring the painstaking task of reading and scrutinising part of this book, whilst feeding and nurturing one of my neglected sons.

A big thank-you goes to Clair Fowles for her exuberant enthusiasm, praise and dogged inspiration. Your text messages pushed me to persevere and succeed. I would also like to thank the receptionist (now known as Rosie) in a doctor's surgery whose enthusiasm inspired me to continue writing; her approval was uplifting – and all the more so because she was a stranger to me.

Thank you Pat Ford for always being there and for making me laugh too much. A heart-warming thank-you to Debra Watts (Flo), who took on the task of reading without hesitation, and even though I hadn't seen her for years.

Thank you to Sharen Compton for showing her support, she's almost as *'lovely'* as me and when she decides to write, I'll return the favour.

Here's to three wonderful people, Jane Hodges, Dawn Hayter and Michelle Jarrold – thank you all for putting up with me, not only whilst writing this book but in general day-to-day life. A huge thank-you goes to Daniel Hayter, and an apology for the constant badgering. Thank you Tracey Rawlings for being my no. 1 fan but I'm sure your dreams of fame and/or fortune will not be fulfilled.

I would also like to thank two beautiful people, Sarah Chambers and Jo Glazebrook for their support through my writing journey. I promise to stop talking about it now and let you get on with your busy schedules. And last but by no means least, Colin Croucher, thanks for an insight in to the future and watch this space.

The biggest thank-you goes to you for taking the time to read this book.

I hope you will enjoy it.

Tara Ford
http://taraford.weebly.com

Alex

How could this have happened?

Only four hours ago I left work to go to the local supermarket to pick up a few things before early closing. I was feeling fine. Now I was lying on a hospital bed.

This can't be happening to me. I'm fit and healthy. I never visit the doctor and I don't take any medications. I'm Alex Frey, a successful, middle-aged businesswoman, a nurturing mum, a devoted wife and a bloody good housekeeper. I quit smoking four years ago; my alcohol consumption is so low that on the odd occasion when I do venture out with friends, I'm known as 'the lightweight' – two vodkas and I need to be carried home in a delirious state. I've never taken drugs (unless you include six paracetamol taken in a day...once) and I have a reasonably healthy diet apart from the Chinese takeaway on Friday nights. Okay, I'm slightly overweight but not drastically. I don't have time to be unwell and now I'm stuck here in a hospital, feeling horribly...*unwell*.

Glancing down at my bare legs and feet I cringed as my imaginative, drug-addled mind played tricks on me. Why had I not paid a little more attention to grooming when it came to the regions below my knees? The long brown bristles stood erect like a hedgehog's back, waving and shouting at me to remove them quickly, before anyone noticed. Weaving in and out of each hair like a raging river, the worrying purple rash cascaded down my legs. Looking further down, I noticed two well-worn feet and ten little toes oscillating and protesting – "Hello...we need a pedicure." A slight understatement: my toes needed a complete renovation. It had been terribly embarrassing earlier when the nurse asked me to remove my clothing and don a pink, flowery gown with a gaping hole all the way up the back. Thank goodness I hadn't worn any of my tattered, 'replacements required' underwear and the gown was long enough to cover ugly cellulite-laden thighs. (The unattractive, bubbly lumps were on my 'to do' list, although liposuction was probably the only option left after years of neglect.)

"You all right babe?" asked a deep-voiced man sitting in the chair next to the high-rise hospital bed. Quickly recovering from my daydream state I realised that Grant had just spoken.

"Yeah, I'm okay," I replied softly.

Grant is my husband. We've been married for 24 years. He is the stereotypical tall, dark and ruggedly handsome man, only the 'dark' has given way to some grey trim. He is gorgeous, he is sexy and I love him crazily. Our friends are two-tone on the subject of our undying love and lust for each other: some say it is 'weird' or 'unusual' after so many years of being together while others think it's 'cute' or 'sweet'. I just think it is great to be married to my best friend. I've been truly blessed with a happy, long-lasting marriage. We have four lovely children and a peaceful life; what more could a woman ask for? Eternal health, maybe? Don't get me wrong, we've been through some tough times in the past. I only hope this won't turn out to be another one of those difficult times that always seem to come out of the blue.

The events leading up to my present situation had happened so quickly that we were somewhat shocked. Life had been plodding on as normal until this afternoon. Now, feeling sure that Grant was more apprehensive about the situation than I was, I wondered if my lack of worry and exaggerated concern about my appearance was due to the effects of the intravenous drip in my hand.

"I'm going to nip outside and call the kids. I'll let them know we might be here all night." Standing up, he attempted a half-hearted smile. "Are you going to be okay?"

"I'll be fine. You go and have your cigarette." I winked at him knowingly.

"I won't be long. I'll tell the kids to lock the front door and go to bed." Grant reciprocated with a twitch in his eye and left the room. I could never work out how he managed to do such a cool and sexy wink by barely blinking.

Bless him, I knew he needed to get outside, have a cigarette and think things through. And of course, phone the kids.

"Is everything okay?" A voice came from the open door. Startled, I looked up to see the nurse who had given me the robe earlier.

"Yes, thank you," I replied.

"I saw your husband leaving. Is he...?"

"Oh yes, he is coming back in a minute. He's just gone out to phone our kids." Suddenly feeling guilty that Grant had also gone outside to smoke on the hospital grounds, I pictured him standing right next to the *No Smoking* sign and offered her a weak grin.

"The doctor should be round to see you soon."

"Oh, okay, thanks." I managed to smile sweetly, wishing she would leave me alone for a few minutes to have a think about this damned situation myself.

"Can I get you anything?" asked the young nurse.

"No, I'm fine, but thank you anyway," I replied, fidgeting uncomfortably on the bed. The nurse paused as she was leaving. "Would you like me to close the door?"

"No, could you leave it open please?" The thought of the door being closed was intolerable as the small, bleak room would then look and feel even more like a prison cell. At least with it open I could watch all the nurses hurrying by at such a fast pace, they looked as if they were about to miss a bus. Now and again people wearing ordinary clothes rushed past the door looking very busy and important. Some were carrying papers, others had colleagues towing along behind them, carrying what looked like notes and files. I guessed they were doctors or consultants. *When are*

4

you coming in here to see me? I wondered impatiently. *I want to get out of here and go home!*

Staring at the bland walls, I lay very still, aching from head to toe. Two large windows covered the wall on one side of the room, each fitted with opaque glass. Unlike normal hospital rooms, there was little medical equipment on display apart from the drip stand and a small hand basin. A door opposite the end of the bed led to an en-suite bathroom. Looking around, I wondered where the TV/telephone console was; it had to be here somewhere otherwise patients would go totally insane with boredom. Maybe this was just an initial treatment room. After all, I had been admitted to the Medical Assessment Unit. Perhaps they needed to assess me first, decide what was wrong and then put me in the appropriate place, or better still, send me home. Maybe once I'd seen the doctor they'd say that I didn't need anything else. After all, the drip in my hand contained a massive dose of bug-killing juice. Those nasty microscopic germs would be paying the price for ruining my Friday night, *zap, zap, zap!* The worst of it was that it was supposed to be 'Good' Friday.

Grant reappeared in the room. "The kids are going to bed, and Joe has locked the door."

"Did you have a cigarette?"

"Yep!" Grant smiled and sat back in the chair. "I take it the doctor hasn't been to see you yet?"

"No, how long have we been here now?"

"Over an hour. They did say the doctor would be here soon. I think you'll probably end up having to stay the night, babe." Grant looked disappointed.

"Great!" Had I only been here for an hour, for goodness' sake? I didn't want to stay here. There were things to do; it was the weekend and I loved weekends. This was a long one due to Easter and Jack was arriving home tomorrow. I could not stay in hospital.

Waking with a jump, I realised I'd nodded off. Looking up at the large, black-rimmed clock on the wall, I noted that it was now 11.20pm. An empty feeling settled in my stomach – Grant was right when he said I'd be here all night. He was curled up in the sofa chair next to the bed, snoring. Hoping and praying he wouldn't start the usual dribbling onto his shoulder or the floor, I imagined the embarrassment if the nurse walked in, or a doctor with a tribe of colleagues. My warped sense of humour pictured them slipping in a slimy puddle that had dribbled and drooled from the corner of my husband's drooping mouth. Smiling at his sleeping form, I reminisced about the tales he used to tell me regarding his commute to London, every day, some years ago. Each evening he'd fall asleep on the two-hour journey home and usually have a damp shoulder when he walked through the door. Repressing a giggle so I wouldn't wake him, I stared intently at the ceiling fan, still intoxicated with medication.

Grant stirred in the chair and I knew it had been a long day for him. I felt so sorry that we had ended up here. It was our favourite night of the week. Our plans had not included this. There was never much planned anyway, apart from the usual end-of-week special fried rice and chicken chow mein; then a bit of channel-hopping to find something interesting to watch, and an early night when we gave up trying to find a suitable programme. Just as I started wondering where the elusive doctor might be and how far down his list of patients I was, Grant woke up.

"You must be so tired, love. Why don't you go home? Nothing is happening here," I sighed.

"No, I'll stay till the doctor comes, find out what's going on." Sleepily, Grant pulled himself up in the chair. "How are you feeling now?"

I thought for a moment. "Just like I have the flu." That wouldn't have been so bad, but the purple rash was rapidly spreading all the way around to the backs of my lower legs and smothering my feet. It appeared to be creeping upwards, too. "Both my ankles are hurting now." I tried to move them but they felt as stiff as a dead hamster.

"The rash is spreading," he remarked.

"Umm...I know," I replied, semi-dazed and abandoned by rational thought.

The rash was a very strange occurrence. Leaving work at just before four o'clock I'd noticed that one of my ankles felt very stiff and achy on the accelerator pedal while I was driving. Thinking that perhaps I'd strained a muscle somehow without realising, I limped into the local supermarket to pick up some bits. I knew then that something was very wrong. Carrying a lighter shopping basket than expected to the checkout, I decided to pick up any other requirements over the weekend. It was frustrating having to go to the supermarket at all, but the shop that I owned didn't sell everything I needed.

Returning to the car, I threw the carrier bag onto the passenger seat and climbed in. Before setting off on the twenty-minute journey home I lifted my trouser leg to investigate – perhaps I had a bruise, or something else that would qualify the pain. To my astonishment my shin was covered in a blotchy, purple rash. I'd never had a rash before in my life. It certainly wasn't a shaving rash; my legs hadn't seen daylight in months so why put them through the arduous task of shaving? Or worse still, the nightmare of the epilator! Being the type of person who had no allergies, as far as I knew (well, maybe just teenagers), what could it be?

On arriving home, I started to feel like a cold was setting in and my neck began to stiffen up. Probably just stress, I guessed. Grant could give me a neck massage later that would make things better. It was about time I got some TLC. The rash was steadily creeping around my ankles, making its angry presence known. Sitting down, I opened my laptop and proceeded to find the NHS helpline on the internet. Ten minutes later, having completed the questionnaire I saw the word *meningitis*. *Please seek medical attention urgently.* Great! I really couldn't be bothered with this, not tonight. I didn't fit the bill completely anyway – I could stare at bright lights, I thought, as I zoomed in on the table lamp next to me, so it must be wrong.

When I informed Grant about the internet diagnosis he looked at me vacantly, and I knew he was thinking the same as me. Did I really have to do this? It was bloody Easter for goodness' sake! Perhaps it would all go away and I'd be better in the morning. But it didn't get any better and it didn't go away, in fact I felt much worse as the evening progressed.

"I'll phone the clinic, get someone to come out, and then we won't have to go anywhere," said Grant, and although the rash was quite unusual for me, I didn't want to become a patient at the General, so I was happy to have a home visit. Hopefully I would be able to take some medicine to clear it up.

As it turned out, I was instructed to go to the nearest hospital to be seen. An appointment was promptly made and we had 25 minutes to get there. On arrival at St. Johns, we were directed to the waiting room and after a minute or two I was called in to see a doctor. Ten minutes later we were on our way to the General, just out of town. I was being admitted!

"You must go straight away," the doctor had said. Was this serious? Everything had happened so quickly, and Grant and I travelled to the hospital in stunned silence.

Anyway, much to our great delight, the elusive night shift doctor turned up to see me at around 8.15 the following morning. We had waited a mere nine and a half hours for his arrival, but we were not bitter. More appropriately, we were utterly fed up...well, actually, we were totally pissed off! We hadn't a clue what was going on during the night. Would I be staying in? What was wrong with me? What was going to happen? Time ticks by very slowly when you are waiting and waiting and waiting some more, for what seemed like the longest night ever.

By the way, during the 'longest night ever' I'd had two observation checks by the young nurse as I drifted in and out of sleep. A consultant of some description (he probably told me who he was but I hadn't listened in my semi-comatose, sleep-deprived state) came in to look at the ever-increasing rash and muttered, "Umm..." Pulling my spiky legs around, he twisted my ankles, which were very painful, and then said, "The doctor will be round shortly." *Well, who the hell are you then if you're not the doctor?* I'd screamed in my head. Then, to our amazement, he just left.

Spending the rest of the night drifting in and out of sleep, once or twice Grant blearily staggered out to 'get some fresh air', right next to the *No Smoking* sign.

So, back to the morning, which had thankfully arrived, and we felt quite wretched and weary.

"Well, it's not meningitis, as we first thought, so we need to do some more tests," stated the doctor as he pressed on my hedgehog legs. The rash was now spreading to the tops of both legs and a frightening paralysis was setting in. Although the invading purple blotches resembled a meningitis rash, which did not blanch under a glass, I really had them fooled as to what it was, and the doctor looked rather perplexed. He mumbled long, medical-type words to his two colleagues while they scribbled notes in a frantic fashion. Then they all left the room.

"Well? What was that all about?" Grant asked tetchily.

"Go home and get some proper sleep. Come back later and I might know a bit more by then." I wasn't sure I would. "There's nothing you can do here." There really wasn't anything he could do but sit around waiting for the next visit from a nurse or doctor. "Tell the kids not to worry. Jack will be home later today, his flight lands in Birmingham at about five, that'll cheer them up." My head was spinning with one of those mental to-do lists. My brain was always overflowing with lists of tasks, most of which never got done. "Can you phone Aaron too, just to let him know I'm here?"

Grant nodded in a defeatist way, he was so tired and ragged. Leaning over the bed he kissed me tenderly on the lips. "I'll be back later."

"Grant, can you bring back my handbag, some clean underwear and toiletries please?"

"I'll get Emma to sort it out. I'll be back this afternoon." Blowing a kiss to me, he turned to leave. Watching him walk out of the door I felt slightly relieved, firstly that he was going home to get some sleep, secondly that the kids wouldn't be left alone, and thirdly that I only had to worry about myself now.

The kids were old enough to be left alone but I wouldn't have trusted them not to get into huge squabbles or fights over the most trivial things, like who should clean up the breadcrumbs on the kitchen worktop or who should open the living room curtains. I also didn't like the thought of them sitting at home worrying about me and not knowing what was going on.

The rest of the morning was spent having more observations, being pulled around by various consultants (who were all scratching their heads in puzzlement at my symptoms), blood tests and assistance with the commode. My legs were completely paralysed by now and wouldn't hold me up. They had seriously failed my dignity. Two nurses arrived for hoisting-onto-the-commode duty each time I called: the young robe nurse, who I was now familiar with, and a very butch-looking woman with a dark moustache and rippling muscular forearms, who grunted and snorted profusely each time she lifted me. Okay, I suppose I was more than slightly overweight but she didn't need to make it that obvious.

Halfway through the morning, once again, I pressed the buzzer and waited a few minutes for a nurse to arrive.

"Could I use the commode, please?" I hated this so much. I was usually such an independent (although very shy) person, but now my modesty was hanging out of the window for all to see and independence had marched off and left the building! A moment later the two nurses arrived, ready for action.

"Right Alex, are you ready?" the young one asked. They both put an arm under my armpits (at least I'd shaved them) as I perched on the edge of the bed.

"Yes," I replied, struggling to stand, with the nurses' help. At the very moment that my backside left the bed a sudden bubbling, squeaky noise expelled slowly and loudly from deep underneath my pink gown. I had blown off under the pressure of the lift! "Oh my God, I'm so sorry!" I cried.

"Oh, don't worry about it, we're used to it," said the young nurse. Well, she might've been used to patients trumping all over the place but I wasn't! My face burned with embarrassment as the aroma drifted upwards, heading straight for everyone's noses with a vengeance. Feeling so ashamed, I knew these unfortunate ladies were sharing the same horrifying experience as me. Their attempts to smile were feeble as they now inhaled what could only be described as the stench of six-day-old, over-stewed cabbage soup! The nurses quickly plonked me down onto the mobile toilet; they appeared to be desperately holding their breaths.

"Okay Alex, gives us a call when you're ready," gulped the young nurse as they left the room hurriedly and shut the door behind them with a bang. I couldn't understand why or how I had been capable of producing such a highly toxic vapour and had to resign myself to the fact that it must be the medication. Suddenly realising that I'd forgotten to prepare my underwear for the throne, I sat staring at the wall, trying to work out how I was going to pull them down now. I couldn't stand up. Somehow I was going to have to rock from side to side and get them down that way. It took 20 minutes to gradually inch my underwear down from one side to another, repeating the process until they were clear of the pan. Relief! It had taken a lot longer to use the commode this time due to the gradual gusset-lowering exercise, and I suspected that the nurses would think it had something to do with the ghastly gas expulsion which still clung to the walls.

The rest of the day ticked by very slowly, and in between the many visitors popping in to examine me like I was some sort of guinea pig with a mystery illness, I continued to drift in and out of troubled sleep. The rash was steadily creeping up and over my body. Completely paralysed from the waist down, the feeling of flu had progressed to the point of feeling like I'd just been hit by a bus.

Strangely, I was not scared.

Grant

It was a gloriously fresh April morning. The sun had shed its winter blues and glowed boastfully as it took its place in the sky. It was going to be an unusually warm day for the time of year. Walking out of the hospital's main entrance, Grant heaved a sigh of relief. He didn't like hospitals but then he supposed nobody did much, especially if they were a patient. The air was cool but the birds were already up, enjoying the rarely seen sunshine and singing in the ornamental trees that lined the pathway to the car park.

The grand General Hospital stood high in the cut of a hill, overlooking the quiet town below. It was Saturday morning. Soon the weekend shoppers would be getting ready for their weekly ritual of hunting down the best deals in town, and this week would be no exception as the traders dropped their prices of Easter eggs to shift the loads. Grant could never understand why anyone would want to spend all day trudging around the shops to see what bargains they could win for themselves. Alex had the same opinion.

Approaching the ticket machine, Grant reached into his pocket for loose change. Retrieving the ticket from his jacket pocket, he inserted it into the slot. The LCD screen hesitated before revealing the shocking news: £11.00.

"Effing joke!" he exclaimed as he returned the change to his pocket and pulled out his wallet. The machine hastily gulped down Grant's debit card and a minute later coughed up a receipt and returned his exit token for the barriers. "Bloody extortionate prices," he grumbled out loud.

There were three cars in the large, newly built parking bays. Grant wondered how long they had been there and how much their parking charges would be. Striding towards his metallic silver Mercedes he admired her beauty in the crisp light of the new day. He loved his new car as much as he loved football. Alex always joked that she was never quite sure where she appeared on his list of affections for cars, football and breasts, but deep down she knew that she was the greatest love of his life. He'd never been an emotionally expressive type and tried to keep his feelings in close quarters, guarded by a male ego but Alex had broken down those barriers and humoured his vain attempts to rebuild them and play the cool 'Macho-Man'.

Fumbling around for his keys, he unlocked the door and climbed into the car, inhaling the familiar smell of the interior which both comforted and reminded him of home. Setting off on the twenty-minute journey to the other side of town, Grant fell deep into thought, driving on automatic pilot. There were so many phone calls to make – should he go home, sleep first and do all the calls later, or get it all over and done with before falling into bed? He couldn't be bothered to spend the next two hours telling everyone the same thing over and over again. He could send a multiple text message to all concerned; that would be the easiest thing to do. Was that the right thing to do though? Grant accepted that it wasn't. He couldn't just send a text to the boys to tell them their mum was in hospital, and he would never hear the end of it if he sent a text to Alex's mum rather than speak to her in person. She'd be on the phone immediately, redialling constantly until someone gave in and answered it. She would then want a minute-by-minute account of the events leading up to Alex's hospitalisation. She would want to know everything that had taken place in hospital so far, what the doctors had said, what the nurses had said, the diagnosis, prognosis and the happily ever after!

No. He decided he would go home and sleep first.

Rolling down Pinewood Avenue, Grant listened to the whisper of the engine, purring like a contented cat on a lap. He had made a wise choice, buying this car. It was luxurious comfort at its best, pleasing to the eye and a proud statement of his success in life. Making a note of the fact that he had driven home again without realising, Grant vowed that he would pay more attention in the future and not rely on his subconscious mind to get him home, like a homing pigeon. The avenue was lined with cherry blossom trees in shades of pink, cream and white announcing the picturesque season of spring. Summer was hiding just around the corner, waiting for the trees to shed their bloom in the breeze and the birds to start collecting nesting materials.

It was just before nine o'clock as Grant unlocked the front door of their large four-bedroom, semi-detached house. It boasted ochre-coloured stone Edwardian decor with five sizeable, shuttered sash windows peering out to the front. A small porch took centre stage on the brindle block-paved drive, showing off a colourful display as the sunlight pierced through the two stained glass panels framing the heavy, Jacobean oak-panelled door.

They had lived in the house for almost 14 years, a legacy from Grant's parents. When he lost both his mum and dad in a tragic car crash almost 17 years ago, he and his sister Josie were left a large sum of money from the sale of their parents' un-mortgaged cottage in Wales. Grant and Josie had made a conscious decision to sell all other valuable assets and investments, thus freeing themselves of any financial commitments in the future. This arrangement had suited them both. Grant had managed to afford a substantial deposit on his new home with the help of the sale of his previous house and a percentage of his inheritance. Alex's shop had swallowed a considerable amount of the remaining savings but had ensured that her lifelong dream of owning a convenience store would be a more secure financial investment. Grant felt safe in the knowledge that Alex had done very well in the management and success of her beloved shop. She had a vast and recurring customer base which had built over the years, thus providing both Grant and Alex with a comfortable existence, alongside his career.

Walking through to the kitchen, Grant noted the peaceful calm in the house. The kids must still be in bed, he thought. Not unusual for teenagers hitting the heights of hormonal pandemonium, as Alex always said. Grant smiled to himself. They didn't usually surface until midday at the weekends. Even then they were completely vacant creatures from outer space until they had slurped and spluttered their way through at least one bowl of cereal and four slices of almost-toasted bread. Only then did they become anything like socially interactive human beings of planet earth.

Flicking the kettle on, Grant reached for his pint mug – he needed an abundance of tea. The long, restless night had taken its toll on him. He hoped that his poor beloved wife was getting a little sleep now. As soon as the tea was made he tiptoed through to the living room, kicking his shoes off and pulling the lever of the sofa leg rest as he sat down and sighed, desperately wanting to finish his tea at least, before the vacant adolescents awoke from their lair and descended upon him, uttering a cereal-deprived language of their own. He knew they would have lots of questions.

Picking up the remote, he flicked the television on – he could always sleep better with it on in the background. Alex would often come in and turn it off if Grant had fallen asleep in the afternoon, and he would then wake up straight away and say, *"I was watching that*!" Alex would roll her eyes upwards and tut as she left the room. Momentarily Grant felt a knot in his stomach as he recalled the events of the last 12 hours. What was wrong with her? Would she be okay? How long would she be in hospital for? It suddenly occurred to him how worried he had been all night, and still was. His macho image was crumbling and he felt incredibly shattered, both emotionally and physically.

"Dad! Dad, wake up!"

Grant opened his eyes. The TV was twittering quietly in the background, and a cold mug of tea sat on the side table. Looking up through a hazy blur, he saw Emma.

"Urgh, you've been dribbling, Dad," she shrieked, staring at the drool in horror. Rubbing his eyes and wiping his chin, Grant's sleepy mind wandered and a flashback made him smile as he recalled his dribble adventures of the past. One evening in particular stood out from the rest because he had returned home that night in quite a flustered state. Sitting next to a large, beastly-looking woman on the train for the whole journey home, Grant had taken a seat first, before the woman came along and plonked herself next to him. She filled the seat entirely with her excessive, overhanging body parts. Grant had already got himself settled and comfortable with his newspaper folded on his lap. He had the crossword page open, a pen poised in his hand and his elbows propped up on both armrests. He was content. Then the large woman turned her bulldog-like head and looked at him disapprovingly as she made a deep puffing noise and slowly pushed her elbow onto Grant's, knocking his off the rest. Smiling to herself, she then had two armrests to spread herself out on.

Feeling very annoyed, Grant had stubbornly replaced his elbow and pushed her heavy limbs off the rest. Their piercing eyes met, like gunfighters enacting a duel at dawn. Looking away, she repeated the action, more aggressively this time, and shoved his arm off again. Grant had felt infuriated at this point. He would have moved his arm in the first place if she had said "Excuse me, please." The elbow war had continued until, with a look of disgust, the portly lady huffed and puffed and resorted to placing both her arms on her lap, which appeared to be as large as a satellite dish, whilst mumbling under her breath how rude he had been.

A couple of hours later the two armrest enemies had woken from their slumbers and adjusted themselves, ready to disembark. Wiping the corner of his mouth, Grant realised that he'd been dribbling again. It then dawned on him that he had just lifted his head from the dragon's shoulder. During the journey his head had rolled over and at the very moment of his realisation, she turned her head and looked down at her sticky, damp shoulder in sick horror. Eyes widening with fear, Grant tentatively looked towards the woman's warm, moist patch. Gasping and gulping, she reeled from the sight, crying out, "Oh my God!" The lump of lard then burst into tears as Grant panicked and hurriedly got up and left the carriage, muttering under his breath how sorry he was. Embarrassment raged through him as he scurried down the carriage, hearing the woman crying out, "Oi, you!" in the distance.

Within seconds the train had arrived at the platform, just in time before the heavy woman came stomping through the carriages like a charging elephant, shouting and waving her thickset arms around. Leaping onto the platform almost before the London Express had come to a halt, Grant ran out of the station faster than a wildebeest bolting from a pride of lions. Now he recalled Alex's words of wisdom, as she always said that he should have stopped and apologised to the woman properly. In hindsight, maybe he should have offered to buy her a new dress, or more suitably, a durable cotton-canvas tent? The incident had been so funny in Alex's eyes that she hadn't been able to contain herself from bouts of laughter during the rest of that evening. On the other hand, Grant was plagued with worry that he may encounter the human-whale again. Or worse still, a policeman might knock at the door to question him and then arrest him on a charge of 'damp assault' (if there was such a thing). Fortunately, neither of these ever happened.

"Dad, what's going on?" Emma sat down, put her arm around Grant's waist, checked for wet patches and then rested her head on his chest. "Is Mum still in the hospital?" she asked as she looked up at him with big brown eyes.

"Yeah, she is, Em." Grant lifted himself up, put his arm around her and kissed the top of her tatty chestnut-coloured hair. Emma would need comforting, he thought; she would be lost without her mum around. Such a caring, kind and sweet-natured girl, the only trait failing her was an extremely naive and gullible side to her personality. Grant often preyed on her innocence to his own amusement.

It was a month away from her 15th birthday and everyone knew it emphatically. She often held court and told everyone that once she was 15, she was almost an adult and should be treated like one, and her dad should not 'pick on her' anymore. Growing up with three brothers and a dad, all of whom tormented and teased her, Emma's dizzy disposition was usually the topic of many jokes and comments whenever the boys were with Grant. She didn't mind really; she quite liked being the youngest member of the family and getting all the attention.

"When is Mum coming home?"

"I don't know, Em. Do you want to go back with me later to see her?"

"What time are we going?" Sitting up straight as if ready to go, her tiny figure poised at the edge of the seat.

"I haven't had any sleep all night. I need to get a few hours first, and then we'll go."

"Okay, Dad." Jumping up, she went to the kitchen. "Do you want a cup of tea?"

"I've got one here, can you heat it up in the microwave for me?"

Emma returned, picked up the mug and went to warm it up. She was so much like her mum, she would do anything for anyone, thought Grant as he watched her leave.

Managing to stay awake, Grant finished his tea before retiring to the bedroom. The alarm clock said ten minutes to ten; a good few hours' sleep was needed before he started the inevitable list of phone calls.

"Do you want me to wake you up later, Dad?" whispered Emma, peering round the bedroom door.

"Yeah, wake me up about two o'clock please, Em."

"Okay Dad, night-night...I mean morning-morning." She giggled sweetly.

Opening his eyes, Grant looked at the blurred red figures on the alarm clock perched on the edge of the bedside cabinet; 12.36. He'd only been asleep for a couple of hours and now his head thumped violently like a rabbit's hind feet signalling a threat. Dragging himself out of bed, he pulled on his dressing gown and hobbled downstairs to the kitchen.

Joe stood in the corner of the room with a bowl of cereal propped up under his chin, shovelling heaped spoonfuls into his mouth as quick as he could.

"Why don't you sit at the table to eat that?" said Grant grumpily.

"Sorry Dad," Joe managed to say between the gulps and slurps. "How's Mum?"

"She's okay mate; we're going back to see her later if you want to come."

"Can I skip it today Dad? I'm going bowling tonight after the match, with my mates."

"No problem, I expect your mum will be in for the weekend though." Taking the paracetamol from the cupboard, Grant tossed two into his mouth and swallowed them down with a glass of water.

"What's wrong with her?" asked Joe.

"They're not sure yet."

Emma hopped into the kitchen and looked Joe up and down. "Are you coming to the hospital with us?" she asked, sneering at him.

"No, I'm going out later. You don't mind, do you Dad?"

Grant shook his head and wished he hadn't as his brain continued to rattle loosely inside.

"Ah, please come Joe," pleaded Emma. She was close to Joe, probably because they were the two youngest and he also made her laugh a lot.

"Grandma phoned earlier," said Joe, finishing the last mouthful of his breakfast/lunch and ignoring Emma's comment completely.

"Oh God, did she?" Grant cringed at the thought of calling his mother-in-law.

"I told her Mum's in hospital; she said you have to phone her as soon as you get up." Joe moved towards the kitchen archway.

"Okay," replied Grant as he mentally prepared for the aftermath of not calling her earlier this morning.

"I sent a text to Jack and Aaron last night. Aaron is coming home early I think. He said he'd call you today."

"Did Jack say what time he'll be back tonight?"

"He hasn't replied yet." Joe edged his way out of the kitchen. "I've gotta go now Dad, we're playing at Tallbridge this afternoon."

Joe, like his father, loved football. He loved watching it, playing it and talking about it. He also enjoyed playing rugby, cricket and basketball. He was very athletic and had secured a place at college in September to do a sports performance and excellence course for two years. His current success had been a long time coming and somewhat doubtful at times. As a younger child Joe had always been the boisterous, loud and outgoing one. Grant and Alex worried about him more than any of their other children. He was a difficult child to understand; that was how the school had described him. He got bored very quickly, which usually lead him into all kinds of trouble. His attention span was zero but he was way ahead of his peers academically. Joe didn't cope well with changes in his life and Alex worried that he also had OCD tendencies. She often fretted over whether he had a form of autism or not, as he also possessed an incredible photographic memory. The doctors, the school nurse and his teachers had shunned the idea and attributed Joe's poor behaviour to a parental handling issue. Alex did not challenge their opinions and spent a lot of time pondering where she had gone wrong with him, when she seemed to have got it right with the others. She now believed that Joe was more than likely on the autistic spectrum, even if only slightly, although it had not been, and probably never would be, officially diagnosed. Joe was impulsive and outspoken, both qualities that could get him into difficult situations, but all in all, everyone accepted that Joe was just Joe and everyone loved his sense of humour and caring nature.

"We may not be here when you get back, Joe. Can you take your key please?"

"Yep, see you later then." Leaving the room, Joe bounced, two at a time, up the stairs to his bedroom like a wallaby in an uphill marsupial race. Emma tiptoed after him like a fairy on hot rocks and retreated to her pink and purple (no boys allowed) girlie sanctuary of a bedroom.

Returning to the living room with another mug of tea, Grant picked the phone up from its base and sat down on the sofa. Staring at the handset, he imagined the conversation he would have with Alex's mum. He did not want to make the call, but he knew he would have to sooner or later.

A shrill sound rang in his delicate head and Grant realised he had nodded off again. The phone rang and rang persistently. Where was the answer machine when he needed it, he thought. Damned kids had probably turned it off again. Reluctantly, he picked up the handset and pressed the answer button. "Hello."

"Grant, did I wake you? What's going on with Alex? Joe told me she's in the hospital. What's wrong with her?"

"Dot, I was just about to call you. No, you didn't wake me," he lied. "Calm down, she's okay. They're not quite sure what's wrong with her yet—"

"What do you mean, they're not sure? They should know what's wrong with her. They're supposed to be the bloody doctors!"

"Look, I'm going back there in a while. I've just woke up, Dot; I'll know more about it later, and then I can call you."

"How can you have just woken up? You said you were just about to call me." Dot didn't miss a thing, he was sure she had an internal tape recorder installed in her brain that scrutinised everything that everyone said or did.

"Where is she? At the General? What ward is she on?"

"She could be moved today; she was in the Assessment Unit last night. I'll let you know later Dot. I'll text you when I'm at the hospital, okay?" Grant's head was still pounding and he wondered whether she could hear it beating down the phone.

"Please make sure you do Grant, I won't be able to sleep tonight if I don't know what's going on. Dad's panicking too."

"Look Dot, as soon as I know something I'll call or text you." Grant began to sweat from the pain in his head.

"Okay, well you must be tired if you've been awake all night. Get some sleep, it'll do you good."

Grant raised his eyebrows in sheer amazement at her stubbornness and wilful lack of tact.

"Will you send her our love?"

"Of course I will. Talk to you later."

"Thank you Grant, I'll wait to hear from you. Bye for now."

The phone went silent, much to Grant's relief. Inhaling a deep breath, he thanked God it was over, although it wasn't as bad as he'd expected. Perhaps Dot was right and he was just overtired. His dull head didn't make things any better.

Ring, ring, the phone went again.

"Hello."

"Grant, sorry I forgot – it's today that Jack comes home isn't it?"

"Yes, he should be back tonight, Dot."

"Oh good, we'll have to see him before he goes back. And how did Aaron get on with the train?"

"Well, he managed to get there in one piece!" Grant smiled.

"Good. Okay, talk later love. Please don't forget to call me as soon as you know anything. Bye for now."

Beep.

Then Grant's mobile phone played a melody from the pocket of his jacket (which he'd slung on the dining room table earlier), indicating that a text message had been received. Dragging himself up, he groped around in the pocket for his phone. There was a message from Aaron.

I'm coming home today. Getting train at 1pm. Hope Mum is all right xx

It was now ten past one; Aaron would be on the train already, thought Grant as he replied to the text.

Your mum's okay. See you tonight when I get back from the hospital, mate. Grant had a feeling Aaron would come home early once he heard the news, although it was only a day earlier. He wasn't actually due back until tomorrow night. Alex hadn't wanted Aaron to go to Wales on his own by train. She'd known, deep down, that Grant was right though. She had to let go of the reins she still held for Aaron, as she had done with Jack.

"But Aaron is different to Jack," she had tried to reason.

Grant admitted that Aaron was very shy and introverted, unlike his siblings, but Alex had to let him start making his way in life on his own. If he wanted to go on an adventure and travel to his Aunt Josie's house in Wales, on a train, on his own, then he should go. He'd saved the train fare from his hard-earned wages working at the weekends in the storeroom of a local supermarket. "He'll be 18 this year Alex, he'll be fine. Let him go," Grant had insisted.

The phone began its familiar ring again. Almost sensing who was at the other end of it, he hesitated, and then pressed the handset to his reluctant ear. "Hello?"

"Grant, I've just been thinking. Is there anything I can do to help you out? Do you need any bread or milk or anything else?"

"Dot...umm, no, everything is fine thanks. I don't need anything."

"Dad said to tell Alex she had better get herself better for next Tuesday." She attempted a laugh.

"Next Tuesday?" Grant couldn't think properly; he hadn't had much time to think at all and the drumming beatbox disco inside his head was getting louder and faster.

"The blasted boat Grant, remember?"

"Oh yes, of course, I'll remind her. I'm sure she'll be okay by then."

Alex would probably rather stay in the hospital and have both her legs amputated, thought Grant as he imagined her on hands and knees, holding onto the hem of the doctor's white coat and begging him to let her stay in the hospital until after Tuesday. Smiling inwardly at his imagined scenario, he knew that she loved her mum and dad dearly. It was just that she felt her dad was really pushing the boat out this time – literally!

"Do you want me to come and sit with the kids while you're at the hospital?"

"No Dot, they're quite capable of looking after themselves now and Emma's coming with me." *For heaven's sake, is she in a time warp? Has she missed the last five years of their growing up or is she completely senile?*

"Give me a call if you need anything Grant, you know I'm always at the end of the phone line."

"Oh, I know Dot, thanks."

"Bye for now."

That was the problem with Alex's mum. She was always at the end of the phone line – always! She believed that the telephone was the greatest invention ever. "It brings people together, no matter the distance between them," she liked to dictate regularly. Alexander Graham Bell had a lot to answer for where the 'Dots' of this world were concerned. Grabbing the phone, Grant squeezed it tightly to stop any more calls getting through as he meandered through to the kitchen and flicked the kettle on again. Wanting to make an important call, he needed to intercept the phone line before Dot could claim a hold on the whole telecommunications network. Calling directory enquiries, he asked for the number of the General Hospital. By the time Grant had finished stirring his tea, he'd conquered the trail of extensions and reached the correct department.

"Alex is doing well," said a female voice, vaguely. "We're waiting for some test results, and then she'll be seen by the doctor again."

"Could you tell her I called and I'll be there soon?"

"Yes Mr Frey, I'll give her the message."

The mail had arrived and still lay discreetly on the front doormat. Mr Postman Pat (a name given by the children, when they were small, to any person who walked up the drive carrying mail) was getting later and later, thought Grant as he shuffled through the envelopes. Bill, bill and a letter from the school. Tucking them under his arm, he carried them outside to the patio along with the phone and yet more tea. It was beautifully bright outside, although the light strained his eyes and irritated his aching head. Increasingly warm for the beginning of April, it had to be 20 degrees by now, he thought. The glowing heat of the sun made Grant's eyelids feel heavy; he hadn't had enough sleep. His mind wandered to an image of dear Alex lying in the miserable, dingy room, while he rested in a high-backed green resin patio chair, taking in the spring newness of their garden.

The peaceful existence in Grant's tranquil, landscaped domain was abruptly shattered.

Ring, ring...

Stalling for a moment, he listed the possibilities; firstly as to the nature of the call and secondly, but more importantly, the caller, as the phone trembled on the plastic table. Concluding that it could be someone important he answered. "Hello?"

"Honey, I'm going into town to get my hair done. Dad's dropping me off; should I pick up some magazines for Alex?"

Resting his forehead in the palm of his hand, propped up by his elbows on the table, Grant replied. "Dot, I think we should wait and see how long she will be there for."

"All right, I just thought that knowing Alex, she would be bored silly."

"When I left her this morning, she just wanted to sleep."

"Well, can I get *you* anything at all while I'm down there?"

"No, I'm fine. I'm going back to the hospital again soon. I phoned them and they're waiting for more test results, but she's okay."

"Yes I know, I phoned them too. They said the same thing to me. I'll let you get on with things then Grant; talk to you later. Bye-bye for now."

"Bye."

The equation was *Dot + phone = blood-boiling frustration* at the best of times. Leaving his disturbed sunny haven, Grant decided to take a shower. At least he couldn't answer the phone while he was standing under the relaxing streams of warm water cascading from the shower head.

Feeling refreshed but still dull-headed, Grant stepped out of the shower and reached for a soft towel. He thought he'd heard the phone ring but he couldn't be sure as it had been left in the garden. He wished that the friendly-faced little garden gnomes (that were Alex's pride and joy) would carry the handset away to a secret hiding place at the far end of the lawn and bury it deeply, where it could not be seen or heard ever again.

"Dad, Grandma's on the phone, she wants to know if she should get some grapes for us to take to the hospital?" came Emma's voice from the other side of the bathroom door.

"Tell her we'll get some, don't worry." *For goodness' sake, that woman is insatiable*, he concluded.

Collecting the forgotten letters from the patio table, Grant made another cup of tea and a sandwich which would temporarily occupy a small area of the emptiness in his stomach. He then sat down in the dining room, one of his favourite places in the house.

Both he and Alex firmly believed that the family should eat dinner together, at the table. It was a time to have family conferences, share news and have a chat about anything and everything. Many good memories had formed within these four walls. The elegant, rectangular glass table stood in the centre of the room, guarded by six high-backed grey leather chairs. A matching sideboard took second place along the back wall. Two statuesque black glass vases reigned in the corners of the room, like Grenadier Guards, with silver and black floral arrangements tumbling and twisting from them in a resplendent display of curliness. Grant picked up the letters and browsed through them. First letter, credit card bill – he tossed it back down on the table. Second letter, electric bill – it joined the first bill, discarded until another day. The third letter was from Joe and Emma's school. What did he have to pay out for now, another trip? Or had Joe acted impulsively again and been punished with a detention for calling the teacher a stupid fat git? Opening the letter, he noted immediately that it was about Emma.

Dear Parent/Carer,

I am writing to you regarding your daughter Emma Frey. Unfortunately, it has been brought to my attention that...CCTV...

£70.00...Police...Prosecution...

Grant scanned the contents of the letter briefly. Then he needed to read it again, more carefully. A heated rage, mixed with tones of disbelief and sadness, began to bubble inside his stomach, working its way upwards to join the battle in his pulsating head. Surely this couldn't be about his sweet little Emma?

Aaron

"Well you've managed to do it once now, so come back soon and stay for longer next time," said Josie as she pretended to pick her nose and wipe it on Aaron's jacket. Impulsively jumping back and away from his aunt, Aaron checked himself for traces of slime and chuckled. "Give your mum our love. Tell her we're all thinking of her and if she doesn't hurry up and get better, I'll be over there to sort her and those doctors out!"

Nodding his head like the Churchill dog on a rear parcel shelf, Aaron beamed as they stood on the platform waiting for the train to arrive. He loved his Aunt Josie; she was an unquestionably jolly and bubbly person and much more relaxed about life than his mum or dad were. There was never a dull moment in Josie's company. Playful, funny and completely crazy, she was 'only' 41 years old. There was a funny side to absolutely everything in her eyes; making a teaspoon appear to be the most hilarious thing in the world was just one of her many talents. Everyone affected by her deranged outlook would stop and wonder why on earth they were all rolling around on the floor, hysterically laughing and crying about a teaspoon that she'd been wearing on her nose. Her special charm could turn practically any situation into a cataclysmic volcano of cachinnation. Whenever Josie and her boys went to stay with the Freys, their home would turn into a fairground funhouse full of laughter and madness. Josie often visited them, at least twice every year, sometimes more. The time she spent there was exhausting for everyone, purely from the constant tears of laughter, strained stomach muscles and aching jaws. Everyone adored Aunt Josie, but no one really knew what it was that had made them laugh.

After her parents died, Josie, like Aaron's dad, had struggled to come to terms with losing her mum and dad in such a horrific and sudden way. The tragedy caused a strain on her already fragile marriage, and just over a year after her parents' death, Josie's husband left her for another woman. Alone and broken-hearted, she had to bring up their young twins on her own. Vowing to do her very best for her sons, her ethos was to always create sunshine and moonbeams in their home, and apparently she always did. Nobody quite knew what the sun and the moon had to do with bringing up children, but she succeeded in turning out two fine young men. A strong and courageous woman, Josie let none of life's little problems (or the blonde bit of fluff she'd been ditched for) stand in her way of accomplishing everything she had set her mind on. As the years rolled by, the twins' father visited them less and less, more intent on making a new life for himself and his new harlot of a partner. Josie decided it would be his loss when the twins eventually became estranged from their father.

Her twin sons, Daniel and Jacob, looked upon their mum in despair at times. They had grown up with a fun-loving, kind-hearted mother who gave all of her time to the careful upbringing and direction of their lives. But as they had got older they made informed decisions and came to the conclusion that she was completely bonkers. Daniel and Jacob were not identical and had very different personalities and goals in life. They were almost the same age as Aaron, but he had always had a stronger relationship with Daniel. Sharing similar interests, they would discuss their experiences through the internet chat sites or via their Xbox games consoles when they were apart, to ensure they kept in regular contact and 'in the know'.

Although it had been less than two days, Aaron had enjoyed his stay in Wales. For some people, two days would be more than enough time to be spellbound by Josie's company and her rigorous timetable of comedy sketches, but Aaron now wanted to get home and find out what was wrong with his mum. He knew it was the right thing to do as he worried about her, although he'd been told not to worry. At least he knew he would be able to travel to Wales on his own again, at another time. Growing up and experiencing the world for himself, he now knew that freedom smelt good.

"Give me a big fat hug then," said Josie as she opened her bulky arms. Looking around the platform and blushing with embarrassment, Aaron felt like a patient in a doctor's surgery waiting to discuss a problem with erectile dysfunction. Luckily there were no onlookers, except Daniel, who was already cringing at the thought of a cuddle in public. It was not a cool thing to be giving your auntie a hug in a public place at his age. Aaron winced and then hesitantly, he put his arms around her wide girth and hugged her. A large and powerful lady, she insisted on crushing him like a python constricting its prey.

"Argh!" squealed Aaron, whose slight frame resembled that of a HB pencil, except he had black, spiky hair on the top instead of an eraser. His friends called him 'Sticky', which was his shortened nickname, the longer version being 'Stick Insect', and he had to admit that it aptly fitted his sleek frame. Struggling to free himself from her mighty grip, he let out a roar of disturbed laughter. Releasing her grasp, Josie looked dishevelled and began to run her fingers through her long blonde hair in slow motion as if she was auditioning for a shampoo advert.

"You nearly broke my ribs, Aunt Josie," said Aaron as he pulled himself together and checked the platform for spectators, just as the train pulled in.

"Nearly? Not quite then. Let's have another go." She chuckled.

"No, I'm going now, you're mad!" said Aaron, edging away from her and smiling cheekily.

"I'll see you again soon mate, yeah?" Daniel stepped forward and patted Aaron on the back.

"Yep, see you soon Dan. I'll talk to you tonight, when I get home." Picking up his rucksack, Aaron turned to board the train. Josie and Daniel stood together on the platform, waiting for him to walk

40

through the carriages and find a seat. The small Welsh station seemed quiet for a Saturday afternoon but Josie had said she would expect it to be busier in Newport, where Aaron had to change trains.

Looking down at his feet, Daniel yawned and screwed up his nose. The sun was pouring through the glass roof of the station, creating warmth and a golden halo above his glorious red, wavy hair. It was not an option: he was definitely going back to bed when they got home. Staying up all night with Aaron, playing games on the Xbox had caught up with him, although he would never admit it. The boys had decided that an all-night Xbox vigil was called for after Aaron received the text message from his brother Joe, saying that his mum was in hospital. Joe had told Aaron that mum was okay and not to worry, but Aaron was a born worrier. When he told Josie he would be going home early to see his mum, she said it was fine, so at least he didn't have to worry about upsetting her or putting her through any unnecessary inconvenience. Aaron just wanted to be at home on Sunday to see his mum, either at home or in the hospital if she was still there.

Josie had gone to bed at eleven o'clock, and Aaron and Daniel made the decision to stay awake all night long. It was a tough competition to battle with their drooping eyelids working overtime through the night, while they waited to see who could last the longest. The dark starry sky sped past and they both won the contest in joint first place; they had made it to the morning and kept their eyelids open.

Daniel's twin brother Jacob had gone to stay at a friend's house for the evening so he was unaware of the other two boys' plans to see the night through, gorging on bags of sweets and enough chocolate to cover a cocoa bean plantation. Jacob said his goodbyes and apologies to Aaron by way of a phone call earlier, as he was unable to accompany them to the train station due to a Saturday league rugby match. The two night owls' nocturnal gaming experience had escaped Josie's knowledge too. Aaron guessed that she assumed they were both up early when she arose at 8.30 this morning. She made them a fried breakfast, one of her specialties, and reminded Aaron that the drive to the station would take at least half an hour. Whilst serving the scrambled egg, Josie told him to hurry up as he needed to get his things together. However, there weren't many things to get together. Aaron believed that underwear and socks could be turned inside out for day two of their wear/wash cycle, and travelling light was his philosophy in his new role as a teenage tourist.

There were few passengers on the train, and seats were abundant. Aaron took a seat in the first carriage he had boarded. Sitting down by the window, he peered out to wave to Josie and Daniel, who were still standing on the platform. Daniel smiled and waved back. Josie frowned, pushed her bottom lip out and rubbed her eyes with clenched fists, shuddering as if she were sobbing. Grinning and shaking his head,

Aaron reflected on her wacky behaviour. A few minutes later the train began to move out of the station and Aaron laughed out loud as he watched Aunt Josie in amazement. Jumping up and down, she waved her arms in the air frantically. She was performing a headbanging, cowlick-flicking, split-ended finale as her Goldilocks hair shook. Josie's goodbye gesture could only be described as the dance of a drug-addled, wailing banshee. Walking away from his mother, Daniel looked decidedly uncomfortable. Reaching the back of the platform he concealed a discreet, less dramatic wave, and then they were gone.

Settling into his seat, Aaron felt weary but amused by the spectacle he had just witnessed. The twins were right: Aunt Josie was utterly bonkers. Checking the time on his mobile phone, he noted that the train would reach Newport in 15 minutes. Once he was on the Portsmouth train, he knew he could have a sleep for the remaining three-and-a-half-hour journey home. Once he was settled he would set the alarm on his mobile phone for the duration.

Newport station was busier than the previous one as Aaron stepped down onto the platform. Relieved he hadn't had to say goodbye to Aunt Josie here – although she probably would have got a rapturous applause for her performance – he glanced around, then followed the other passengers towards the main station. Suddenly a toilet was top of the agenda for Aaron, and pretty quick! The motion of the train and the fresh air filtering through the station had spurred on Aunt Josie's cooked breakfast which was working its magic, along with the copious amounts of splendiferous confectionery he had consumed during the night. It wasn't long before his next train was due, but hopefully there was enough time to find the public conveniences before going to the correct platform to catch his train home. Unsure of this part of the journey, Aaron remembered that there were only four platforms and he came in on number three, so how hard could it be? Racing along with buttocks clenched tightly, he followed the signs that displayed two little people, one with a skirt and the other wearing trousers. Hopefully he would make it in time to the lavatories before anything touched cloth!

As Aaron sat in the cubicle, feeling relieved, the long waking hours since Thursday night suddenly overcame him like a cloak of heavy, dark leather placed upon his head. Fatigue and a feeling of being unwell in the bowel department kept Aaron anchored to the toilet seat for longer than he had expected. Listening to a voice from the tannoy faintly floating around the smelly men's room, Aaron just managed to hear the rambling announcements between toilet flushes and running taps. A moment later the bodiless voice inside the speaker system caught his attention, and sitting upright and rigid, he listened intently.

"Platform three; train leaving...1.30." One thirty? That was the time his train was due to arrive. He was here only two days ago on platform three – *shit!* Panicking, he tried to hurry himself and get to the train.

The third carriage had the least number of passengers. Desperately needing some sleep, Aaron wanted to sit away from other people so he stumbled through to the end of the coach and found that the last two rows of seats were empty. At last he plonked himself down and sighed, *that was close*, he thought, before reaching into his jeans pocket and retrieving his phone. The train gently pulled away from the station and the mesmerising sound of the wheels on the track lulled him into a sense of peace and calm. Setting the alarm on his mobile for three hours later, Aaron knew that would give him plenty of time to wake up before arriving home. Wedging the rucksack under his legs for safekeeping, he removed his jacket and covered his head as he curled into the seat and drifted off.

"Tickets please." A voice filtered through Aaron's dreams and momentarily brought him back to consciousness. Turning over, he put the jacket back over his head, hoping the inspector would pass him by.

Startled, Aaron awoke with a sense that somebody had touched his shoulder.

"Come on lad, time to get off," said the ticket inspector. "Have you got your ticket please?"

"Sure," he mouthed, fumbling around for the piece of card and wondering why his alarm hadn't gone off earlier. The stout man took the ticket and clipped it without examination. "Come on then, off you get."

Aaron gathered his coat and bag, feeling puzzled by the apparent escort off the train. Hopping down to the platform with a fuzzy head, he looked up and froze. Where was he? Turning around, he opened his mouth to ask the inspector where they were, but the man had gone. The station was the largest he had seen throughout his young adventures (although he hadn't seen many), and it was frighteningly large. Aaron's feet were rooted to the ground like a well-established oak tree. He didn't know what to do or where to go. All around him, passengers made their way to the exit signs and disappeared up the escalators. Rescuing his anchored feet from the platform of sinking sand, Aaron followed a young couple to the exit sign with a sense of foreboding. At the top of the escalators, he could see a large sign in the distance saying *Welcome to Birmingham New Street*.

"Oh my God!" he cursed under his breath. Birmingham? How did he get here? Questions raced through his head like a high-speed train. How was he going to get home? He didn't have enough money left to buy another ticket. How much would a ticket cost? "Shit!" he muttered under his breath as he walked hesitantly towards the centre of a gargantuan concourse. Flowing through the station in a stream of people, he was overwhelmed by the sheer size of the building. The number of platforms, subways, escalators, signs, shops and the crushing waves of human traffic of all nationalities made him dizzy and homesick.

Drawn to an unoccupied marble bench, Aaron sat down. *What an effing idiot,* he thought while surveying the unfamiliar surroundings, feeling scared and disturbed by the enormity of the place. The escalators on the right carried the passengers and shoppers to a retail arcade above the main station. Watching the procession of bobbing heads gliding up and down like penguins on a conveyor belt, he gathered his jumbled fragments of thought. Pulling the phone from his pocket he stared at it intently, trying to compose a message in his mind. What text could he send to his dad? *I'm lost Dad, help!* No, that sounded ridiculous. Would Dad be mad? What was Mum going to say? Aaron could almost hear her voice – "I told you he shouldn't have gone, Grant!"

Dad, I got the wrong train and I'm in Birmingham! Aaron pressed send and waited, clutching his lifeline to a ticket back home. *Ticket!* Why hadn't he looked at his ticket earlier – surely it had details of the journey he had booked? Removing the hole-punched card from his pocket, he noted that it had *Platform 3* written in one corner, so he had got on at the right platform. He had not, however, got on a train at the right time.

The escalator transporting a never-ending flock of penguins continued its tireless journey as Aaron endured the mindless observation and contemplated his next move. Being patient and waiting for his dad to reply or call him, five minutes of his life ticked away slowly and three hundred penguins ascended or descended. Ten minutes, fifteen minutes... Examining his phone several times, willing it to ring or chant an unusual techno sound, announcing a text message, nothing came. Burying his head in his hands, Aaron closed his eyes and prayed that his dad would call soon.

Fumbling to hit the answer button, Aaron spoke apprehensively. "Hello?"

"How the bloody hell have you managed to end up in Birmingham, Aaron?" His dad sounded pretty peed off.

"Dad, I'm so sorry, I got on the wrong train."

"You couldn't get much more wrong than that, could you?" His dad huffed down the phone. "What am I supposed to do about it?"

"I dunno, Dad. I haven't got enough money to get another ticket."

"Where are you in Birmingham?" The question came angrily.

"In a train station."

"I know you're in a bloody train station, for Christ's sake! Which one?" Aaron could hear the irritation rising in his dad's voice.

"Sorry Dad, it's called Birmingham New Street, I think."

"You think? Is it or isn't it?"

"Yes, that's what it's called." Aaron began to feel angry at his failure to complete his first ever one-man adventure.

"Look, I'm up to my eyeballs here mate. Jack arrives in Birmingham at five o'clock. I'm going to call him and ask him to pick you up, so just wait there and don't move. I've had one problem after another today Aaron, and this just adds to the list. I'll contact the airport and make sure Jack gets the message; leave it with me, we'll get it sorted." Aaron's dad hesitated, and his tone lowered to a gentle utterance. "Are you okay?"

Instantly Aaron felt a pang of despair; he wanted to get home to his family. "Yeah, I'm okay." He sounded submissive. "Thanks Dad."

"Don't worry son, we'll get you home but you need to stay there for a couple of hours and wait for Jack. Have you got enough money for something to eat or drink?"

"Yeah, I've got a tenner."

"Okay, I'll talk to you in a while, don't worry. I'll sort it out before I go back to the hospital to see your mum."

"Okay, thank you Dad. Tell Mum I love her."

"I will son, just don't worry about anything, okay?"

Pressing the off button, Aaron noticed the battery level was running low. He would have to conserve what little energy was left in case Jack or his dad called him. The time was a quarter to four, so he wouldn't have too long to wait, he hoped. Leaning back against the marble bench, he watched hundreds of people passing by. They probably all knew where they were going and how to get there, he thought to himself, as he watched and waited.

Jack

Speeding along the runway, the airplane reached the point of lift-off and departed from Düsseldorf, soaring into a cloudless sky. Jack was on his way home. The plane was at full capacity, carrying mainly English and German passengers. Jack was seated towards the back of the plane on the aisle side of a three-seater row. An elderly couple occupied the other two seats next to him, and the old man had the window seat. *Lucky sod,* thought Jack as he listened to the routine announcements and safety procedures that piped out over the tannoy. Two air hostesses delivered a display of hand and arm movements, facing each other at opposite ends of the gangway. Studying the girl nearest to him, Jack admired her beauty. Her long, dark hair was swept up and back into a bun and she spoke through full, bright red lips that held a natural pout. Guessing she was of similar age to him, maybe slightly older than his 23 years, he studied her voluptuous figure as she moved her torso during the demonstration. Lustfully observing her curvaceous breasts, which were of ample size, Jack's mind wandered for a moment. He hadn't slept with a woman in over six months and it was starting to play on his mind. The stewardesses completed their presentation and moved towards the back of the plane. Jack altered his brain waves and shifted in his seat uncomfortably – it was just as well that no one could read his mind.

The elderly lady next to him had been twittering away incessantly since Jack had taken his seat. There had been a short delay for some unknown reason before the crew closed the hatch and prepared for flight, hence Jack had been blessed with an extra 20 minutes of rampant babble from the moaning old hag. The old man to the right of her looked like he had been henpecked for many years – the furrows in his forehead could probably tell a story or two, thought Jack.

"I'm not sure we will *ever* be going back there again, Cyril," said the little white-haired lady. "It was a disgrace!"

The bald man nodded in agreement, probably having learnt over the years to agree with everything she said. He seemed like the type of man who would rather go two rounds with Tyson than argue with his wretched, wrinkled wife.

"And that toilet, it was horrific Cyril. You were nearly sick, I heard you retching."

Cyril nodded again and pursed his lips.

"We didn't bring her up like that, so why has she turned into such a disgusting little madam? It doesn't take much to keep a toilet clean, for goodness' sake!"

Cyril shrugged his shoulders. Jack questioned to himself whether the man could actually talk at all.

"When I asked her about it she said she hadn't had the time to do any cleaning in the last week. The last week? There was more than a week's worth of shit encrusted in that bowl, I can tell you!" she complained as Cyril cringed with awkwardness. "I've a good mind to call her when we get home Cyril, what do you think?"

Jack concluded that Cyril must use his shoulders a lot to shrug his way through conversations.

"And those flea-ridden cats were everywhere, I counted 23 of them Cyril, how many did you count?"

He shook his head and looked at her with a glint of animosity in his old, blue eyes.

"There was as much cat poo scattered around as there were cats, it was filth Cyril, what's wrong with her?"

Jack leant slightly towards the lady, intrigued about the cats and the 'her' she was ranting about. Assuming it was their daughter, he continued to listen in amusement. Watching from the corner of his eye, Jack noticed Cyril gazing straight ahead into nothingness.

"Why won't she just come back home? She doesn't need to stay out there anymore."

Cyril shrugged again: he obviously didn't want to have this conversation.

"Half of those poor cats had legs or eyes missing and chunks of fur falling off their bodies. It's cruel to keep them alive isn't it?"

"Umm," muttered Cyril.

Jack smiled to himself. The man did have vocal chords after all!

"She can't take any more strays in, it's ridiculous!" The woman was getting quite agitated. "Cat breeder, my arse. More like feline zombie farm." Her gravelly voice raised as she looked towards Jack, grinning a plastic smile at him. "Surely she's not going to breed Cyclops, three-legged cats with selective fur patches?"

"Daphne, that poor lad doesn't want to listen to this all the way to England." Cyril had really stepped up to the mark. He'd spoken!

Looking towards them both, Jack smiled. "That's fine mate, don't worry about me."

Daphne eyed Cyril distastefully and sucked her wrinkled cheeks in, pursing her lips in a frown.

The flight home took an hour and a half. Jack adjusted his army-issue watch to allow for the crossing of time zones – nearly there, he thought, feeling a rush of excitement shoot through his body. However, his trip had been an interesting one. He had learnt a great deal over the past 90 minutes, and he felt like he almost knew Cyril, Daphne and their daughter Trudie. He was almost sympathetic about the clowder of cats, the hovel Trudie lived in, her morbid fascination with death, the ex-husband who had left her for a homeless bisexual tramp, her own colourful past and the present poo pandemic in her small flat. The outcome looked grim for the future of German cats!

Jack was exhausted by the time they landed in Birmingham. Once through customs, he had to find a phone and call his dad. A text message delivered in the middle of the night, from his brother, had informed him that his mum was not well. The queue to exit the plane was long and tedious. Jack pulled his rucksack from the overhead storage and stood in the aisle waiting with Cyril as Daphne continued to moan on several new topics, namely the British queues, rude people and excessive hand luggage.

The airport was bustling like a smoked beehive. Elated to be back on English soil, Jack smiled at the thought of almost being home. Initially he'd booked his flight back to Birmingham, planning to spend a night with a lady he had met some time ago. Unfortunately the brief relationship had petered out before it ever got going. Jack realised he had a close escape with that one, but Facebook had its uses, good and bad. He could have changed his flight plans and gone straight back to Gatwick, which would have been closer to home, but decided against it, saving himself the hassle of changing flight details. The army had sent him out to Germany from Birmingham, so he saved himself any confusion by sticking to the way he knew. He quite liked the idea of travelling home on a train, taking in the English countryside and chilling out with a beer. He now had four weeks' leave to enjoy, and boy, was he going to enjoy it. The old cliché 'wine, women and song' sprang to his mind, although more appropriately for Jack it would be 'beer, birds and bars'! Jumping into the booth before anyone else could occupy it, Jack fed the payphone and dialled his home number.

"Hello?"

"Hello Pops! I'm in Birmingham, what's up with Mum?"

"Jack, I was just about to call you; thought you must have landed by now mate." A pause. "Your mum is okay. I'm going back to the hospital to see her soon. I needed to talk to you first though. I was supposed to contact you through the airport to give you a message in case you hadn't received the text but I've been caught up in all sorts of other things."

"Why, what's up Dad?"

"Well, for a start, there is someone that you know lost in Birmingham!" His dad's voice increased in volume at the word 'Birmingham'...

"Who?" Jack asked, trying to think of the possibilities.

"Your stupid brother, Aaron!"

"How's he lost in Birmingham?"

"He got on the wrong bloody train coming home from Wales!"

Jack laughed out loud. "How the hell did he manage that? He's gone completely in the wrong direction for a start – where is he, do you know?"

"He's waiting for you at Birmingham New Street. Can you get over there and pick him up on your way back? Sorry mate, I know it's a bloody nuisance."

"Yeah, sure Dad. What an idiot he is, eh?"

"Yep, you said it! Look, he hasn't got any money for a ticket home, so can you get him one and we'll sort it out when you get home?"

"No worries Dad. Can you ring him and tell him I'm coming to get him? I ain't got any credit on my phone yet."

"Sure I will son." Grant was so proud of his firstborn son. A soldier in the army, Jack had finally made something of himself and he had enjoyed every minute of it. Based in Germany for the next two years whilst he continued his advanced training, he had also taken advantage of the numerous courses on offer. He had achieved many things in the last two years with the army, utmost respect being number one on the list.

"Okay Dad, I'll go now and get him; don't know what time we'll be back. I'll text you later when I've got credit."

"Thanks Jack, look forward to seeing you mate."

"*Auf wiedersehen*, Dad."

The train station connected directly with the airport via monorail. Jack's new mission was to find out where New Street was and get there. He liked taking on missions; they were what he had joined the army for. Over an hour later, he was on the train to New Street, and looking at his watch, he noted that the time was 6.45pm. The journey to New Street was only 15 minutes, so he would be there by seven o'clock. What would he do if he couldn't find Aaron? Jack had topped up the credit on his phone with a debit card, which was so much easier to do in England, but Aaron's mobile must have been turned off because it rang once and then went to a recorded voicemail message.

Right, if I was Aaron where would I go? thought Jack as he arrived in the New Street concourse. Worrying whether he would find his little stick insect of a brother, he paced around, scanning the terrain like a soldier on a missing persons operation. It was possible that it could be like looking for a needle in a haystack as Aaron would not be the most obvious one in a crowd, in fact he would be the very least conspicuous. *Operation Stick Insect, search and rescue mission – Private Frey reporting for duty, Sir!'*

Jack's tall, muscular physique stood out amongst the crowds of travellers scurrying around like ants on a hot summer afternoon, trying to get to the right platforms. Stepping onto an escalator, he travelled to the upper floor and was amazed to see a small city of shops and cafes. He paused as he stepped from the escalator and moved over to one side to prevent a pile-up. *Where the hell am I going to start looking for Aaron?* he wondered as he felt himself getting annoyed. Scooting around the centre without entering a single shop, he suspected Aaron would not be enjoying a Saturday evening shopping spree during his unexpected visit. Satisfied that Aaron wasn't on the retail floor, Jack returned to the main station below. It was more likely that he would find Aaron cowering in some corner somewhere. Straining his eyes as they constantly darted around from person to person, desperately seeking the familiar figure of his little brother, he wondered if he should just stand in the middle of the largest part of the concourse and shout as loud as his sergeant did on parade duty. As he surveyed every area in view he saw a figure standing in a phone booth over the other side of the station.

Was it Aaron? Stepping toward the booth without taking his eyes off the male figure propped up inside, he accidentally bumped into passers-by, but Jack remained homed-in on his target.

"I've been looking everywhere for you," said Jack as he tapped the teenager on the back. *Operation Stick Insect, mission accomplished, Sir!* Aaron turned quickly with the earpiece still held to the side of his face. His eyes lit up in recognition as he spoke to the receiver.

"Jack's here now; tell Dad not to worry. Can you send him a message, Joe?" Aaron paused, listening to the phone while he stared at his soldier brother with the widest grin of teeth he could muster. "Yeah, see you later." Replacing the handset, he turned round and took a flying leap out of the booth to land on Jack's already turned back.

"I've been waiting for you for ages!" Aaron screeched as he flung his arms around his hero's shoulders. It's cool to hug your brother in public, just not your aunt, he thought, hugging Jack for what seemed like a long time. Aaron was relieved and very emotional to have been rescued, and also to see Jack after such a long time.

"You bloody idiot! How did you manage to get the wrong train?" Jack laughed as he hugged his little brother back, making sure not to crack any of the stick insect's ribs.

Deciding that they were both hungry, Jack and Aaron headed out of the station to find a local Indian restaurant. Aaron was starving; he hadn't eaten since his Aunt Josie's special fried breakfast with pine nuts, and he'd saved the little money he had left in case it was needed to make a phone call in a kiosk. The alarm on his mobile had indeed sounded at the correct time of three hours later, as he sat in the station waiting for a *Mission Impossible* army-style rescue, but the last heave of battery power required to sound the alarm had rendered it dead and useless.

A short walk from the station the duo found an Indian restaurant, thanks to the directions of three jaunty men who they passed. The town was lively, as the hour of 'nightlife' had begun and already the pubs were overflowing with groups of young people who were hoping for a good time. Jack and Aaron were fortunate enough to get a table for two by the window of the delicious-smelling restaurant. They ordered a large set meal for two, a beer and a Coke. Aaron was warm and happy; he felt safe now his brother had found him.

"As long as we're back by about ten, we'll be able to get the train home," said Jack confidently. Leaning back in the chair, he stretched his arms above his head, hoping his over-filled stomach would ache a little less. Two additional pints of beer had made him feel very weary, and along with his bloated tummy, he was now ready for a sleep on the train. Looking at his watch, he said, "Come on mate, hurry up, we've only got 15 minutes." Aaron shovelled down the last few mouthfuls and felt exactly the same as Jack, except he had not had any of that 'disgusting beer stuff'.

"Two tickets to Portsmouth please, one way," Jack called through the perforated hole in the glass screen.

"Next train leaves at eight minutes past ten, platform 1A. Four changes, arriving in Portsmouth at 6.22. That'll be 146 pounds please."

"Six twenty-two? What? In the morning?" said Jack as he stared in amazement at the man in the ticket box. "Have you got any direct trains?"

"No mate, last direct one was ten past nine. It's Easter you know."

"Great!" said Jack, as he turned to look at his brother standing behind him. Aaron just stood there with his hands in his pockets raising his eyebrows and shoulders in unison, looking pretty vacant. Reluctantly, Jack paid the fare, knowing they had a long night ahead of them and an eight-hour journey. The most annoying thing was the changing of trains, not just once, but four times.

"I'd better send Dad a text to let him know we won't be home till the morning!" said Jack as they sat down in the first train of the night. Aaron nodded sheepishly, worrying whether their long journey was entirely his fault...and it was.

Alex

The situation was worse than I initially thought, yet I was still not overly worried or scared. Should I be? I wondered as I lay in the lonely, cube-like room. It had been a tediously long day. I slept for brief moments, answered random questions from several doctors, had tests, then extra tests and yet more tests. There were regular observations and the inevitable commode moments, but always remembering to pull down my underwear first. Entertaining myself, I had spent the rest of my time watching the sun's rays trying to creep in through the opaque glass, casting patterned shadows across the walls and slowly moving around the room as the hours drifted by.

"Have you been abroad lately Alex?" asked Dr Theresa Pond from the doorway.

"No," I replied, knowing they didn't have a clue what was wrong with me. She smiled, and then left. She would be back soon enough with another random question. They had spent so much time and effort pursuing numerous ridiculous enquiries. I was aware that three doctors were outside the room sat at a desk, poring over medical records. I expected they had the medical dictionaries out too, trying to come up with a diagnosis. The trio had all been in to see me, one at a time initially, and then all three at once.

"Have you been scuba-diving at all in the last few months?" Dr Pond was peeping round the door again.

"No. Never," I replied. They were clutching at straws, trawling through every possibility in the book. It didn't look very professional. The doctor disappeared again, and seconds later the handsome, tanned and seemingly very caring senior male doctor came back in. I guessed he was senior to the other two because he didn't ask silly questions. He just came in and spoke about the serious bits.

"We have some concerns about your condition Alex," he said gently. "I'm going to be honest with you. We are worried that the paralysis will spread to your diaphragm and cause you to stop breathing."

My eyes widened in horror. Was I going to die?

"We have arranged a ventilator to be on standby." He looked genuinely troubled, which made me start to feel more uneasy. Maybe I wasn't indestructible after all. "There's a condition called Guillain–Barré syndrome that we are looking at in your case, but you don't quite tick all the boxes for symptoms." He sat down at the end of my bed, looking pensive. Hoping and praying that he was not going to examine my legs and feet (even if I was going to die), I pulled my body upwards and away. He was far too handsome to be gawking at my legs! However serious this was, I still had my dignity and didn't want to die of embarrassment. A constant practical joker, I never could take anything seriously, but actually this was starting to strip me of humour and my optimistic outlook on life.

"Your rapid state of paralysis could be linked to an aggressive form of GBS, which is why we have concerns about your breathing. We'll monitor your condition closely in case you start to struggle." Looking at me intently, he appeared to be expecting some sort of reaction, but I was void of any emotion and lay motionless, staring in his direction. "Alex, we are going to get you over to the specialist neurological unit for an MRI scan today. They may also decide that you need to have a lumbar puncture."

"Okay," I said, surprised by the urgency in his voice. "Can you contact my husband and let him know where I'm going?" I was trying to think what a lumbar puncture was – I'd heard of it before and worried about whether it would hurt. I don't like 'hurt' but if I was given the option, I would probably choose hurt over death.

"You'll be back tonight; we'll get you transported over there and back, but I'll make sure your husband knows."

I desperately wanted to, but did not dare ask what a lumbar puncture was. I didn't want to look dumb in front of this admirable man.

"Thank you." I sighed, feeling relieved that Grant would be told where I was going. I would prefer it if he came with me, just in case I had to have a lumbar puncture and it hurt. It sounded like something would get punctured in the lumbar region, wherever that was. It was almost five o'clock, and I expected Grant would be back soon to visit me. I had hoped he would've been here sooner, but maybe he hadn't got to sleep until late due to the phone calls he had to make and then sorting everyone out at home. No, that wasn't Grant's forte; I was the one who always sorted everything out in the Frey household, if only I was there. In hindsight, I decided that he had more than likely spent most of the day in front of the TV, thumbing through sport channels or washing his beloved car.

"Okay Alex," said the doctor, patting my lower legs which were hiding in disgrace under the waffle blanket. "Do you have any questions?"

Umm, what's a lumbar puncture? "No, nothing," I replied, as he smiled, nodded his head gently in acknowledgement and left the room.

Slightly stunned by the doctor's demonstration of genuine concern, I realised that I obviously was not going to get out of the hospital over the weekend. Grant would have to brush up on his efficiency talents and take on a new role as businessman, househusband, agony uncle, cleaner, mediator, meal provider, call centre operator (where Mum was concerned), timekeeper, calendar organiser, gardener, good neighbour, community spirit coordinator and an active curator of my gnome sanctuary. Oh, and then he would also have to do some shopping at the same time as taking mobile calls from Mum, and try to remember what he needed because he had forgotten to take a list. The fact of the matter was that I had always done everything for everyone in our family, looking after all the household chores, arrangements and situations to the extent that everyone relied heavily upon me to be there and know what was what, all of the time. My overly efficient 'I am the mother of all things' attitude caused Grant to get uptight at times. He said I did too much for everyone else and didn't help the kids to gain any kind of responsibility or independence. I knew deep down that he was right but it was just the way I was – I enjoyed taking care of my family and controlling a smoothly-running, happy household.

Some 40 minutes later Grant walked into the room with Emma trailing behind him. My face lit up like a Chinese lantern, a burning sensation pricking my eyes – *Don't cry*, I told myself, *not in front of Emma*.

"All right, how are you feeling?" Grant bent down to kiss me. "They told me you're going to the neuro unit." He looked very worried. Emma shuffled towards the bed with her fingers fumbling in her mouth.

"Are you gonna die Mum?" Moving around the side of Grant, she leant over to kiss my cheek.

"Em! You don't say that when you come to a hospital for Christ's sake!" Grant sounded overly angry.

"It's all right Grant, she's just curious." I tried to calm him. "No I'm not Em. Glad you could come honey. Are you all right?"

A pouting lip and frown suggested that Emma was not all right, as she wore the typical 'totally misunderstood teenager' look on her young face. Trudging round to the other side of the bed, she plonked herself down on a chair and let out a loud 'I want attention' huff. Sitting down on the sofa chair where he had spent most of the previous night, Grant sighed as I looked to him questioningly. Sensing the dark grey cloud looming above them both, growing in intensity and predicting a thunderstorm, I puzzled the forecast as Grant twisted the corner of his mouth and shook his head nonchalantly.

"Right, what's the matter?" I searched from one face to another, trying to pick up some clues. Emma looked down at her shoes and Grant raised his eyebrows and stared at the ceiling. "Grant, tell me what's wrong please!"

"I'll tell you later, it doesn't matter now."

"Yes it bloody well does. Tell me! Come on, I want to know now!"

"Go on then, Emma." Grant looked towards her as she continued to sit with her head hung low, fumbling with the carrier bag she had brought along with her. I hoped it contained my toiletries and underwear. Glancing both ways, from Emma and then back to Grant, I felt like a spectator at Wimbledon.

"I want to know what is wrong Grant. Tell me." My voice had risen slightly, but not enough to attract any attention from outside of the room.

"I got a letter from the school today, about Emma."

"What did it say? What's the matter?" I turned to Emma but she had not lifted her head and remained still and quiet.

"She's been vandalising school property Alex. We've got a bill for 70 pounds which has to be paid by the end of the month otherwise they will refer it to the police for prosecution."

"You're joking! How do they know it's Emma? Are you serious?" The display of emotion was the most I had expressed in my whole hospital stay, which was less than 24 hours but felt like 24 days.

"They've got CCTV footage of her doing it. She kicked in a locker door," said Grant as he stared at Emma with fiery eyes. My mouth fell open as I watched him in horror – no wonder she was sat in the corner with her head held low like a praying nun.

"Emma, what have you done? Why?" I pleaded for a reasonable answer but she said nothing as she twiddled the carrier bag handles in her fingers. She had teenage attitude written all over her face.

"She's grounded for a month and she'll be doing extra jobs around the house until she's paid the fine," said Grant, looking to me for backup.

"Absolutely!" I agreed. "I can't believe you have done something like this Em, it's not like you."

Emma continued to tie the handles in knots, slowly strangling the carrier bag without looking up.

"Is there anything else?" I sensed there was more that Grant was not telling me.

"No, only that Aaron got lost on his way home." Grant waited for the familiar '*I told you so*' but it never came. I smirked and asked, "Oh dear, did he miss his stop?"

"You could say that!" Grant huffed. "He got the wrong train completely. He's in Birmingham! Jack's trying to find him."

Pulling myself up in the bed as best I could under the circumstances, I thought, *I bloody knew it. I said he would get lost*. However, I decided that Grant did not need to hear this.

"Oh God, how is Jack going to find him?" I needed to get out of this damned hospital, but how could I? It wasn't like I just had a bit of flu and would get over it. I felt totally useless lying in bed and it frustrated me, although the feeling did not last too long as I had no energy to hold onto any thoughts of escape. The bus that I felt had hit me earlier had morphed into a high-speed train as the day had progressed.

"Don't worry babe, Jack will find him, it's all under control." Grant knew that I would be pulling my hair out with worry, even if it wasn't visible. I resigned myself to the fact that I had to let Grant get on with things. I couldn't burden myself by worrying about what was going on at home. I needed to concentrate on getting better...somehow.

"Here you are," said Emma sulkily as she passed the strangled carrier bag to me.

"Thank you hun. Why did you do that at school, Em? Who was with you when you did it?"

"There were three of us, Kasey, Morgan and me. They did it as well." Emma stated the last sentence as if it would make things seem better. If her friends had done it as well then it wasn't so bad.

"For Christ's sake Emma, you don't copy others just so you can fit into the crowd. I know what you've done." She continued to look down as I spoke. "You've tried to look clever in front of them haven't you? I know what you're like!" She was just like me actually, when I was at school. I would have done anything to gain respect and acceptance from my peers. "I do hope we will never hear of anything like this again Emma. I agree with your dad that you will pay for this yourself." There, I had said my bit. As far as I was concerned, hopefully it would be a lesson learned. The punishment fitted the crime well and Emma would have to work hard at home to compensate our loss.

Opening the carrier bag, I took my handbag from it, leaving the other items inside. Looking into the dark bottomless pit I could see the fluorescent pink case which held my mobile phone peeping up from the depths. Good, at least I could keep in contact with everyone now I had my phone. Reaching over, I placed both bags in the cabinet by the side of Emma. I would change my underwear later, having worn the same pair for 24 hours, I felt horrible, but it could wait a little longer. "Is my toothbrush in there Em?"

"Yeah," she huffed.

"Jump in, there's a seat over there mate." The paramedic pointed to a small fold-up chair in the ambulance. He was a jolly, robust man and cheerfully referred to the other paramedic as 'his missus'. I was placed alongside Grant on a stretcher, then the medic pulled two straps across my torso and legs to hold me down like a trussed-up chicken ready for the oven. Emma was going to sit in the front with the woman, who was just as good-humoured as 'her old man', as she called him. I assumed they were a couple or even married by the way they interacted with each other.

"Last one today, then we've got four days off, haven't we Kate?" 'The old man' shouted through to the front of the vehicle.

"Yeah, can't wait!" Kate replied from the driver's seat where she was helping Emma to put on a fluorescent paramedic's jacket. Curiously, I wondered whether Emma was allowed to ride in the front of an ambulance, or was the jacket a disguise to hide the unqualified teenage medical assistant? Grant held onto my hand as he sat poised opposite me and grinned from ear to ear like a little boy with a brand new bicycle. Sensing his excitement, I just about managed to smile back at him to convey my recognition of his pending world-class, high-speed adventure. Unfortunately my enthusiasm lacked any kind of energy but Grant was already on another level of consciousness by now and didn't notice.

"We doing blues all the way Kate?" the man shouted from his seated position at the end of my stretcher.

"Righty-ho!" she replied jovially.

As the ambulance pulled away from the hospital I watched the siren through the roof, flashing a blue light overhead. Looking at me, Grant beamed again. "I've never been in an ambulance on blues!" He was so excited and the tone in his voice sounded very childish. I stared at him despondently. I couldn't have cared less that I was in a 'blues' ambulance racing towards another hospital, 20 miles away.

Emma and 'the missus' sat in the front listening to music blaring from the CD player as we headed out onto the main road and the siren started to sound. The vehicle picked up speed, weaving through the traffic that had pulled over to the curb, allowing passage for our apparent emergency. Peering through the glass partition to the front windscreen, Grant reached ecstatic euphoria as he watched the ambulance cut through red traffic lights with ease. Lying on the stretcher I felt relieved that I had been strapped down. Tossing from side to side, I bumped and banged against the sidebars of the stretcher as the ambulance veered from left to right like a snake winding through grass. I could hear Emma and 'the missus' singing at the tops of their voices to an Ed Sheeran song in the front cab, like they had known each other for years and were having a day out. Grant held on tightly to the sidebars and spoke ardently to the paramedic at my feet about football teams and ambulances.

"Bet you love this job, mate!" he said to 'the old man'.

"Yeah, it's a legalised form of joyriding!" The man laughed as we seemed to go faster and faster. Everyone appeared to be enjoying heightened, high-speed entertainment while I continued to feel like a tossed salad.

Wheeling me into the neurological unit, 'the missus' and 'the old man' held one end of the stretcher each while they continuously babbled away about their four-day break and what they were going to do, which seemed to be practically nothing. Silently, Grant and Emma trailed behind in a daze, carrying my bags and wearing ridiculous looking G-force smiles on their faces. After several minutes a nurse greeted us and showed us the way to my new bed. The zany paramedic couple expertly hoisted me onto the bed with ease and removed the stretcher from underneath my limp and battered body.

"Right, all the best to you," the uniformed man said as he looked at me pityingly.

"Yeah, hope it goes okay," said Kate, 'the missus'. She was itching to go and start enjoying her short break.

"Thank you Kate," said Emma shyly through her G-force smile.

"You're welcome love." Kate looked towards 'the old man'. "I've got a new karaoke partner here, Jim."

"You can have her!" laughed Grant, shaking Jim's hand. Emma looked down at the floor and tried to crack a vicious scowl into her cemented smile as Grant put his arm around her shoulder in repentance.

"Get off," mumbled Emma, scooting out from under her dad's arm, attempting to retain a moody teenager appearance but to no avail.

"Thank you," I managed to say, although I couldn't be bothered to smile and didn't have a semi-permanent etched grin, caused by the high velocity ambulance ride, like Grant and Emma did. I was losing energy and interest in everything rapidly. I had to try and pull myself together somehow, even if it was only mentally, as I couldn't control my physical attributes. This unknown illness had taken hold like an all-encompassing cloak of depression.

The paramedics left; they had now finished work and looked forward to enjoying some lazy days in the sun. Lying motionless, I watched Grant and Emma pull two chairs around to the side of the bed and plonk themselves down wearily. The smiles on their faces were imprinted and semi-permanent, like a clown's oversized painted mouth. Having just experienced the ride of their lives, they were now contented, placid and slightly pathetic.

Two of the top neurosurgeons spent almost an hour with me while Grant and Emma went to the cafe to revive themselves after their rocket-riding daredevil adventure. The 'top docs' asked lots of questions, poked and prodded, twisted and turned my body, tested this and tested that and came to a conclusion. The conclusion was that they didn't know what was wrong with me. They had managed to rule out certain illnesses and diseases and the aggressive GBS possibility, but they were scratching their heads like nit-infested children.

"We want to keep you here tonight Alex, and run more tests."

I couldn't exactly say, 'No, take me back', but I knew this would cause a problem for Grant and Emma as the car was parked back at the other hospital 20 miles away. I didn't think for one minute that they would be able to call an ambulance, like a private taxi service, to take them back, although they probably would have liked to.

Moving me onto another ward, the porter placed my bed at the far end of the room next to a large window. It was dark outside and I couldn't see if I had a nice view as the curtains were closed, leaving just a small gap in the middle, but at least I could see that the glass was clear. I'd have to wait until the morning to see the world outside and hopefully the view would make me feel a little more human again. It was getting late and I knew Grant and Emma would have to find a way to get home somehow. Their return journey would certainly not live up to their arrival, that was for sure. We had not expected that I would have to stay here overnight.

"How are you going to get back, Grant?" I said as they returned from the café a second time, and no doubt, another 'breath of fresh air for Grant.' The G-force smiles had dissipated from their faces at long last, leaving weary, glazed eyes and hot chocolate moustaches.

"I've just called Dave, he's going to come and pick us up in an hour and take us back." Our friends Dave and Julie could always be counted on in an emergency. We would do the same for them too; we just hadn't ever had the opportunity to help them out as they were blessed with good fortune in every conceivable way, unlike us.

"Oh good, were they surprised?"

"No, I texted Dave earlier today and told them you was in hospital, they said they hope you get well soon."

It suddenly dawned on me that I hadn't thought of anyone else and whether anybody knew about my predicament.

"Do Mum and Dad know?"

Grant raised his eyebrows and opened his mouth in surprise.

"You haven't told them, have you?" I questioned as he smiled warmly.

"Yes I have. Your mum has been on the phone all bloody day, I've hardly had any sleep!" he said, holding my hand in his.

"Oh dear, has she?"

"Umm," he replied. "Your dad is worrying too that you won't be able to make it on Tuesday."

"Oh no, I forgot about that. You'll go though, won't you?" I looked at him with a glint in my eye and squeezed his hand. Tuesday was a big day for my dad; he had spent four years of toil to get to this exclusive event and somehow Grant and I had got roped into the day's schedule along with Mum.

"Suppose I'll bloody have to as I've booked the day off!" Grant sounded a bit stressed. I decided to change the subject.

"Have you told Zoe and Carol?" I asked urgently. It had just occurred to me that there was a possibility I would not make it into work on Monday. It was more than a possibility – it was almost a certainty! I couldn't imagine turning up for work in a motorised wheelchair; I wasn't ready for that yet. That would really be serious stuff if I was chair-bound. Deep down,

I still thought this would all go away or that I'd wake up and find it had all been a bad dream.

"Yeah, I sent them both the same message, and then Zoe called me. Don't worry; everything is sorted out for Monday. They're not expecting you in, and they'll all be covering your shifts between them."

"Oh good, it's only just occurred to me about the shop Grant. Are you sure they don't mind?"

"Babe, stop worrying, it's all sorted. They're all concerned about you. Zoe said you must make sure you get better before you go back."

I knew they would be concerned – they were my employees, but also my friends. Carol had worked for me from the very beginning, giving almost 13 years of dedicated service. I had employed a number of staff over the years, some good and some bad, but I praised Carol for her loyalty and genuine conscientious dedication to my shop. She had a brilliant rapport with the customers and they adored her sense of humour. When I offered her the position of assistant manager some six years ago, in the year of her 50th birthday, she had turned it down, preferring to remain as just a shop assistant. She'd stated that she was really happy staying as she was and didn't want to take any more responsibility. Her honesty was admirable. I'd been looking for someone to take some of the burden of running the shop from me when Zoe came along. She was young, vibrant and clever. After two very successful years with her on board, I offered her the position, which she gladly accepted.

Now, taking comfort from the knowledge that the shop would be in good hands, I accepted that I was unable to keep an overview of things from hospital. The two weekend staff would probably get some overtime too if I was going to be 'out of the loop' for any period of time. Melvin and Ruby helped to run the convenience store at the weekends. They had originally been customers until they jointly took early retirement and subsequently decided they wanted a little extra sparkle in their lives. At first they had helped out at a moment's notice whenever I needed them, but as time went by I realised that I depended on them more often, and so a year after their retirement, I offered them both some weekend work which they gladly accepted. Living just across the road, it couldn't have been more convenient for them. Melvin and Ruby loved the shop, knew nearly all the local customers and enjoyed working weekends. They liked to keep their weekdays free to enjoy their pastimes and hobbies; they loved dog walking and shopping sprees. Weekdays were their best days, when there were less people around and fewer kids to get in their way. This was when they liked to spend long days browsing the charity shops and antique alleys.

Admitting that my shop was in very good hands, I had to try and forget about it (at least until I was out of the hospital) and stop worrying about everything, as I always did. Between Grant and Zoe, any problems would be dealt with. Unfortunately I was not as indispensable as I would like to think I was – would this be the case at home too? After a lengthy discussion with Grant about my condition and the possible scenarios and expectations of diagnosis, we breathed simultaneous sighs and resigned ourselves to the morbid reality of the hopeless situation as it currently stood. Always reserving crosswords for difficult or uncomfortable conditions, Grant opened the outdated newspaper he had collected earlier from the cafe and requested a pen from my constant source of junk.

"Em, can you pass my bag over please?" I asked, pointing to the Next handbag which boasted an excessive amount of pockets and secret hiding places. I liked bags that had so many pockets and pouches in them that it was a complete mystery as to what they could all be used for, however I always did find a little something to put in each compartment, even if it was just an old broken pencil or an empty lip balm covered in fluff. Emma was busy on her phone, which was usually attached to her right hand, and if it wasn't in her hand it was hooked up in the side of her bra. Managing to grab my bag without looking, she was able to send a text message at the same time as she passed it over to me. Luckily my belongings had been brought along with us, so I could soon get changed and ask a nurse to take me to the bathroom so I could wash and clean my teeth. Dignity desperately still held strong and I did not want to rely on Grant to help out with all my personal hygiene issues, at least not until it was an absolute requirement. Faith and prayers might help to avoid that type of needy situation arising. I groped around in the endless bottom of my handbag and found a pen for Grant, and my phone-dead as a dead thing!

"Grant, can you take this home and charge it, or bring my charger here please?" I said, waving the phone under his nose.

Looking up from his crossword he replied, "I'll take it back with me." Clasping the phone, he slid it into his jeans pocket, and at the same time Grant's phone vibrated in his other pocket. It was Dave.

After lots of hugs, kisses and goodbyes, Emma and Grant left and said they would come back tomorrow. Watching them walk out of the ward I felt sadness engulf me; I wanted to go with them. Picking up my emotions, I injected some fake high spirits into them – I knew it was just a matter of time before I went home. It was getting very late and the ward lights had been switched off, giving way to dimmer night-lights. The ward housed just four beds, each occupied by sleeping patients, apart from mine. Working on a computer under the beam of a desk lamp, a nurse sat at a desk at the front of the ward. Deciding it would be best to wait till the morning to wash, change and clean my teeth, I hoped no one else would come and see me to do more tests. I could then rest easy in my dirty underwear, as I had no inclination to change right now. It had been a very long and eventful day. Reaching for the carrier bag that Emma had lovingly packed for me, I proceeded to have a quick look through the comforts from home. To my surprise and horror, the bag contained:

One pair of old, holey thong knickers which had half of the lace trim hanging off. (I never wore them anymore; my thong days were well and truly over and they didn't even fit!)

One toothbrush.

No toothpaste.

An empty pot of anti-wrinkle night cream which never did what it said on the box.

A nail file. (Did she think I was in prison and needed to escape the iron bars?)

The bathroom cleaning cloth, still covered in Flash and posing as a flannel. The bathroom cleaning cloth didn't even look remotely like our soft and fluffy turquoise flannels.

Grant's old, empty pack of Curanail ointment. (My toes weren't that bad!)

The Joy of Sex handbook. I blushed. Emma must have found that at the bottom of my knicker drawer along with the tattered thong! Why she had put it in the bag, I had no idea, or was she being facetious?

A pack of slim panty-liners, which were completely useless with a thong anyway, and a dried-out, crusty, travel-size bar of Nivea soap which had split in two. I remembered seeing it in the bathroom cabinet and it had been there for about 12 years, left over from one of our holidays. At least she had made the effort, bless her, even if she had got it all completely wrong, yet again.

Grant

"Cheers mate, I owe you one."

"No you don't Grant, anything we can do to help, let us know." said Dave, remaining seated in his car. Grant and Emma jumped out and waved goodbye as Dave turned around outside the car park and drove away.

"You hungry?" asked Grant.

"Yeah, suppose." Emma spoke quietly, grumpiness towards her dad still being foremost on her agenda, as they walked to the parking meter. Choosing to ignore Emma's little protest Grant approached the pay shelter, dreading what the greedy ticket machine would foretell tonight. Cautiously, he fed his ticket into the slot. It was almost midnight; perhaps it would turn into a sabre-toothed, money-munching, monstrous transformer, thought Grant as he waited anxiously. Seven pounds and twenty pence. Not as bad as last night, he thought, taking his credit card from his pocket and feeding the hungry, square beast.

"Get two plates out, Em," said Grant, hastily opening the wrapped chip shop goodies. The smell of vinegar wafted up his nostrils and made his mouth water like a leaky tap. Hunger pangs abounded as the aromas teased Grant and Emma with chicken burgers and salty chips. Hurriedly seating himself in the dining room, Grant noticed a carrier bag that had been left on the table. Peering inside, while cramming a handful of chips into his salivating mouth, he saw two large bunches of grapes and four magazines. *Dot!* he thought. *Why did she bloody well ring to ask, if she was just going to buy them anyway?*

Alex's parents had their own set of keys to the house, a token gesture reciprocated many years ago after Dot and Charlie had asked Grant and Alex to check their home while they were in Canada for three weeks. Big mistake. Making a point of getting two keys cut, one for Alex and one for Grant, Dot had adorned them with countless jangly, sparkling key rings (to ensure they would be heard if they fell on the floor, or so they could be found easier, should they get lost). Dot had no qualms about using her door key to enter Grant's house, particularly if she had phoned and no one was home. Having to deal with things straight away, Dot couldn't tolerate waiting for people to arrive home. She often bought gifts for the family and her impatient streak meant that she had to bestow them to the lucky recipients – yesterday. On many occasions, the children had found their birthday presents left in the house six to eight weeks prior to the actual day. This often caused storage problems for Alex as her parents had no shortcomings when it came to presents for birthdays or Christmas.

The Freys dreaded the festive season each year. Fearing absence from home and unable to protect their living room from resembling the elves' toy-assembly production line – even now, the kids still got toys! Throughout December their home gradually filled with beautifully wrapped boxes, ribbons galore and metallic bows stuck to the sides of concealed objects of every conceivable shape and size. Twenty-three Pinewood Avenue resembled Santa's grotto even before the glitzy decorations had taken up temporary residence.

"They're men's toys!" Dot would profess. "Boys to men, they never grow up you know. And us ladies always like to own a collection of cuddly, cute teddy bears, don't we?" (Do we?) Unaware that the local Sunday morning car boot sale had been generously supplied by Alex and Grant with unwanted toys and homeless bears for the last decade, Dot continued her lavish gift regime regardless. And of course, now it was Easter once again. That cringeworthy time of the year when they all still received a chocolate egg each and a pack of six Creme Eggs. Also, Grant and the boys got novelty socks bearing a yellow Easter chick print, or worse still, bunny socks, and Alex and Emma got fluffy chick cuddly toys or rabbits with long floppy ears. Alex tried every year to dissuade her mum from continuing the lavish gifting, but to no avail.

Seated at the opposite end of the dining room, Emma maintained her 'sulky expression' into a glass of squash before proceeding to devour her meal. Hurtling down the stairs, three at a time, Joe reached the dining room door.

"I see your grandma has been round, then?" questioned Grant rhetorically, as Joe entered the room sniffing the salty air.

"Yeah, I didn't see her though, she must have come in when I was out," he replied, ogling the chips. "Ah, give me a chip Dad!"

"Sorry mate, didn't think to phone you and ask if you wanted any. Here, take some."

"No it's fine, only joking, I had a McD's when we left the bowling alley. It took us an hour to get home though!"

Pulling out a chair, Joe sat down at the table and watched Emma grumpily stuffing the whole chicken burger in her mouth as far back as her tonsils would allow.

"Why?" asked Grant as he too noticed that Emma was looking quite undignified, with half a quarter-pound chicken burger protruding from her lips. "Em, can you eat that a little more civilised please?" barked Grant. Withdrawing the oversized burger from her mouth, she sarcastically took a small nibble from the edge, barely removing a crumb from the sesame seed bap. It was apparent that she was still reminiscing about the letter and her punishment.

"We walked back from bowling through the field." Joe sounded concerned. "There were cows in it; they'd been left out for some reason. They aren't normally out at that time of night." His voice started to race. "Dad, the cows ganged up on us and wouldn't let us get through the gate!"

Almost choking on a chip, Grant let a roar of laughter fill the room as he pictured a picket line of cartoon cows holding onto the gate with their hooves, mooing, "You're not coming through here!"

"What do you mean, they ganged up on you?" he managed to squeak between chips and chortling.

"They did! We were scared. Kyle's got it on video. The cows saw us and moved closer together, then they stood in a line staring; they had evil in their eyes!"

Almost crying onto his plate, Grant continued to shake his head and roar. "Bloody hell Joe, you idiot!" he managed to say between wheezy breaths.

"I'm not an idiot! You don't know what it was like. They started heading straight towards us. They were going to charge at us and kill us! We didn't know where to run. They had us trapped in a corner!" There was panic in Joe's voice and his brown eyes searched desperately for acknowledgement in Grant's contorted face. "Kyle lost his shoe in a load of mud and I had to go back and get it because no one else would. And the cows kept coming closer! There were about eight of them stood in a row, they were definitely ganging up on us. They were scraping their hooves on the ground like they were going to charge!" Inhaling a deep breath, Joe continued. "You don't know what it was like – those cows are psycho cows!"

"Joe, calm down," Grant managed to blurt. "Have you ever heard of anyone being mauled to death by a killer cow on the news?"

"It wasn't just one though Dad, they were definitely going to get us, I could tell they felt safe in a pack!

That's why they all stood close together in a line. They knew what they were doing."

Grant almost fell off his chair, while Emma hid behind her glass of orange squash and tried desperately not to laugh – it would not fit well with her stroppy image.

"You don't know what it was like!" Joe said angrily. "We've got it all on film – they stared us out with big bulbous eyes; I could see them clearly even in the dark!"

"Did they have red dots lit up in their eyes like the Terminator?" asked Grant, trying to compose himself as best he could.

"You're just taking the mickey, aren't you Dad?" scowled Joe, seated at the table with his arms folded and an air of resentment about him.

"Joe, trust me son, there are no callous, murdering gangs of cows that I know of. Or maybe they are a new breed, called something like the Hereford Homicidal Heifers!" Grant only just managed to get the words out before he spluttered into another guffaw and Emma played her part by choking as she swallowed a mouthful of chips.

"Well you didn't see the look in their eyes; you're not a cow expert," Joe replied angrily as he got up from the table. Stomping up the stairs to his room, he slammed the door loudly. The atmosphere in the dining room changed to a serious one just for a second, and then Grant and Emma looked at each other across the table and burst into shrieking belly laughs.

Guilt wore heavily on Grant. He knew he should try and talk to Joe; to explain that cows really wouldn't have hurt him. Trying to think of an explanation as to why they had watched the boys like they did, he concluded that they may have been expecting some food. *And don't cows just follow people anyway?* he wondered. Deciding to talk to Joe in the morning, Grant knew he would have to hold his composure, because Joe felt that he was being laughed at...which he was! Eventually Joe would see the funny side of it and be able to share it with the rest of the family, Grant hoped, giggling again. Alex would have loved this if she'd been here.

"Goodnight." Pecking Grant on the cheek, Emma went up to bed feeling bloated like a puffer fish after her large meal. It was almost 1.30, and dawn would soon be peeping in through the window at this rate, thought Grant as he sat gazing blankly at the TV. Knackered and aching, he couldn't even be bothered to climb the stairs, and he didn't really want to anyway as Alex wasn't there. Hauling himself up out of the cosy chair he proceeded to lock the doors and turn all the downstairs lights off, as thoughts of Alex pricked his mind.

Smiling to himself, he began to reminisce about the night he'd met her, over a quarter of a century ago. He'd been struck by her beauty, her alluringly sweet smile and her daringly provocative style of dance in the heaving nightclub. When Alex realised she had an admirer watching from the edge of the dance floor she began to tease him with the half-empty bottle of cider she held in her hand, gently pushing it in and out of her mouth, like she was sucking a lollipop. Grant hadn't been able to take his eyes off her, but nervously plucked up the courage to ask if she would like a drink when she left the dance floor. Thankfully, she accepted, much to the annoyance of her two friends who had already decided that they wanted to go to a different part of the club. Alex told her friends to go without her as she wanted to stay and chat to him.

By the end of the evening, Alex had become very drunk, while spending her time with Grant, talking and occasionally dancing. After her two friends had gone off somewhere else, Alex had to make her own way home and proceeded to join a taxi queue that looked like it would be hours long, as hundreds of people poured out of the club.

"I could give you a lift home, my car is over there in the car park. My mate's here somewhere; I've just got to wait for him," said Grant shyly, realising his offer was turning into a chat-up line for a date.

"Bet you haven't got a car really. How can you drive when you've been drinking?" slurred Alex, swiftly putting her arm through his to steady her uncoordinated legs.

"I haven't been drinking. I don't drink."

"Oh, okay. Let's go," she'd giggled, dragging him in the direction of the car park. Approaching the car with a wobble, Alex laughed. "This isn't your car!"

"Yes it is," he said, pulling a bunch of keys from his pocket. "You can get in if you want to, while I wait here for my mate, Matt."

Wearily, Alex climbed in the back seat and looked around the neat interior of the Ford Capri. *Hmm, bet it belongs to his dad*, she'd thought to herself, and then told Grant later on in their relationship.

Smiling again, he switched another light off and snorted a short laugh as he remembered her words of warning that first night they met. Foolishly, Alex had come to find herself sat in the back of a car with two beefy young men in the front, who she hardly knew, in the early hours of the morning.

As Grant set off on the journey to her house to drop her off, she said, "I can fight you know, so don't try anything funny 'cos I'm tougher than I look."

The two men laughed at the endearing, vulnerable woman, saturated with alcohol, who could have potentially made a very big mistake when it came to her safety. Luckily for Alex, Grant thought he'd fallen in love with her at first sight and therefore she would be safe for as long as she wanted to be. That was the start of what turned out to be a beautifully romantic relationship which went from strength to strength as the months and years went by, culminating in a lifelong, loving pairing. Most importantly, they became best friends.

Returning to the lounge, Grant flipped the handle of the reclining chair and pressed the remote control until he found an old western film. The 1950s movie was perfect material for his eyelids to view as he started to doze in the dim and flickering light of the television.

What the hell was that? The awakening thought injected shock into Grant's body and he bolted into startled consciousness. A loud bang from the back garden roused him like the firing of a starting pistol. Pulling himself up, he crept through to the dining room as his pupils adjusted to the darkness. Peering out of the patio doors, Grant was infected with an adrenaline rush as a dark figure of a man moved stealthily through the garden. Immediately Grant stepped back behind the curtain, his heart leaping to his throat and a cold sweat leaking through the pores of his forehead. Edging backwards into the darkness of the kitchen, Grant slowly opened the drawer and pulled out a carving knife. Inching back to the patio door, his heart pounding heavily in his chest, he cautiously turned the key in the lock – *click!* The startled hooded intruder turned towards the patio, caught site of Grant's fearful, glaring eyes, and shouted an incoherent word across the garden as he darted to the fence and scrambled over. Grant halted in terror on the patio with the glinting, razor-sharp knife held menacingly in his fisted grasp. Fear and anger surged through his veins as his body began to tremble. To his left, another loud bang resonated along the fence panels from the side garden. This time Grant was sure he knew where the sound was coming from. Dashing around the side of the house, he caught sight of a second hooded figure leaping from the shed roof down on to the wheelie bin on the other side of the wall. The trespasser turned his head back towards

90

Grant and their eyes met momentarily before he scurried away silently.

Launching himself through the side garden to the six-foot gate, Grant scaled the wrought iron bars and pulled himself up and over the top, gripping the knife in his teeth like an action hero. Jumping down into the drive, he caught hold of the blade and sped out to the middle of the road. The two figures were fleeing from the scene a hundred yards up Pinewood Avenue as Grant stood motionless, catching his rapid breath. The knife held firmly by his side, thoughts racing through his head, Grant's conscience battled over whether he should pursue them. Suddenly aware of his menacing appearance, standing in the middle of the road like a psychotic maniac brandishing a threateningly large knife, Grant came to his senses and returned to the driveway. Blood charged through his veins like an electrical current as his adrenal glands continued to seep a fight, flight or freeze chemical concoction. Historically, Grant's past experiences and failings had always been due to the fight response kicking in, culminating in many unnecessary and foolish situations.

Realising that he was locked out of his own home, Grant climbed back over the padlocked side gate, praying that no one would see him or suspect him of being an intruder, brandishing a carving knife. Staggering into the back garden, he noticed that Joe's bike wasn't in its usual place. *Not another one, for God's sake!* Entering the house, he closed the patio door and paced up and down the dining room, powered by the adrenalin and pent-up fury. The thought that someone had dared enter his private grounds consumed him as he continued to tremble uncontrollably. Pausing on the laminate flooring, Grant had a burning question: where was Joe's bike? He had not seen the two men running off with it, yet the bike was gone.

Gently at first, Grant shook Joe's shoulder in an attempt to wake him, and then jerked him more vigorously.

"Joe, wake up mate. Joe!"

Stirring and turning to look at his dad with half-closed eyes, Joe woke up, somewhat puzzled. "What?"

"Where's your bike?" Grant whispered.

"In the garden."

"No it's not mate, I've just seen two fellas in the garden. I chased them off. Your bike's gone. I'm going to call the cops."

"What?" Joe called as Grant tiptoed back out of the room and down the stairs. Heaving himself out of bed, Joe groped around clumsily in the semi-darkness and got dressed. By the time he reached the lounge, Grant was already on the phone to the police.

"I nearly caught them, can't you send someone out now? I know they took it." Grant paused. "Look, this is the third time this has happened to my boy... No, I don't want a bloody crime number. I want you to do something about it!" His temper was rising. "Well if you're not going to do anything about it, I'll go and find them myself!" He slammed the phone down onto its base so hard that the table lamp wobbled before Grant caught it.

"Come on Joe, we'll go and find them. I saw one of them clearly, I would recognise him again. They've got your bike, I know it! I'm not sitting back and waiting for the cops to do nothing about it."

Sneaking into Emma's room, Grant could see she was fast asleep. He pulled her door to and crept down the stairs, leaving a scribbled note on the kitchen top for her in case she got up and wondered where everyone had gone. Grant and Joe left the house, the front door locked safely; then hopped into the car and pulled out of the drive at speed in the dead of night.

Trawling the streets in a two-mile radius again and again, Grant knew he would recognise them if he saw them again; he was sure of it. At 2.45 in the morning there was no traffic and no pedestrians anywhere to be seen, not even any drunken late-night clubbers trying to remember their way home. The only vehicle they had seen was a police car passing by. The two police officers closely examined Grant's car and the passengers within as they slowly slipped past.

"I'm sorry about laughing at you earlier Joe." Grant's apology was now sincere after the ridicule earlier in the evening.

"That's okay. Suppose it was funny, but I was scared at the time."

"Yeah I know mate, but seriously, they wouldn't have hurt you." He leant over and ruffled Joe's hair as they continued the rest of their circular journey in contemplative silence.

Twenty minutes later, Grant said they should give up the pursuit and return home. On the way, they encountered the same two officers trawling the streets in their panda car. Grant was flagged to a halt as they approached and pulled up alongside him.

"Are you lost?" asked the round-faced woman.

"Erm, no. We're just looking for someone," Grant replied guiltily.

"Who are you looking for at this time of night?" The policewoman looked puzzled.

"I caught two men in my garden and they've nicked his bike." Grant pointed towards Joe in the front passenger seat, who looked bleary-eyed. "We were looking for them to get his bike back." Realising that he was being far too truthful, Grant then started to worry that he could be getting himself into trouble.

"What's your name, Sir?"

"Grant Frey." Damn, was he in trouble?

"I think you need to head home, Mr Frey. We will survey the area, don't you worry. Looks like you should be getting that young man home to bed at this late hour. Call the station and report the bike stolen."

"Yes, I will, thank you. We were just on our way home anyway," replied Grant hastily as he pushed the gearstick into first and slowly started to pull away. The two cars parted and went their separate ways. "Phew! That was close mate, wasn't it?"

Joe didn't reply, assuming it was a rhetorical question as he smiled through a yawn.

Exhausted and miserable, Joe went straight back to bed upon their return from an unsuccessful road trip. Back in the comfort of his armchair, Grant slurped some calming sweet tea and thought just for a moment that he sounded like a teenager eating breakfast. Retracing his steps and the events of the last 12 hours, Grant mused over just what a night it had been. One minute he was travelling at high speed in an ambulance and then in the same night he was climbing his gate with a weapon gripped in his teeth like an Indian fruit picker climbing a coconut tree. What would he have done if he'd caught one of the men? Not even wanting to contemplate that, he looked at the clock and wondered just how much sleep he'd really had in the last two days, as the time approached 3.25. Finishing his tea, Grant turned off the TV and curled up on the sofa. His mind darted around, retracing his heroic steps frame by frame. Had he been brave or stupid? The pent-up anger began to rise again as he felt both pity at yet another of Joe's bikes going missing, and fury at the invasion of his privacy – his castle. As sleep prevailed, Grant's turmoil subsided and gave in to unconsciousness.

Was someone knocking at the front door? Opening his eyes, Grant caught sight of a stream of light beaming through the fabric of the curtains. Was he dreaming? *Bang, bang, bang.* The front door shook again. Staring up at the clock above the mantelpiece, he could just see the large hands of the clock face in the gloom. Who the hell was knocking on the front door at 4.30 in the morning and shining torches through the window? A bolt of anxiety raised Grant to his feet as he thought of the two hooded men. Surely they wouldn't knock on his front door. Maybe they wanted to borrow a bike lock so they could secure Joe's bike safely for themselves, he thought sarcastically. Hesitantly he advanced to the porch and peeped through the stained glass window. Fragmented images of two police officers wearing fluorescent jackets stood outside. Opening the door slightly, he peeped out and remembered the two officers from earlier.

"May we come in, Mr Frey?" asked the plump policewoman who had spoken to him only an hour ago.

"Umm, yeah, sure, come in." *What the hell are they doing here?* he asked himself. Showing them through to the dining room, flicking the light switches on as he went, Grant fumbled and mumbled in a sleepy, confused state.

"Have a seat. Do you want a cup of tea?" he asked, turning the corner into the kitchen and flicking the kettle on. Perhaps tea would be a good peace offering, should he need one. Overriding guilt filled Grant as he tried to convince himself that the police had turned up to tell him they'd caught the thieves, and not to tell him off for his telephone manner earlier.

"No thank you," said the man with a long, crooked nose. His piercing blue eyes sent a shiver through Grant's aching body. The assault course over the gate earlier had highlighted his diminishing fitness levels since he'd given up playing football two years ago.

"No thanks," replied the policewoman as she held her hand up like she was stopping traffic.

"Do you mind if I get one? I've just woke up." Grant desperately needed a cup of tea. His addiction was quite extreme, he realised, but it could have been a lot worse; he could be an alcoholic or a heroin addict! He popped a teabag into his mug before either of the officers replied.

"No, go ahead Mr Frey, we just have a few questions we would like to ask you. My name is PC Oakes and my colleague here is PC Gallimore" said PC Oakes, pulling a notebook from her pocket and smiling at PC Gallimore.

"No problem, what can I do for you?" Grant stood in the kitchen waiting for the kettle to boil, leaning back slightly so that he could see around the corner of the wide archway between the dining room and kitchen. The overworked kettle had just reached its climax as Grant grabbed the handle to pour.

"Mr Frey, I'll come straight to the point. We have reason to believe that both you and a minor accomplice have been involved in vigilante behaviour this evening," the policewoman stated bluntly.

The shocking news stunned him into absent-mindedness.

"Argh!" A momentary halt of brain function had caused Grant to continue pouring boiling water from the kettle into his mug to the point of overflow. The blistering hot liquid gushed over the rim of the mug, flooded the worktop and poured down the units to his socks. "Ouch!" he yelled, thumping the kettle down and hopping away from the units like a one-legged kangaroo bounding around the kitchen. PC Gallimore stood up and peered around the corner of the arch in surprise.

"Are you all right, Mr Frey?" he asked.

"Yes – no!" Grant bent down and hastily grabbed hold of his socked foot as the water continued to seep across the kitchen floor. "Argh!" he moaned, squeezing the scalding hot sock and almost burning his hand. Crouching down, he carefully peeled the soggy, hot cotton mix away from his skin to discover that three toes on his left foot were bright red like a baboon's bottom and blisters were already forming.

"Can I get you anything?" asked the policeman, as he moved towards the kitchen area, stopping at the archway and looking rather uncomfortable at the embarrassingly ridiculous situation.

PC Oakes rose from her seat and joined the fiasco in the kitchen. "Have you got a bowl?" she asked as she quickly and efficiently gauged the burnt toes. Grant pointed to the cupboard. "Argh," he complained, hopping into the dining room and plonking himself down on a chair.

"Dad, what's going on?" A little sleepy voice turned everybody's heads. At the same time, PC Oakes came rushing out of the kitchen, precariously carrying a large mixing bowl half-full of cold water.

Grant sensed that his daughter could really be starting to panic at the sight of two police officers in the dining room, in the middle of the night. Knowing Emma, she probably thought that the police were waiting to see *her*. She had frozen to the spot. Grant imagined the things that would be running through her head. Was she going to be sent to prison? She hadn't meant to damage the school locker. Slowly she edged forwards into the room. "I'll clean cars for the rest of my teenage years," she whimpered, before her eyes began to fill. Her face turned a sickly pale colour as she was just about to burst into a sea of tears.

"Em, it's okay honey, go back to bed. Everything is all right, don't worry," murmured Grant as PC Oakes placed the bowl on the floor next to him and planted his foot into the cold water. "Argh!"

"What have you done, Dad?" Emma looked horrified and puzzled at the unusual scene before her eyes. "Why are the police here then and why are they looking at your foot?"

"Em, just leave it please. I'll explain later," replied Grant huffily.

"I just want a drink, can I get one?"

Grant nodded, and Emma stared at him, bemused. This rather crazy situation wasn't about her and the crime she had committed after all. Her Dad had hurt his foot somehow. "Did you accidentally call the police instead of an ambulance?" She asked innocently. Grant glared at her and Emma knew it was time to shut up. Stepping over the woman who was examining her dad's damaged toes and picking black sock fluff from the soothing water, Emma headed towards the kitchen.

"Be careful, there is water everywhere," said PC Gallimore, leaning against the archway like a groom waiting for his bride.

"I'll clean it up," said Emma shyly, unaccustomed to having a police officer standing in her kitchen and another one bathing her father's foot in a mixing bowl in the middle of the night. She grabbed the tea towel and started to mop up the warm water from the floor.

"Dad?" Joe towered in the dining room doorway. Grant looked up, PC Oakes looked up, PC Gallimore looked across and Emma stopped mopping and peered around the arch. "What are you doing?"

I'm having my foot lovingly bathed by a sexy lady dressed up as a police constable, who is on her hands and knees at my feet. It's just a fetish midnight treat!

"Don't ask mate!" Grant shook his head and raised his eyebrows at Joe.

"I think you will have to get that looked at, Mr Frey," said PC Oakes as she stood up and went to the kitchen to wash her hands, tiptoeing along the tiled floor. Returning to the dining room, PC Oakes took the chair next to Grant. "It looks like three of your toes are burnt quite badly," she advised him, as the delicate skin on his little toe continued to bubble and blister in the mixing bowl. PC Gallimore left his marriage post and joined the party at the table.

"Can I sit down, Dad?" asked Joe rhetorically, pulling another chair out. He was slightly less bemused than Emma as he too had encountered these police officers earlier and guessed that their presence was connected to the bike theft.

"Yeah, of course mate," Grant replied as he noticed that the oppressive darkness was starting to lift outside in the garden; dawn would be upon them in an hour or so. What a crazy situation this was, he thought for a second. Alex would not like it if she could have seen what was going on in her home tonight.

"Mr Frey, we would like a quick chat and then we'll be on our way. Is this your son?" PC Oakes looked towards Joe and smiled. "I believe he was with you tonight, in the car?"

"Yes, he was."

"You stated earlier that you were looking for someone?"

Grant shifted in his seat awkwardly as his foot remained below the water level in Alex's favourite cupcake mixing bowl. "Erm, yes."

"Mr Frey, as I said before, we have reason to believe that you have been taking the law into your own hands. As you are probably aware, conducting your own vigilante patrol is quite unacceptable behaviour, and more importantly, illegal."

Wandering through from the kitchen with a soaking wet tea towel in her hand, Emma gawked disbelievingly at her dad. "What's a vigilant patrol, Dad?"

Shaking his head in despair, Grant glared at her with one of his *'Shut up – now!'* looks.

"It has been noted that you called the station to report a stolen bike, is that correct?"

"Yes, I'm sorry; I was frustrated. I got a bit angry on the phone. I felt like nothing would be done about it. Joe's had two bikes stolen in the past. He works very hard at his paper round to scrimp and scrape every penny he can together to buy a new one, and now we've had the third one stolen tonight."

"Mr Frey, you cannot take the law into your own hands," PC Gallimore said quietly.

"I don't know why I went out looking for them; probably because I'd nearly caught them in the garden. I was so angry!" Grant pleaded.

"Did you get a good look at them, then?" asked PC Oakes as she jotted notes into her pad.

"One of them, yes." Grant replied nervously, pondering whether he would get away with it? What was Alex going to say? He looked at Joe, then to Emma. Was this all really happening?

"Perhaps you could give us a description." PC Oakes sat poised with her notepad.

"They both had dark clothing on and they wore hoodies. The one I saw at the end of the garden had stubble on his face, and he had dark hair," Grant guessed, judging by the colour of his unshaven jaw.

"Height? Build? Could you estimate their sizes?" asked PC Oakes.

"Both around my height and build, I would say," he replied, hoping he was steering the officers away from the 'vigilante' accusation.

"Mr Frey, I'm going to give you an informal caution about your behaviour tonight. I do not advise you to patrol the streets in this manner again." PC Gallimore sounded serious; he wasn't speaking quietly anymore. "You did the correct thing by calling the station, reporting the crime and receiving a crime number. The matter should have then been left for the police to deal with. I'm sorry if you feel that we haven't been very helpful in the past, but you must appreciate that we have numerous bike thefts every single night!" PC Gallimore was actually quite scary. They always say you should watch out for the quiet ones, thought Grant. "How old are you, lad?" the officer asked Joe.

"Sixteen," he squeaked. Nodding in acknowledgement, PC Gallimore continued.

"Mr Frey, may I suggest that you pay more attention to the upbringing of your sixteen-year-old? You have not set a very good example to him."

Grant lowered his head in shame knowing he had acted irrationally. "Look, can I explain? My wife was rushed into hospital last night (*was it only last night?*), and I've hardly slept in two days. Then this evening she was taken to Southampton Hospital in an ambulance to have a brain scan. Everything is going wrong and I just lost it when I woke up to find two men in my back garden," Grant pleaded.

"Okay, Mr Frey, we can see that you are having some problems. May I suggest that you get some sleep after you have had your foot looked at?" PC Gallimore had returned to being the nice, quiet officer.

"Yes of course." Grant felt relieved. Could this be the end of it?

The police got up to leave. "Please, stay there, we'll see ourselves out," said PC Oakes raising her 'Stop!' hand again. "Make sure you get that looked at," she said, pointing to the mixing bowl of soggy foot and musty, cold water.

"No it's okay, I'll see you out." Joe jumped up and followed the police officers to the front door, saying goodbye and thank you to them. Grant worried about Joe escorting the officers to the door as he wasn't the most polite, well-mannered person and usually spoke out before his brain had engaged. He hoped and prayed that Joe wouldn't blurt out something silly like, "Ciao, piggy-wiggies!"

"Dad, what have you been doing?" asked Emma, as she took on nurse duty and tried to dry Grant's foot with the soggy tea towel she had used to dry the floor.

"Oh, it's a long story Em. I'll tell you later. Make me a cup of tea darling, I'm gasping!"

Emma tutted as she got up and went through to the kitchen, wishing her mum was home; then she wouldn't have to make so many cups of tea for her dad. Probably none of this would have happened if her mum had been home, she decided as she filled the kettle.

"I thought you were going to get nicked, Dad!" Joe chortled, returning from escort duty. Grant looked up with raised eyebrows and rolled his eyes, as he shook his head in acknowledgement of the close call.

"That would have been all we needed, son."

"Umm," laughed Joe. "Mum and Grandma would go mad!"

The new day was rapidly arriving, and once again Grant felt shattered emotionally and physically. What a weekend this was turning out to be, he thought. If he told everyone at the office about it on Monday, he doubted they would believe him. Looking down at his swollen, pulsating toes, Grant recalled the moment when Emma had arrived in the dining room. It must have looked like a scene from a comedy movie to her. He lovingly studied her as she searched through the medical box to find an appropriate dressing. She loved looking through the first aid box because it was full of lots of interesting bits and pieces. For the last few years, Grant and Alex had said she should be a nurse when she grew up.

"This will do." Emma unwrapped a small piece of muslin. "Shall I put some cream on first?"

"What have we got in there?"

"Hand cream?" She held it up.

"No Em, that's for your hands."

"Well we haven't got any foot cream. Aren't hands and feet the same?"

Grant looked at her and decided that she had just given him more ammunition to taunt her, but he would save it for another day.

"Hand cream is not medicated, Em. Let me see in there." He laughed.

"What are you laughing at?" Emma frowned.

"Nothing honey." He smiled. He couldn't be bothered to explain it to her now. "Here, look – this is for burns. That'll do." Grant passed the tube to her.

"Dad, this went out of date in 2005!" she exclaimed, carefully reading the instructions on the tube.

"That's okay, it'll do," he replied. Then Emma made a very professional job of binding Grant's three toes, although he could hardly fit his slipper over the extensive wadding, let alone anything else.

"You would have made a great job of those Pharaohs in Egypt, Emma. You should take up mummification for a hobby!"

"People don't get mummified anymore, do they?" she asked innocently.

"No Em, they don't!" He grinned.

After the events of the last few hours, Joe now had time to think through the night's affairs and his stolen bike, as he sat in his room sulking. He'd lost yet another bike. He'd saved all his paper-round wages to pay the three hundred pounds for it and it had taken him months and months to save up. His dad had said he would have to buy it himself as the last two hadn't been locked when they were stolen and he would not pay for another one if Joe couldn't look after them properly and lock them up. But he had locked his new bike! It had been locked to the rotary washing line, where he always left it. So how could they have stolen it? Joe lay down on his bed, feeling annoyed and tired, and drifted off to sleep.

It was another clear, crisp morning as Grant carefully stepped out to the patio and looked around the garden. The glistening grass slept peacefully under heavy dew, waiting for the sun's rays to creep slowly around the garden, warming on its way. Limping round to the side of the house, he inhaled the 'breath of fresh air' deeply – he always referred to his cigarettes in this way. Recalling the events of yet another long night, he looked at the gate and was surprised that he had actually managed to climb over it. He couldn't do it now with his toes bandaged together and an aching back, and he knew he would pay for his nocturnal agility antics. Hobbling back towards the patio, he noticed Joe's bike lock lying on the floor under the rotary line. The chain had been cut in half. *So that's how they got it,* he thought angrily. However, he was still puzzled as to how he could have seen the criminals running away *without* a bike in tow. Bending down to pick the damaged lock up, he stopped abruptly: it might have fingerprints on it. He decided to leave it there and call the police later, not that they would be interested, he thought.

"Cup of tea, Dad?" Emma stood on the patio, grinning like a Cheshire cat.

"Yes please." Grant didn't know why she was so cheerful now after her sulky all-day protest yesterday. Maybe she had already accepted the punishment. She didn't usually hold a grudge for long, unlike Joe. The whole family would soon know about Joe's bike (or lack of it) and he would mope around for weeks and weeks. Or perhaps it was because it was Easter Sunday and she wanted to devour a large chocolate egg in one sitting (which wasn't uncommon for Emma to do).

Grant's mind wandered to Alex; how he missed her this morning and wished she was with him. He was so worried about her mysterious condition and could not contemplate the thought of her not getting better very soon. He wanted her home, he wanted normality and he wanted her love.

"Dad, what time are Jack and Aaron getting home?"

Grant looked at Emma in surprise. He had forgotten about them arriving home this morning.

"I would've thought they'd be here by now," he replied, trying to remember the one text message he'd received from Jack last night. He hadn't even read all of the messages on his phone yet; he felt like he was drowning in a sea of communications. Usually this was Alex's department.

Quarter to eight on a Sunday morning and the phone is ringing – it can only be one person, thought Grant as he stumbled into the house and was met by Emma holding the phone.

"It's Grandma!" she whispered. Grant tutted.

"Morning Dot, you're up and about early."

"Grant, Evelyn tells me the police have been round. What's happened?" Panicky tones rang through her voice.

"Dot, no panic – Joe had another bike stolen last night, that's all." *That bloody woman Evelyn across the road is a ninety-year-old, stick-stomping stalker!*

"Oh no, not another one. But why were the police round so early this morning?"

"I called them late last night, so they just came round to take a statement as they knew I was up," Grant lied. *There's no way I'm telling her everything that happened last night! She'd set up a stakeout across the road at Evelyn's house to make sure I was behaving myself!*

"Very efficient! They haven't done that before, have they?"

"No, I think it's because it's the third time it's happened," he lied again.

"Poor lad, I bet he's heartbroken, and at Easter too."

Umm, not sure that Easter makes any difference to how he's feeling, Dot.

"How is Alex? I popped round yesterday evening; did you get the bag I left for her?"

"Yes thanks, I'll take it over with me this afternoon. She's in Southampton – they took her there last night for an MRI scan."

"What? Bloody hell Grant, why didn't you call me? What's wrong with her?"

"They still don't know yet. She's in good spirits and the doctors are doing everything possible."

"How long will she be there?" Dot sounded quite stressed.

"I think she's only staying there until she's had the MRI today." Grant shuffled back to the sunny patio, desperately needing another 'breath of fresh air'.

"Where do we go then if we want to see her?"

"I'd leave it for today Dot. I'm really not sure what will be going on." He took a long draw on his cigarette and relaxed as the calming rush of nicotine kicked in.

"Grant, we are so worried about her, you must keep us informed please."

"I will Dot, I promise. It was past midnight when I got home. I was going to give you a call this morning to let you know. You beat me to it again," he lied yet again. Suddenly Grant felt an overwhelming sense of empathy for Dot and Charlie; after all, Alex was their only child. They were great in-laws when life was running smoothly, but Grant was struggling to cope himself at the moment, let alone worry about the feelings of anyone else. He too was desperately anxious about Alex and everything just seemed to have gone tits-up since Friday.

"I know Grant, sorry, you must have a lot on your plate at the moment, looking after the kids and rushing around everywhere."

Erm, the kids can look after themselves, it's me that needs looking after!

"Please let us know where we need to go to see her as soon as you can and make sure you look after yourself too. You know we're always here if you need anything Grant. It's very hard for you too, I realise that."

Touched by her acknowledgement of his predicament, Grant felt sad and sorry for himself. This weekend couldn't be over quick enough.

"Thanks Mum." Grant had usually relented when he called Dot 'Mum'.

"Is Jack home now?"

"No, he should be back anytime soon, with Aaron." That was another story he did not want to get into now.

"I'll call back later on then; maybe we could have a chat with Jack and arrange to see him as well." She hadn't picked up on the Aaron story, luckily. Grant did not have the energy or inclination to explain anything at the moment.

"Okay Dot, I'll talk to you again as soon as I know anything about Alex."

"Thank you. Bye-bye for now." She hung up.

Gazing across the lawn in a daydream, Grant thought about many things and generated a tick list in his head. Perhaps this was the type of thing that Alex did. She always said she had 'to do' lists floating around in her mind, waiting to be ticked off. His list was relatively short and consisted of five bullet points: buy a packet of fags, get some petrol, sort toes out so I can wear shoes, get Emma to wash my car as one of her 'payback' jobs, and sleep; the latter being the most favourable job to tick off first. This time he would go to bed and hopefully he wouldn't be disturbed by anything or anyone.

"Here's your tea." Emma startled Grant and he jumped back into the here and now. Placing the cup on the table, she went to head back indoors, but halted on the step. "Can I open an Easter egg, Dad?"

Grant smiled to himself – he knew she would want to open one as soon as possible and he'd been waiting for this. "Have some breakfast first, at least, please Em."

Stubbing his cigarette into the ashtray, he leaned back in the chair and basked in the early morning sunshine. Jack and Aaron would be home any minute and he could retire to his bed once he'd caught up with them. Really looking forward to seeing Jack after such a long time, Grant grinned at the impending reunion and 'lads' chats' he would have with him. Having a close relationship with all his children, Grant had come to enjoy them more and more as they'd grown older. He was able to relate to them much better as teens and young adults than when they were younger. Learning so much about himself when the kids were very young, Grant had also had to come to terms with the loss of his mum and dad, which took a considerable length of time and a lot of heartache on his part. He felt that he'd missed some of the vital years of their development due to his inability to cope with anything. There were two years of his life that had drifted by almost unnoticed as he tried to come to terms with his loss. Continually there and forever understanding, through the good times and the bad times, Alex had been his proverbial rock. Unable to turn the clock back, Grant now had all the time in the world for his children and would always make every precious moment count.

Being the firstborn, Jack had been dealt the roughest ride as far as Grant's emotional state had been concerned. An unrelenting desire to be the best father possible to him and the others kept Grant on tender toes. (And even more so now!) Alex had said many times that Grant should not feel like he owed the children anything just because he hadn't always been there emotionally for them. He was a great dad, a loving husband and a successful and distinguished man. Alex was usually right about almost everything and she liked to remind him of that from time to time. Memories of his married life and fatherhood filled him with pleasure momentarily, until the sickening truth of the present situation fell heavily on his heart again.

Jack and Aaron

"Right, let's have a good look at these tickets. Don't want to make any mistakes, do we?" Peering out of the corner of his eye at Aaron, Jack knew how his little brother was feeling. They could both think of far better ways to spend their Saturday night than train-hopping together. A nightclub would have been on the menu for Jack, meeting up with a few mates and chatting to some unsuspecting ladies. As for Aaron, he would have been happier to sit at home in his bedroom, merrily typing meaningless messages to friends on social networks, on his top-of-the-range laptop (his prized possession) or playing PC and Xbox games.

"We've got to wait for three hours in Southampton!" Jack frowned as he studied the details.

"We could get a taxi from there, couldn't we?" Feeling more and more uncomfortable about the whole cock-up, Aaron turned to the window and stared at his own reflection as the darkness that sped by on the other side caused a mirror effect on the glass.

"No bruv, I'm not paying another 50 quid for a taxi when it cost nearly 150 for train tickets!"

"I'll pay it then," Aaron replied weakly.

"No you'll not, mate. Tell you what..." An idea had sprung to Jack's mind. "I'll give Karen a call. She lives five minutes away from the station. We could go round there for a couple of hours if she's at home. I haven't seen her in ages."

"What? At two o'clock in the morning?" queried Aaron anxiously.

"Yeah, she's a party animal. She will have only just got home from the clubs at that time, knowing her. Come on mate, let's do it, it'll be a laugh." Jack was always up for a laugh. "I don't want to spend three hours sitting in a train station and we're not paying out any more money to get home."

"I'd rather get a taxi and go straight home."

"Well, we can't afford it, especially if it's double time!" reiterated Jack. His mind was made up, and they were going to see Karen. "I'll call her and see if she'll be at home, okay?"

"Okay," replied Aaron, feeling very unsure as his subconscious worry-demon surfaced.

A rush of excitement raced through Jack's veins as he sought Karen's number in his phone's large directory. He hadn't seen her for two years, and it would be great to pop in and say hello after such a long time. So much had happened over those two years, and so much had changed.

Karen and Jack's friendship had started in college over six years ago. She stood out from the crowd on the bricklaying course, which tutored 17 students; 16 of those were men and then there was Karen. Jack and Karen had become inseparable during their time at the college, and their personalities just seemed to click together. Having the same sense of humour, the same outlook on life and enjoying the same things only strengthened their mutual respect. After a very brief dating encounter, they'd decided they would prefer to stay just good friends rather than lovers. Their sameness was too much the same to allow a deeper relationship to blossom. Dialling the number impatiently, Jack waited and listened to the ringtone as the train cut through the English countryside.

"That's it, then." The beam on Jack's face gave Aaron a sense of dread. "She's out tonight at a party but she said she'll be back by two. She can't wait to see us!" The excitement in his voice skipped along at a pace. "She couldn't believe it was me. She thought I was gone for good." Jack laughed. Sitting quietly, deep in thought, Aaron tried to look happy for him but he really did not want to go to Karen's house in the early hours of the morning. Waiting patiently in the station was a more favourable option, having only met Karen once before. He hardly knew her and his shyness would be awkward. But that was the difference between the two brothers: Jack was as outgoing, adventurous and inquisitive as an excitable puppy while Aaron was more like a tortoise, meandering along, minding his own business and living in his own cosy little shell.

"She's got a boyfriend now as well, so we'll probably meet him too." Jack grinned.

"Are you sure they don't mind us going round there at that time in the morning?" Aaron fretted.

"No, she can't wait. Stop worrying about everything mate – chillax!" Sensing Aaron wasn't happy, Jack spoke more softly. "I'll look after you mate, it'll be fine. We'll just stay for a cup of coffee and then get back to the station. Then that's it; we'll be on our way home to see Mum."

"Okay," Aaron said, resigned.

Several hours of catnapping and train-hopping later, they arrived in Southampton. Having spent most of the journey sending text messages to Karen, Jack had kept Aaron awake by laughing and giggling to himself, hence neither of them got any sleep, much to Aaron's annoyance. As they stepped off the train, the cold night air pricked their droopy eyelids, waking and alerting them as it sent shivers through their fatigued bodies.

"Come on then, follow me." Crouching over, Jack whispered, "Mission accomplished, Sergeant; we have landed. Preparing to dispatch to Checkpoint Karen."

"Shut up, you wally," sighed Aaron, peering around the station to see if anyone was looking, but there wasn't a soul to be seen anywhere. The only signs of life were the sleepy pigeons nestled high in the rafters.

"Cheer up mate." Rubbing the top of Aaron's hair, Jack realised just how tall he was getting. "How come you've managed to grow taller than me now?"

"Dunno," replied Aaron, feeling sorry for himself and wishing he could get home to his safe and comfortable bed. "You're just a little squirt," he added, trying to look cheerful as he forced a fake smile onto his innocent young face.

"This way, young Private Frey – marching orders!" Guiding Aaron out of the station and onto the main road, Jack held onto his brother's small shoulders and walked behind him, pushing him forward.

"Get off me, you nutter," Aaron laughed.

"There, I knew I would make you laugh sooner or later." Stepping alongside Aaron, Jack flung an arm over his shoulder as they strolled along the road, heading towards Karen's flat.

Holding his finger on the dimly-lit doorbell, Jack waited eagerly for a voice to answer through the intercom. Standing closely behind him, Aaron studied the names of the other residents in the block of flats that were displayed and lit up on the speaker panel.

"Mr W. Kerr – I wonder if his first name is Wayne," whispered Aaron.

"What?" questioned Jack as he turned and gave his brother a puzzled stare.

"Wayne Kerr!" Aaron giggled.

Jack rolled his eyes and tutted. "You're witty tonight."

"Hello?" a female voice came from the speaker.

"It's me, Jack," he called, grinning like a Cheshire cat.

"Hi hun, come on up," the faceless voice spoke quietly. Strangely, Karen didn't sound her usual bubbly self. Her voice was different from earlier in the evening when Jack had called from the train. Perhaps she hadn't had a good time at the party, he thought as the front door clicked open.

Standing out on the landing of the first floor, looking as beautiful as ever, Karen greeted Jack with open arms.

"Look at you! How are you doing babe? Come in." She pointed to the open door. "Hello Aaron, bloody hell you've grown, haven't you?" Placing a hand on his shoulder, she offered him the doorway, after Jack. "Go through to the front room, I'll put the coffee on in a minute." They all sat down on the two leather sofas, both angled towards a flat-screen TV mounted on the wall above an old-fashioned fireplace.

"You're looking well, Kaz." Jack couldn't help but notice her familiar curvy figure.

"Thanks babe, you look great yourself," she replied, flattered by his remark. She knew she could always brush up pretty well, and particularly so this evening. Determined to impress her new boyfriend with her natural good looks; long, dark, wavy hair and voluptuous figure, she'd sensed that her low-cut black shift dress had been a winner at the party, but not only for her partner Jay. Karen often attracted lots of attention from male admirers and jealous glares from less attractive, insecure females, but she was made of tough stuff and could deal with the scowling from other women. Living her daylight hours in black trousers, steel-toed boots, a high visibility jacket and a hard hat, Karen's feminine side would only manifest itself in the evenings and at weekends.

"What's the matter Kaz, you don't seem to be your old self. Are you upset about something?" asked Jack bluntly.

"I've just had a big row with Jay, my boyfriend. He's pissed on vodka. He thinks I'm having an affair with you." She shrugged. "He will regret it in the morning, I can tell you!"

"Where is he?" enquired Jack sensitively.

"Don't know, he walked out and left the party. He's probably walking the streets somewhere. He can think twice about coming home here!" Karen was a tough woman on the surface but Jack knew that deep down she had a kind heart and beautiful feminine qualities about her. The fact that she could drink more pints of lager than anyone Jack knew was just one of Karen's many abilities. Having successfully completed the bricklaying course alongside Jack six years ago, she had managed to secure a summer job in the construction industry. The opportunity had been crucial in gaining experience and knowledge, thereby advancing her prospects to a university degree in building management. Karen now had a secure managerial job in the construction business and favourable career prospects for the future.

"He bloody well knows that you and me go back years, Jack. I'm always talking about you. I told him you're like my brother." Two tears trickled down and over her soft cheeks, racing for first place to her chin.

"Do you think we should go? If he comes back and we're here it could provoke him." Surprised at his sensible attitude, Jack knew the army had changed him and he'd matured. In the past, he wouldn't have been quite so thoughtful and would have probably hung around just to see some 'action', or a fight.

Aaron perched cautiously on the opposite sofa like an owl, turning his head from side to side; from Jack to Karen, without saying a word. Wide-eyed and ears alert, he teetered on the edge of the seat, waiting to take flight, as soon as he heard the words, 'let's go!'

"No, it's all right Jack, don't worry about that idiot. I'll make you both a coffee; you've come a long way so it's the least I can do. I'll sort Jay out later." And she probably would 'sort him out', surmised Jack. "Are you okay, Aaron?" she asked, wiping the tears from her face and pulling herself up to a proud standing position.

"Yes, I'm good, thank you." He grinned politely.

Smiling sweetly, she left her two seated guests and went to the kitchen to turn on the coffee percolator.

"How long are we staying?" whispered Aaron.

"Just for a coffee and a chat. Not long, stop worrying about everyth—" Jack stopped short as the doorbell buzzed repeatedly like an angry swarm of bees.

"Is that her boyfriend?" hissed Aaron.

"Shush!" Rising from his seat, Jack peered through the window to the pavement below. "I can't see anyone," he whispered. Shifting on his perch, Aaron felt guilty, but wasn't sure why.

A few moments later Karen could be heard talking in a raised voice at the front door and then came the slurred speech of a man. Jack and Aaron strained their ears, trying to hear what was being said. It was obviously a heated conversation.

"Shall we go?" asked Aaron, quite alarmed by the verbal battle echoing on the landing outside.

"No, wait here a minute," Jack huffed, hearing his name being mentioned by the deep voice. Creeping towards the door, Jack turned around to Aaron and mouthed, "Don't move I'll be back in a minute." He had to try and calmly diffuse the situation. Alternatively, he would leave with Aaron quietly. Not wishing to cause any trouble between Karen and her boyfriend, Jack certainly had no intentions of causing a scene for the sake of a cup of coffee with an old friend. Approaching the turn in the hallway, he took two strides towards the front door. The intruder in a lovers' tiff, he calmly advanced and spoke softly as he approached the doorway.

"Look, I think we had better leave, Karen."

Focusing his inebriated eyes on Jack, Jay shouted, "Is this him? Ha! Can't you do any better than that?" His tall, stocky figure filled the doorway as he drunkenly propped himself up on the frame with his hand.

"For God's sake, please stop this, you are pathetic," said Karen. Fearfully glancing towards Jack, she shook her head in an attempt at an apology.

"I think we should go and let you two sort this out," suggested Jack, feeling slightly embarrassed about being in the middle of a situation like this.

"No, you stay Jack, Jay can get lost. Come back tomorrow when you're sober and we can discuss this," she advised him angrily. Trying to close the door on him, Karen heaved and pushed with all her might but

Jay burst his way through, knocking her sideways and headed straight towards Jack, spitting expletives as he towered over him.

Smack!

Throbbing pain rippled straight through Jack's nose and filled his right eye, knocking him hard against the wall. Instantly, his quick reactions rendered Jay immobile on the opposite side of the hall. Pinning him to the wall, Jack overpowered him with a firm grip around his tormentor's throat. Emotionally overdosed, Jack held back the urge to hit the man fully in the face as his disciplined army training served him well and he switched into 'bring the situation under control' mode. Fluid began to fill the space around his eye as his body went into instant repair-and-protect mode and padded his eye socket like a blister building on a rubbed foot.

"Think you had better leave now," said Jack calmly and quietly as he loosened his grasp on Jay's scratched and reddened neck. Spluttering and gasping, Jay reached for his throat and rubbed the sore skin gently, in a state of shock.

Deciding he had handled the situation pretty well, Jack envisaged a Clint Eastwood film where he acted out the placid persona of a cowboy in the old westerns. Jay had frozen against the wall in Jack's powerful grip and sobered up instantly as the mighty hand loosened. He raised his hands in a gesture of surrender and looked desperately at his captor as he inched away, stumbling, to the door. Transfixed and gripping the front door, Karen's wide eyes reflected both sorrow and fear; she was overwhelmed by the speed and ferocity of the act she'd just witnessed between two of her most favourite people currently in her life.

Overhearing a scuffle and the shouting and swearing, Aaron had tentatively fluttered through to the hallway and halted mid-stride as he beheld the horrifying scene before him. His soldier brother was actually killing another man! The man's reddened face and bulging eyes were being pressed and squashed into the hall wall by Jack's strong hand. Fearing the possibility of a new wallpaper design in Karen's hallway (a montage of ex-boyfriend's brains), Aaron felt very faint. Collapsing on the floor, his racing heart sent him into his imaginary shell where no one would see him or hear him and he would not have to be a witness to a murder.

"Come on Karen, try and calm down." Jack held her tightly in his arms as she shook with grief. "He'll be back here tomorrow, begging for forgiveness."

"I don't think I can forgive him for hitting you," she sobbed. "I didn't want it to turn out like this. I've seen him in a completely different light now."

Aaron lifted himself up onto the worktop and sat down waiting for his coffee to cool. The extra-sweet drink would aid his recovery from shock, he had been told, after Jack picked him up from the hallway and shuffled him into the kitchen. Aaron looked like a limp lettuce – a homesick limp lettuce to be precise – and his ashen face had worried both Jack and Karen.

Jay had made a hurried exit, ahead of the front door slamming shut and had left the building quietly. Feeling really unhappy now, Aaron desperately wanted to get back to the train station. What would Dad say when he saw the state of Jack's face, and more worryingly, what was Mum going to say?

"Here, put the ice pack back on it. You're going to have such a shiner there." Karen managed to pull herself together and placed the frozen sausages, wrapped in a tea towel, back over Jack's swollen eye.

"Don't be concerned about me, Kaz. Look, we really have to get going soon or we'll miss the train. Are you sure you'll be all right when we go?"

"Yeah, I'll be okay. I could probably do with a good night's sleep."

"I'm sure you will be okay and sort it all out, you're a big girl and I know you won't let things get the better of you. He was very drunk. He'll regret what happened when he wakes up," replied Jack as he withdrew from the icy sausage compress numbing his cheek. "Text me later and let me know how things are." Bleary-eyed, Karen nodded and gave him half a smile.

Thankfully for Aaron, it was time to go. He drained the coffee mug and jumped off the kitchen worktop. "Thank you for the coffee," he said, edging towards the hallway and his escape. Flinging her arms around Jack, Karen apologised sincerely for her boyfriend's behaviour and his black eye.

"Don't worry about it. I'm a big boy now. I can handle it. Just get things sorted out for you, babe."

Nodding her head, Karen showed them to the door and watched as they hurried down the stairs.

Luckily, the next train was due to arrive within 30 minutes as Jack and Aaron had only just missed their ticketed ride home. Seated silently on a metal bench they watched the sun rise slowly in the distance, way down the train track on their left. Proud and amazed by his composure during the brawl with Jay, Jack prodded the outer edges of his swollen eye socket and winced. Karen had a bit of a problem with that new boyfriend of hers, and Jay's jealous streak could only lead to further problems in the future, he concluded. Hoping she would be able to sort it out, Jack wished that happiness would one day fall upon her – she deserved nothing less. The track record for 'Karen meets boy' was not a proven one and Jack had always believed that some women could just be too good-looking for their own good.

The last 12 hours had felt like an oppressive cloud looming above Aaron (by his standards of eternal peace and tranquillity), and one that he never wished to repeat. His plan to get home early and see his mum had not worked and now they would be getting home even later. Sleep was top of the agenda for both of them and Aaron guessed that he would spend a good deal of the day doing it now. As for Jack, he was the proud owner of a whopping black eye, which continued to sting as an assortment of colours blossomed in the socket. Whatever else happened, at least they could be home in an hour and a half and

Aaron would then be able to satisfy the physical craving for his safe, warm and cosy bed. His shell.

Grant

Sipping tea on the patio, Grant eased his slipper off and wriggled his bandaged toes. They were much more painful than they were earlier, and guessing that perhaps Emma had bound them too tightly, he decided to investigate the burns when he showered later, before he went back to the hospital. Wondering which hospital he should go to, he decided to phone the General first and find out when, or if, Alex would be returning there. He had quite a story to tell her but would she regard him as a hero or a fool? Probably the latter, he guessed. She wouldn't be impressed by his rash behaviour or his lack of parental skills and guidance if she knew he'd taken Joe on a vigilante mission in the middle of the night.

Familiar voices drifted into the garden from within the house and Grant knew that Jack and Aaron had arrived home. Smiling to himself, he remembered that they'd had to endure a long journey back during the night. Stubbing out another cigarette, Grant made his way through to the lounge as well as he could manage with sore toes and aching gate-climbing limbs.

"Hello Dad!" Jack waited for the shocked look on his dad's face as he peeled Emma from his back. Trying to jump up on him again, Jack stopped her in her tracks. "Get off, you lump," he said. Emma had enjoyed piggybacks around the garden for as long as she could remember, and huffily, she stopped and got off him.

"Bloody hell, what have you been up to?" asked Grant, shaking Jack's hand and pulling him towards his chest as he hugged his firstborn.

"Don't ask," replied Jack, peering over his shoulder at Aaron standing behind him, grinning.

"Don't tell me Aaron did that," laughed Grant in surprise.

"No, no, he didn't." Jack smiled. "I'll tell you about it later, Dad. Anyway, what's up with you limping around like an old man?"

"Don't ask!"

"On a serious note, how is Mum?"

"Emma darling, can you put the kettle on? Come on, we'll sit in the garden and have some tea." Grant patted Aaron on the back as the two boys walked through to the patio, leaving their rucksacks scattered on the floor in the middle of the lounge.

"That's not fair! Why do I have to do everything just because Mum's not here?" Emma protested, wanting to be outside with her dad and the boys. Curious about Jack's black eye, she flicked the empty kettle on and trotted out to join the trio. "I'll make it in a minute, Dad," she informed him as she joined them at the table, while Grant was giving them all the details he knew about their mum's illness. Three of the foursome took turns to tell their weekend stories and spent over an hour discussing what had gone wrong for each of them since Alex had been admitted into hospital. Emma kept quiet, still sulking about her punishment. If there was a 'the world is not fair' expression, she would have been wearing that too. The only person who had escaped any unfortunate mishap (apart from his bike) was Joe, but Grant had forgotten about the killer cows.

"Oh, I've got to tell you what happened to Joe last night," sniggered Grant as he recalled the tale. "Or maybe we should wait until he wakes up and then he can tell you." Grant winked at Emma. "By the way, where's that tea, Em?" Stomping off, she threw herself through the patio doors, went into the kitchen and flicked the kettle on again before returning quickly to the garden – Emma didn't want to miss anything, especially given that they might talk about her.

"No, tell us now Dad," pleaded Aaron. Any bit of ammunition against his younger brother could only be a good thing.

"No, it wouldn't be fair. He did get a bit annoyed last night when he told us because we couldn't stop laughing, could we Emma?" Grant cracked up as he looked at her.

"Umm." Emma was bored now. She wasn't getting the usual attention, just because she had been the naughty one getting a letter home, so she sulked some more.

"Well Jack, I'm sure nothing else can go wrong now. Good to have you back home, son." Patting him on the back, Grant beamed: he had a superb family. "Is that tea ready?"

"Huh," Emma huffed, as she went back indoors. "Dad, the kettle's not working," she hollered.

Entering the kitchen, Grant looked puzzled. "Bloody hell Emma, you've boiled it dry," he shouted peering into the bottom of the kettle. "Why didn't you put any water in it? For goodness' sake Emma. It's bloody ruined. You've burnt out the element."

"I thought there was water in it already. I didn't know," she grunted, folding her arms and leaning on the sink, pouting.

"We'll have to go and buy a new one now; you should always check there's water first," said Grant, getting more annoyed, knowing he couldn't have his tea-fix now until he'd been to the supermarket.

"We need Mum to get better and come home don't we?" piped Aaron as he sauntered through and stopped in the archway. "She always makes the tea." Desperately missing her, he needed to hear it from his dad that Mum was going to get better and she was going to come home.

"All right, you don't have to rub it in, Aaron!" shrieked Emma and stormed out, pushing past him with an elbow shove to his ribs as she went.

"No, you're right mate," whispered Grant, "and she will be home soon, don't you worry." Grabbing a saucepan from the cupboard, he began to heat a pan of water to make his much-needed cup of tea.

It was already warming up, although the day hadn't really got started yet. The kitchen clock reached 9.30 and appeared to tick much louder than usual as Grant crouched awkwardly over his burnt toes. Hiding behind the archway in the kitchen, he could hear his body screaming at him to get some rest, or at least have a soak in the bath to help heal the aches and pains. But losing was not an option; he would get the last hit. Flicking and twisting his tea towel, he prepared himself for the next onslaught of towel-flickers approaching from the rear garden.

"I'm not playing anymore!" shouted Emma as she stomped through the dining room, looking for her dad. Motionless, Grant continued to squat behind the arch: this could be a ploy, he thought, to get him out of hiding and receive a good thrashing from them all.

"Dad, what jobs have I got to do?" Emma didn't sound like she was the bait to catch Grant out.

"Shush, I'm over here, Em. We'll sort it out in a minute."

Emma turned and headed into the kitchen. "I want to start doing the jobs I've got to do," she huffed.

"Just wait a minute, you'll blow my cover," whispered Grant. Rolling her eyes and tutting, she leaned back against the worktop with her legs crossed and arms folded. Racing back into the house, Joe shrieked as Jack came hotfooting after him, spinning his tea towel in readiness for another super-slick stinger. Joe wound round the table and back out to the garden as Grant stood up and appeared from behind the arch to catch the tail end of Jack's legs as he too turned to exit the dining room.

"Last hit!" exclaimed Grant as Jack stopped dead in surprise. "That's it I've got things to do now. I've won, mate."

"Ah, come on Dad, that's not fair, you can't bail out," Jack retorted.

"That's not fair daddykins, you can't bail out, boo hoo, blah blah", mimicked Joe as he poked his head around the patio doors teasing and tormenting Jack. Then Joe shot away, laughing out loud, as his big brother heaved himself towards the door, after him.

Grinning victoriously, Grant folded his tea towel and returned it to the cupboard. "Right Em, your job today is to clean my car. I suppose we had better do your mother's yet again as well."

"Ah no Dad, I can't do that. What if my mates see me?" Emma was horrified at the thought.

"Your mates won't be up at this time in the morning. Wait a minute and then I'll show you what you have to do," he replied, grabbing the bread from the roll-top bin and placing two slices in the toaster, his tummy growling like a rabid dog. Checking that the dial was turned to the highest setting, he pressed the lever and down went the bread. It never failed to amaze him how the kids always had it set on the lowest setting to produce barely recognisable toast, but that was how they liked it: warmed through, limp bread. Yuck. The thing that annoyed him and Alex the most was that they would then put their limp buttered bread into the microwave to warm it up.

"Right, come on then and I'll show you what to do quickly while my toast is cooking. It won't take you long."

Emma followed behind him like a depressed caged animal, all the way around the side of the house, through the gate and out to the drive. Passing Jack and Joe on the way, she noticed that Joe was starting to get angry as usual. Incapable of losing a fun family game, unfortunately Joe's lack of sleep had made him more of a sore loser than normal.

"I'm going to football. Let's stop now!" shouted Joe as he turned and walked away. Following close behind, Jack caught up with him at the kitchen archway.

"All right mate, last hit," laughed Jack as he flicked Joe on his behind. Reaching for his kit bag and scooting round to the other side of the table, Joe threw his towel across the room at Jack.

"Missed." Jack burst out, ducking the flying tea towel, which landed in the kitchen.

"Come on then, I'm not playing anymore anyway. We're gonna be late," snapped Joe as Jack too, threw his towel onto the kitchen top.

Leaving through the back door, the brothers walked round to the drive and said goodbye to Grant and Emma. Joe's tournament would last most of the day and Jack had promised he would go with him, although he was extremely tired and somewhat headachy from his throbbing eye.

Aaron had the more sensible idea of going to bed after his catch-up with his dad and Emma earlier. He'd discussed the possibility of seeing his mum today but his dad had explained the complications of not knowing which hospital she would be in and had suggested that both Aaron and Jack leave their visit until tomorrow. Hopefully by then, they would all know where Alex was going to be.

Emma carried the bucket to the outside tap on the side of the house, filled it with water and returned back through the gate to the drive. The look on her face made it plainly obvious to Grant that she hated every minute of it. She looked up and down the road, checking no one was around that might possibly see her cleaning cars and then she plonked the bucket on the floor next to her dad, splashing cold water over the sides of the container, drenching his feet.

"Emma, will you be careful?" he hollered as she stood nonchalantly, chewing her bottom lip. "I've got bad toes, remember!" Busily preparing a soapy cleaner, sponges and cloths he'd found in the shed, Grant made sure the job would be as stress-free as possible for Emma. He sensed her distaste and didn't want to prolong the agony any more than he had to.

"Yoo-hoo!" Grant froze as he heard the croaky voice crackling across the road. "Good morning Grant!" The whining tongue of Evelyn crept closer and closer. Looking up from the bucket that Emma had just filled, he was so tempted to turn and run. "How is Alex?" asked Evelyn as she finally reached the drive, a mere 30 yards from her own home.

"Morning Evelyn, Alex is okay. She's doing well." He smiled weakly. Emma had quickly crouched down on the opposite side of the car, just out of Evelyn's view. Sniggering, she began to crawl round to the gate and was going to try and make a dash back into the garden without being seen. Emma's thoughts were the same as her dad's; she didn't like Evelyn either. At times she'd spent over an hour trying to edge herself away from Evelyn's idle gossip.

An expert in entrapment, Evelyn would hang around in her front garden, across the road, waiting for an unlucky passer-by and then she would pounce. There was no escape for anyone. She was like the avenue's personal, woman-sized spider, sat in her web, waiting and watching for the next innocent fly to cross her path. Sometimes she would venture out to spin further webs in the neighbouring gardens, capturing unsuspecting homeowners who were going in and out of their houses. The unassuming gardeners of Pinewood Avenue had no chance of absconding as they tended their front lawns and hanging baskets. Now she had caught Grant, he knew there would be no one to bail him out for hours. He had to come up with a cunning plan to get rid of her.

"I hear poor Joe has had another bike stolen. Those little beggars, I hope the police catch them," Evelyn sneered as she entered the drive and propped her gnarled body against Grant's car.

"Yeah, it's bloody annoying to say the least. The police don't seem to do much about it either," he sighed, wishing he could walk away from the silky threads she was beginning to wind tightly around him.

"Have they said what is wrong with Alex yet?" she asked as she scanned up and down the avenue for more potential victims.

"They're not sure at the moment" Peering over the roof of the car, Grant could just see Emma's head bobbing up and down as she crawled her way round to the back.

"I spoke to her mum earlier. Poor Dorothy and Charlie are so worried about her."

"Yes I know, we all are," stated Grant as he watched from the corner of his eye at the tail end of the car, trying to catch a glimpse of Emma's epic escape.

"Where's young Emma gone? I thought she was with you a few minutes ago," the arachnid asked.

She has arachnophobia Eve, she's the lucky one; she has fled from your evil fangs.

"Think she went indoors." Grant's eyes swivelled round to the gate while he smiled sweetly at Evelyn. Catching sight of Emma's backside, he could just see her crawling through the gateway on all fours, he knew she had fled and would not return until the black widow had disappeared.

Propping herself up by the gate, Emma sat quietly and listened to the conversation on the drive, giggling softly to herself. She knew her dad detested Evelyn's snoopy behaviour, and it served him right for making her do horrible, degrading jobs like cleaning cars. Resting against the wall, she tipped her head back and closed her eyes as the warmth of the sun kissed her face that wore a big smirk.

"She is growing up quickly, isn't she?" droned Evelyn. "I hear your Jack is home today too, what a courageous young man he has turned out to be. You must be so proud of him."

"Yeah, he came home this morning but he's gone out with Joe now." Grant tried his hardest to be polite and civil but his mind was saying, *Go and rot somewhere; slowly!* Usually Grant was a calm and caring person who could listen to anyone, help anyone and talk to anyone, but not this weekend. He'd experienced quite enough traumas for one weekend and Evelyn was a trauma in her own right.

"I'd better get this car cleaned before I go back to the hospital to see Alex," he said, picking up the bucket of water.

"Why are you limping? Have you hurt your leg?" queried the eight-legged spy.

"No, it's my foot, it's just a bit sore but it's no problem." *Fuck off!* he screamed inwardly. He didn't often swear but this was a cursing occasion and he would have happily said it out loud if he thought there would be no repercussions from Eve's best friends, Dot and Charlie (but mainly Dot). What made it all the worse was the thought of Emma watching him and probably laughing her head off at his entrapment.

"Ooh, there's a police car coming down the road," said Evelyn straining her ragged neck to watch the vehicle heading along the avenue. Barely visible at the very top of the road, the car steadily moved closer – Grant was sure that she had eagle vision to go with her web-spinning capabilities. Popping her head around the side of the gate, Emma peeped at her dad as he turned and spotted her hiding. Giggling, she moved back again so that the spider wouldn't catch sight of her with one of its many eyes. The police car drew closer and slowed to a halt, as it parked directly outside Grant's drive. *What now?* Placing the bucket on the floor, he approached cautiously and recognised the two officers from earlier.

"Oh Grant, I think they have come to talk to you," said Evelyn, delighted like a spider that had just caught two flies. Rubbing her hands together in anticipation, she moved closer to the car to listen to the conversation. At the same time Emma appeared from behind the gate, surprised to see the police car parked right outside the house. Stepping through the gateway, she hesitantly sneaked down the drive and stood behind Evelyn.

"Good lord. You made me jump Emma," shouted Evelyn, as the two officers got out of their car.

"Yes, please do, come on through," said Grant, extending a hand towards the gate. PCs Gallimore and Oakes nodded an acknowledgement at Evelyn and Emma as they passed by and entered the side garden. Seeking eye contact with Grant, Emma sidestepped in front of him as he tried to limp past.

"What now, Dad?" she asked nervously.

"Come on, don't panic!" Grant put his arm around her shoulder and pulled her towards him. "We'll have to catch you later Eve, sorry." *Sorry, my arse!* he mouthed as they left her standing by the police car looking puzzled and disappointed that she wouldn't be required to sit in on this latest award-winning gossip story.

"Shall we sit here or would you prefer to go inside?" Grant pointed to the 'morning' table and chairs, as Alex called them. The side of the house was the first place to catch sight of the full rays of the sun, early in the morning. Alex loved to sit there with a cup of tea in the summer and ponder the day ahead. The flash of an image shot through Grant's mind as he thought about her and what a beautiful day it was again; she would be sitting there right now, if only she could.

"Yes, here's fine, thank you," replied PC Oakes, who was looking decidedly tired as she pulled out a chair and sat down. Joined by PC Gallimore and Grant, PC Oakes continued. "If you're happy to make a statement Mr Frey, then we can go ahead."

"Of course," he replied, looking up at Emma and grinning. "They've caught the bike thieves, Em."

"Oh good!" She smiled, relieved once again that the police hadn't come back to get her and lock her away in a dungeon. "Shall I make a cup of tea?"

"Would you like tea?" Grant asked the two guests. PC Gallimore smiled and shook his head.

"No thank you," laughed PC Oakes. "I would have thought the events of this morning would have put you off tea for life."

Grant recalled the pre-dawn fiasco and smiled too. "It would take more than three burnt toes for me to stop drinking tea." He smirked. "Although I have to make it in a saucepan at the moment, as dear Emma here boiled the kettle dry this morning." Scowling at him, she poked Grant in the back. "Just one tea then, Em. Thank you." Emma left and hopscotched round to the back of the house, looking slightly annoyed again.

Removing a folder from her briefcase, PC Oakes placed it on the table. "The two men you say you saw last night are suspected of being part of an organised gang of eight bike thieves. We have recovered three stolen bikes this morning but none of these fitted the description of your son's bike unfortunately. If you could give us a statem—"

"Dad, Dad – argh!" screamed Emma at the top of her voice. "DAAADDD!" Tearing round from the back garden, Emma hurled herself at the table, almost knocking it over. Grant jumped up and stood to attention, "Dad, the house is on fire!" spluttered Emma, jumping up and down in a frenzied state.

"Bloody hell!" he yelled, launching himself awkwardly towards the rear, followed by both police officers. Turning the corner of the house, Grant hopped and hobbled past the kitchen window and turned abruptly as he caught sight of the bright flickering flames in the kitchen.

"Mr Frey, have you got a fire extinguisher? Please don't go in there." shouted PC Gallimore, as he too turned the corner and stopped dead at the kitchen window.

"No I haven't!" shouted Grant, reaching the patio doors. "Call the fire brigade!" he hollered to PC Oakes as she stared in through the window and could not believe her eyes.

"Toast!" shouted Grant as the policewoman radioed through to the emergency services.

"Aaron!" screamed Emma and burst into tears.

"Holy shit. My son is upstairs!" cried Grant, leaping through the patio door. "Aaron!" he yelled as loud as he could.

Upstairs, Aaron had woken to the sound of Emma screaming in the garden. Annoyed at her lack of consideration when people were trying to sleep, he dragged himself out of bed to investigate the commotion. Opening the bedroom door, he breathed the smoky air as he wondered why on earth his dad would be lighting up the barbeque at this time of the morning. It was at that moment that Aaron heard his dad screaming his name. He then knew something was seriously wrong and he would not be getting a hot dog for breakfast, as first thought.

Stepping into the dining room, Grant could see that the fire was contained within the kitchen area and more specifically, to the place where the toaster once lived. Flames licked the units above and flickered across the work surface, aided by what used to be a pile of tea towels and a kitchen roll holder. It appeared that the fire had been burning for some time; probably since Grant had put his toast in, which he then left to help Emma set up the car-cleaning kit. He'd forgotten about his rumbling tummy because the evil spider had pounced – oh no, this was entirely his fault.

"Mr Frey, step out and let the firemen deal with this when they get here. Have you got a ladder? We can access the first floor from that window." PC Gallimore spoke authoritatively.

"Aaron!" screamed Grant again, as he paced his way into the smoky dining room, disregarding the warning. Confirming the address on her walkie-talkie for the fire brigade, PC Oakes comforted Emma with an arm around her shoulder.

"Dad," Emma hollered, watching him disappear into the house. Distraught that her mum wasn't here, Emma knew this wouldn't have happened if she'd been at home. Everything was going wrong because Mum was in hospital. Emma sobbed into PC Oakes' armpit.

"Quick, get out!" called Grant from the dining room as he saw Aaron trotting down the stairs, frowning and sniffing the air. "There's a fire in the kitchen, come on!" Grabbing Aaron by the arm, he pulled him past the dining table and out through the patio doors.

"What the hell has happened?" asked Aaron as he gazed disbelievingly at the police officers.

Standing by the kitchen window, Grant watched helplessly as the large flames ate into the cupboards directly above the toaster. PC Gallimore exited the garden and walked out to the drive to flag down the pending fire engine. Turning her temporary loyalties from PC Oakes to Aaron, Emma hugged her big brother tightly as they stood on the lawn watching their dad peering through the window despondently.

"Is everything all right, officer? I'm a family friend," said Evelyn as she hobbled back across the road to Grant's driveway.

"We have a situation that will be under control in just a matter of minutes, Madam," replied PC Gallimore, eyeing the top of the road.

"Ooh! What is happening?" she asked as she began to spin her latest web.

"There is a fire in the house. The boys will be here in a few minutes."

"A fire? Oh my goodness, is it serious?"

"Serious enough," he said, trying to move away from her spinnerets.

"Where in the house is the fire?"

"In the kitchen Madam."

"Can I help at all? Where are Grant and the children?"

"They are all safe. Please don't worry yourself; we have the situation under control. There's nothing you can do to help." PC Gallimore was getting agitated by the old lady, who seemed to be just sticking her nose in where it was not wanted.

"I'm going to make a phone call. I live just there." Pointing to the house opposite, Evelyn eyed the policeman suspiciously. "Tell Grant he can come over to my house with the children if he needs to. What a terrible situation for them, poor little mites. My name is Evelyn Archer, should you need to know."

"Thank you Evelyn, I will pass on the message." The two new acquaintances looked to the top of the road as a fire engine hastily made its way through the parked roadside vehicles. Hobbling as fast as her rickety legs would carry her, Evelyn left the drive and scuttled up the road to the house next door but one. Curious neighbours had noticed the police car parked outside Grant's house and now a fire engine was pulling up alongside the panda car.

Gazing through the window into the kitchen in a daydream state, Grant watched the flames rising and growing in ferocity, as one of the cupboard doors caught alight in the intense heat. Patchy, dense, grey smoke filled the kitchen space like a heavy evening fog. Dazed and numb, he knew there was nothing he or anyone else could do to quell the flames until the firemen arrived. This weekend was turning into his worst nightmare and his backbone – Alex – had no idea about any of it. Moments later, two burly firemen trudged around the corner of the house, carrying equipment.

"Where is your electrical cupboard?" asked the younger uniformed man.

"Umm, it's under the stairs; through the living room." Grant couldn't think straight as he realised how serious the whole affair was becoming. The taller of the two firemen escorted Grant and the others around to the front of the house. PC Oakes rejoined her colleague in the driveway where a small crowd of spectators had gathered. Evelyn held court and provided a running commentary as the firemen went about their important and brave work. Her earlier quest to go home and make a phone call had been quashed in favour of an audience with the residents of Pinewood Avenue. The faint smell of acrid smoke drifted on the light breeze and peppered nostrils as it made its way through the onlookers.

"Are you all right Grant?" called Tina from next door as she peered over the tops of the gathered crowd. "Can I get you anything?"

Grant shook his head. He seemed to have lost his voice. The surreal situation became a blur of babbled noise and staring eyes as he slumped himself down in a corner of the driveway. Already the dictating black widow (appropriately named, given her long black hair which was tied up in a bun and a dead husband-whom she probably had wrapped up in a cocoon and hanging from the rafters in her loft) had trapped two flies by twisting her spindly arms around their backs. Looking stressed and uncomfortable, Emma and Aaron stood speechless on the pavement in Evelyn's embrace.

Within an hour of the initial discovery of a roaring fire in Alex's cupcake kitchen, Grant surveyed the carnage in horror. The fireman in charge concluded that a tea towel covering the toaster had indeed caused it to ignite. Before their departure, the fire officer gave Grant a lecture and some good advice on safeguarding his home from fire risks in the future.

"The extent of the damage could have been minimal if you'd replaced the batteries in your alarms, Mr Frey. I recommend you purchase a small fire extinguisher and fire blanket for the kitchen too. I trust Sir, that the shock and the fire damage have made you realise the importance of fire safety in your home."

Nodding his head, Grant felt like a naughty little boy being told off by a parent. PC Oakes overheard the one-sided conversation and gently nodded her head too, in agreement with the fireman, as she looked despondently at her earlier patient.

Coming to terms with the fact that his house insurance would not cover him for the extensive damage, Grant slumped against the kitchen archway. A melted plastic blob and surviving metal parts bore the evidence of what had once been a four-slot toaster. The twisted rod of charred wood still stood upright on its base, but there was no sign of the cupcake-patterned paper towel roll that once lived there. Blackened hinges desperately clung to the remains of two wooden cupboard doors that were hanging from the wall units. Charcoal-coloured soot dusted every available surface, extending to the dining table in the adjoining room. A sodden, black mess of barely recognisable kitchen cupboards, worktop and appliances remained in the area around the source of the fire like gravestones in a cemetery. With his sunken heart in the very bottom of his slipper, Grant returned to the garden to join Emma and Aaron, who had just escaped from the spider's web.

"Evelyn has gone home, she said she needs to make a phone call," Aaron huffed. "She's probably going to phone Grandma."

"Without a doubt!" Grant groaned, reaching to put his arm around Emma's shoulder. The very notion of Dot finding out about the fire sent shivers through his body.

"Grandma will go mental," sighed Emma, snuggling further under her dad's arm. Distraught and tearful, she desperately wanted her mum to put everything back straight and return the household to normal. Dad was just Dad and although he was good at a lot of things, he was no good at being the organiser of the family and household. She had come to this conclusion after just the last six hours.

"Well, she's the last person I want to see today!" stated Grant, peeling himself away from Emma and reaching into his pocket for a 'fresh air stick'.

"Can we go in and have a look?" asked Aaron, knowing his dad would be sitting in the garden for a while, enjoying a long smoke.

"Yeah, sure you can. Don't touch anything, it's filthy in there." Grant breathed out a wispy grey trail of cigarette smoke. Following behind like a shadow, Emma grabbed hold of the bottom of Aaron's dressing gown and they both entered the house like a pair of performing elephants walking trunk to tail.

Both PC Gallimore and Oakes had decided to leave the Frey household during the commotion and asked Grant to call in at the station as soon as he was able to do so, to make a statement.

"We are well over our shift times, Mr Frey, and we've got homes to go to," smiled PC Oakes as they were leaving. Grant's mouth took another downward turn as he watched his two new friends climb into their car and drive away. Strangely, he felt safer with them around and more able to cope with the crazy situation he had come to find himself in on this glorious Sunday morning. Joining the other spectators held in the sticky fibres of silk thread on Pinewood Avenue, Grant watched the police officers drive away. Luckily their colleagues from the station had caught two men last night who, it was later discovered, were part of an organised gang of eight bike thieves. Unfortunately, the police hadn't had any success in recovering Joe's bike, but had managed to seize three others that had been stolen at the same time. Joe was going to be more upset than he was earlier.

Before he became entwined in the pavement web, Grant had managed to escape the hoard of flies unnoticed and return to his sanctuary, the home of Alex's gnomes. Wandering onto the lawn, he studied the comical little men (and a couple of women) and wished he could morph into their perfect world of landscaped garden, tranquillity and sunshine. *Boy, am I going to be in the shit,* he realised as the image of Alex's horrified expression materialised before his eyes. Shaking off the disturbing portrait, Grant entered the house and carefully stepped through to the carnage of the kitchen.

"Grant, are you there?" the shrill voice pierced through the open front door. Bolting upright in his chair, he heard the dreaded call from the garden where he had been sat pondering over what to do. "Grant! Where are you?" It came again, as he rolled his eyes, stubbed another cigarette out and levered himself from the chair.

"Dot...Charlie, you've heard then?" mumbled Grant as his eyes adjusted to the gloom of the dining room. Fading into the background, Aaron mouthed a hello and disappeared to his room quicker than a hounded rabbit running to its burrow.

"Bloody hell Grant! How on earth did it happen?" asked Dot pulling her white cardigan off and hanging it over the chair back.

"Be careful, I wouldn't put it there Dot. There's soot everywhere," muttered Grant. Pulling the cotton-mix garment off the high-backed dining chair he carried it through to the living room and threw it on the sofa. "It's not too bad through here," he called back, hoping they might return to the living room. Charlie and Dot stood by the arch, gawping at the charred remains of one half of the kitchen.

"Oh no, what a mess," sighed Dot as she looked to Charlie, who was scanning the damage and muttering something under his breath.

"Can you claim on the insurance, son?" asked Charlie, as Grant returned to the dining room feeling hopeless.

"No, it was our fault that the fire started," Grant replied morosely. Proceeding to explain the chain of events that had led to the fire, he pulled a dining chair out and plopped down on the seat wearily. Joining him at the table, Charlie listened intently. He was a great listener and usually came up with the best solutions to life's problems. Admiring him deeply, Grant felt that he was in safe hands now this clever old man was on the scene. He would know what to do.

Spending most of his life being a listener and thinker rather than a talker (which fitted well with his wife), Charlie had enjoyed a very successful career in pioneering projects and engineering. Some people thought he was a mad professor as he invented many weird and wonderful creations throughout his lifetime. Several patents later and Charlie had created an innovative product that was still used worldwide now.

"Let's try and get this mess cleaned up then," prompted Dot as she heard footsteps upstairs. After the constant tears and a troubled, sleepless night, Emma had gone to her smoke-scented room for a lie down. Unable to sleep, she heard Grandma arrive and lay on her bed for a further 20 minutes before deciding to go downstairs and meet the 'wrath of Granny'. Luckily things were settled and calm in the dining room where Charlie and Dot were seated when she got there.

"Hello Grandma and Grandad," she sighed as the sight in the kitchen reminded her of the long trail of events stretching back to the early hours of the morning, when she had woken to find her dad with his burnt foot in a bowl, being nursed by a policewoman. *Crazy!* She wondered how much her grandparents really knew. Her Grandad smiled and beckoned her to him for a hug without saying a word.

"Hello love, are you all right? Your dad's a silly beggar isn't he?" Rising from her chair, Dot pulled Emma to her and squeezed her around the ribs until the usual crunch and grind of bone meant that she had been cuddled to death by Grandma. "We're just going to start cleaning up. Do you want to give us a hand, darling?" No wasn't an option in Grandma's rule book, so Emma smiled sweetly and nodded.

Knocking the plastic casing of the toaster harder, Grant eventually peeled the melted mould away from the burnt worktop. "That top will have to go too," injected Charlie as he examined the surface.

"Umm, I think I've pretty much lost half a bloody kitchen here Charlie!" panted Grant. Nodding his balding head, Charlie collected the toaster remains and discarded them on the patio along with several other pieces of kitchen equipment. The April sun still shone bright and strong in the garden where Dot, Emma and Aaron (who had been coaxed back down by his sister) scrubbed plates, pots and pans in the buckets which had been prepared earlier for car-cleaning. Row upon row of cutlery, bowls, cups, dishes and any other salvageable kitchen inhabitants lined the lawn as they dried on bed sheets in the midday heat.

"Dad, Evelyn is at the door, shall I invite her in?" grinned Aaron, upon his return from an authorised toilet break. Peeping through the window of the front room he could just see her twig like figure almost crouching, ready to pounce through the door as soon as it was opened. The proximity of Evelyn's good friend Dot, Grant's mother-in-law, meant that Grant had to oblige and agree to let the arachnid in.

"Yes, of course!" he shouted from his incinerated empire, as he tutted and rolled his eyes.

A good hour of interrogation and ridicule later, Grant had gathered enough clean mugs to attempt to make a sooty cup of smoked tea for everyone. Great – no bloody kettle and the saucepans were on the lawn, ready for scrubbing!

Returning from the supermarket, Grant rushed indoors and unpacked the brand new, gleaming chrome kettle (at least there was one new item in the kitchen now, but Grant knew there would be many more by the time Alex had finished buying a new kitchen). Silently, he thanked whoever it was that came up with the idea of around-the-clock shopping, for although it was Easter Sunday, some shops were open for a few hours. Five minutes later, Grant burnt his lips trying to sip the hot elixir and then its magical powers renewed his vigour-somewhat vigorously. *Ah, that's so much better,* he thought, leaning against the sink unit, before putting it on again to make everyone else a cuppa.

Thoroughly engrossed in the ill fate bestowed upon the Freys, Evelyn revelled in the glory of knowledge that she would dictate to any web captives later.

"Ooh, you must be excited about Tuesday, Charlie." Evelyn beamed. "What are you going to do if Alex isn't any better?"

"Dot and Grant will be there. They can do it between them." Charlie glanced from the corner of his eye at Dot, who pretended not to hear him as she continued to scrub an unlabelled tin of baked beans, until it was sparkling clean.

"I'm sure they will manage perfectly between them," smiled spidery Evelyn. "I can't wait to see it, Charlie." Rolling his bottom lip, Charlie tried to edge away from her (like Grant, he knew what she was like and he was well aware that his wife was just as bad) and found reason to return indoors to help Grant with the tea.

"Oh dear, Evelyn might come to watch on Tuesday," said Charlie forlornly as he towered in the archway, watching Grant testing out his new kettle.

No, surely she'll stay at home and watch my house. It's far more interesting to her. "Great, that's all we need, eh?" Grant replied sarcastically.

"I think you should use these tins quite soon, Grant. They may have been heated up already, in the fire. I've cleaned them up but most of the labels have come off. I could number them if you'd like me to," called Dot cheerily. Doing a good deed for anyone always made her feel more self-righteous than she felt on a normal self-righteous day.

"Don't worry about them Dot, I'll throw them away," barked Grant in frustration through the open kitchen window. "They're only a few tins of beans or peas."

"Well I've just spent the last half an hour cleaning them!" she replied, disgruntled.

For fuck's sake, why don't you just go home and leave me to it; it's my fucking house! thought Grant, feeling his temper start to rise as he falsely grinned at Charlie.

A tall figure of a man, Charlie had aged extremely well. For his 70 years, he stood as upright as anyone else and could still do most things that he wanted to do. White wispy hair curled from the lower parts of his head, skirting a brown, shiny bald top. His nickname was 'the nutty professor', given to him many years ago by work colleagues who witnessed his inventions developing and heard about his lifelong hobbies. His placidly quiet demeanour and clandestine hobbies at

153

the end of a long day only stood to enforce his nickname. The small ground-floor room at the front of his house was accessed only by himself. Every two or three years (sometimes even longer), he would allow the family to visit his sacred room of magnificent machinery to peruse his latest creation.

"We'll be gone in a bit," whispered Charlie, sensing the mood in Grant's voice. A crinkled wink of his eye, and then Charlie carried the tea tray out to the garden.

"Ooh, a nice cuppa, just what we need out here," crowed Dot, who was still scrubbing tins and packets of cereal. Lounging in the deck chair, Evelyn kept a close watch on the cleaners with her four pairs of eyes, as Grant followed Charlie out to the patio. Grant had to be honest and admit to himself that a good job had been done by all parties in the efforts to clean up the kitchen. Obediently washing and cleaning plates and all the other kitchen paraphernalia, Aaron and Emma sat on the sunny lawn looking like two orphaned children in a Victorian workhouse.

"Are you two okay?" asked Grant, realising they were not. Teenagers could not be expected to sit on the lawn and continue to look happy while filling bed sheets with wet pots and pans in the company of their irritating grandma and a predatory spider.

"Yeah," replied Aaron without looking up. Sitting close by, Emma didn't say a word but the scowl on her face spoke for her.

"Why don't you both have a break now, you've done a brilliant job," smiled Grant, feeling sorry for them both having to sit under the evil glare of Evelyn, which was always well hidden behind a partially toothless grin. Without a moment's hesitation they quickly jumped up and scooted indoors to the living room to watch television and eat soot-flavoured Easter eggs.

Four o'clock and the sun had shined all day, although the heat on the patio was wearing thin as the April evening started to creep in. Stubbing out his first cigarette in the last few hours, Grant heaved a big sigh and went indoors to survey the kitchen once more. Well, he supposed they could do with a new one; it had just come at the wrong time but Grant knew he would have to arrange something pretty quick for when Alex returned home. Alex! A guilty streak ran through him as he realised he hadn't thought about her at all in the last few hours. It was getting late in the day, and she would probably wonder where he was. She would also be distraught and positively angry when she found out what had happened, and more poignantly, how it happened. Another thought hit him; he hadn't even phoned to find out which hospital she was in.

The front door opened and Jack and Joe strolled in with tired, burnt faces and muddy knees. The bulging eye glowed blue and purple having been enhanced by the sun, but Jack was too fatigued to care.

"Have we got a barbeque for tea?" shouted Joe in an elated, hungry voice (he was always hungry) as he threw his kit bag down and slumped in a chair.

"I'm going to get a shower before tea...then it's bed for me," Jack stated firmly as he began to head for the stairs. Apart from a couple of brief catnaps on the trains the previous evening, he hadn't had any sleep (well, apart from when he was a sleeping spectator on the sidelines of the football pitches).

"Hang on a minute boys," said Grant, "I've got something to show you." Beckoning Jack and Joe with his index finger, Grant led the way through to the dining room.

Alex

A kind, old-fashioned, elderly woman, Nurse Gower had assisted me in the bathroom in a most respectful and dignified way. Wondering whether she was on borrowed time for her pension rights, I gratefully accepted her help in getting onto a chair under the shower head. The warm, refreshing water cascaded over my entire body as I smoothed over the Hibiscrub I'd been asked to use.

Initially, I had been somewhat offended when Nurse Gower gave me the small container and told me to have a wash with it. Looking like a bottle of disinfectant in my hand, I worried that maybe I smelt so bad that the staff wanted me to sterilise myself. As paranoia started to get the better of me I decided to take control, convincing myself that it was routine to wash with a gel form of sterilising fluid. With an ever-present risk in hospitals of the MRSA virus, I assumed it was a precautionary measure rather than my body odour being so unbearable to the ward staff and other patients.

Dried and warm, I dragged the tattered, clean underwear up my legs. Coming to a halt above my knees, I realised they would not comfortably go any further without cutting off the blood circulation. Nurse

Gower said I could pull the cord if I needed any help in the bathroom, but I was not going to ask her to wrench the pathetically small piece of fabric, otherwise known as a thong, any further. Admitting defeat, I pulled them back to my ankles and reached for the two-day-old pair I'd recently peeled off. I stretched over in the chair and just about managed to grab them.

Startled by a tapping noise on the door, I seized the old underwear and dragged it up as quickly as possible.

"Are you okay in there, Mrs Frey?" called Nurse Gower.

"Yes I'm fine, thank you!" I replied, inching the material past the seat of the chair. Becoming an expert in underwear dressing while seated with dead legs, I concluded that I'd had enough practice while using the commode on numerous occasions, in the hospital, to warrant calling myself an expert. The drugs injected directly into my veins had ensured that my bowels had no problems whatsoever in emptying themselves in a very unprofessional way, and therefore, copious amounts of commode usage had given me my new proficiency status.

"Remember to pull the cord if you need anything."

"Yes I will, thanks," I articulated through the wide bathroom door. Nurse Gower was wise enough to sense that I desperately needed some dignified privacy, after the last 36 hours of personal invasion by countless medical staff. The fresh smell of disinfectant rising from my skin became a pleasant and comforting experience as I sat on the plastic chair behind the shower curtain, refreshed and clean.

Surely things could only get better from this point of renewed vigour and optimism, I pondered, rubbing the remaining traces of pink Hibiscrub from my arms. Even wearing the same underwear again had a fresh, renewed feel as my skin tingled and glowed after the warming shower.

The fear of getting my hair wet, had ensured that I just managed to fling my head backwards and away from the shower head enough, to keep most of it free from the pre-frizz-bomb water.

"Don't wash your hair with this," Nurse Gower had informed me earlier when she handed the bottle over. *Have no fear! I have no intention of washing my hair at all!* I'd replied inside my head. My hair, water and no straighteners in the hospital was an inconceivable idea. I would make Hair Bear from the *Hair Bear Bunch* look like a decidedly well-groomed member of the trio. There would be carefully considered expletives added to their famous catchphrase, 'Help! It's the Hair Bear Bunch!' if I had to endure a wet mop.

Sliding myself back across and onto the wheelchair, I was ready to leave the bathroom and return to the ward, wearing a fresh hospital issue, rose-print gown. It was heaven-sent that I was still able to use both arms and the rash was starting to fade on its travels upwards past my navel. Hopefully, today would be judgement day and I would finally discover what was wrong with me, get some tablets, borrow a wheelchair and go home. Sunday was my favourite day of the week; it was cupcake day and by the look of the weather outside, it would also be barbeque day at home, so I didn't want to spend any longer stuck in the hospital. More importantly, I had Easter eggs to eat!

Returning to the ward, riding on my new form of transport, expertly driven by Nurse Gower, I noticed that the curtains had been drawn on the ward. The sun glared through the large windows, highlighting the view I had been eagerly looking forward to. Disappointingly square, the landscape outside bore sections of the hospital, built in all shapes and sizes dotted across the skyline.

"Do you want to sit in the chair by the window?" asked Nurse Gower sweetly as we approached my bed.

"Yes please." I smiled. "It's another beautiful day out there, isn't it?"

"Oh yes," she replied, beckoning the other nurse over to help lift me onto the padded, old-fashioned chair.

Breakfast was a glorious affair! Hunger grew inside me as soon as the sound of the clinking trolley came onto the ward, followed by the potent aroma of hot buttered toast. Having voluntarily skipped every meal over the last day and a half, much to the annoyance of the medical staff, I now devoured every crumb of toast on offer, every flake of cereal and every last drop of tea. I actually felt a little better today! The proverbial bus that had hit me and then morphed into a high-speed train had now been demoted to a three-tonne lorry.

Listening to classical music in the earphones, which had been provided, I lay motionless as the giant magnetic machine whirred and knocked, sometimes loudly. Claustrophobia was a sixth sense for me, and one that I struggled to deal with.

"It won't take too long," the radiographer said calmly through the earphones before returning my ears to the delights of Andrea Bocelli, noting the fearful gaze in my eyes as I lay on the bed. "Just keep very still in there," she said from the kiosk.

Well I'm hardly going to get up and walk away, am I? I smiled back, as I surveyed the tunnel.

On my return to the ward after the caving expedition with Andrea Bocelli and Sarah Brightman inappropriately singing, *Time to Say Goodbye,* to me, Nurse Gower assured me that the doctors would be doing their rounds shortly. (I'd heard that one before.) The furry film of what I could only surmise would be a battlefield of bacteria on my teeth had faded away during breakfast but now it was returning with a vengeance. Daydreaming on the chair, I cogitated over the idea of cleaning my choppers with Hibiscrub and then quashed the thought instantly, reaching into my handbag in search of a mint. Maybe Emma would realise she had forgotten the toothpaste and tell Grant to bring some in – fat chance of that happening! Inwardly giggling, I concluded that if Emma's last package was anything to go by, she would probably end up bringing K-Y Jelly in for me to clean my teeth.

Oh, how I missed them all and could only guess what they would be up to on a Sunday morning. Grant would be reading his Sunday paper and then complete the crossword whilst eating a cooked breakfast (but I wasn't there and I couldn't imagine anyone else bothering to cook breakfast, so maybe not). Perhaps he was cleaning his car – and mine! Grant always told me off for the state of my clapped-out old Mondeo. I was a house cleaner, not a car cleaner!

"For heaven's sake, Alex, filth and utter mess is one thing, but then there's your car - which is another. It's ridiculous!" I could hear him saying. Of course, he was right. It was an embarrassment really, compared to his pristine model, but I couldn't part with my faithful, ancient 'Blondy-Mondy', as I'd named her for her champagne colour. "You have got to stop parking under the trees Alex, the paintwork is going to rot away and I'm not paying out for another re-spray!"

I had tried desperately to find somewhere else to park but it wasn't always possible, especially when I had a bootload of stock from the wholesaler. Convinced that the trees around my shop had pterodactyl-sized birds watching and waiting in them, I attempted to park strategically between two trees, but this just meant that my car got bombarded by low-flying bird poo from both sides. It always managed to splatter artistically all over the bonnet and windscreen. The interior was another story-well, it was my mobile office, restaurant and launderette. I was a busy businesswoman and a multi-tasker!

Thinking of Jack and Aaron, I guessed they would be home (I hoped) after the fiasco of Aaron getting lost, but they would probably stay in bed until way past midday. Joe would be at his football tournament for most of the day and arrive home tired, muddy and temperamental. As for Emma, she would spend the morning (what she would see of it), in her bedroom, listening to music and experimenting with make-up. Then she would go out with her best friend Annie for the afternoon, maybe swimming at the new sports centre or hanging out at the local park. (Actually, I'd forgotten that she was now grounded, so maybe she was just going to spend the whole day scowling.) Would they all be doing normal Sunday activities, or were they all missing me and moping around the house under a cloud of heavy hearts? Deciding on the latter lifted my spirits, for I needed to be wanted and wanted to be needed.

A group of medical practitioners appeared early as Nurse Gower had prophesied. Inspecting the records of my visit, Dr Thomas agreed with himself, muttering under his breath. After a short deliberation with the rest of the group, he decided that I should be transported back to the General Hospital.

"The scan results will be ready soon," I overheard him saying to another doctor, leaning on the end of my bed. Then the curtains around my bed were pulled, cocooning me inside with the two doctors who proceeded to examine my legs and feet. It was the same routine as before. Firstly, I had to close my eyes while the doctor stabbed me repeatedly with a sharp metal pin-like object, up and down the length of my legs, along my feet and on the top of each toe (I knew this because Grant had watched them do it previously and was amazed that I felt nothing). Secondly, the extensive reflex tests on my unresponsive legs and feet, which really puzzled everyone. Thirdly, and I enjoyed this part, I had to play strange games with my hands, either following along with the doctors' hands or using my fingers to touch my nose. Worryingly, I couldn't find my nose with my fingers, which was one of the many reasons for the MRI scan. My coordination had become very much uncoordinated. The last part of the examination was to inspect the rash which continued to travel upwards, but had actually lost some of its colouration and potency as it went higher and higher.

"That is good news," the doctor said cheerily, not looking at anyone, so I presumed he was talking to all of us. The bit of good news was that there was a glimmer of movement in my right foot, triggered by the reflex tests; my big toe had reacted to the foot-stroke. However, the mystery still remained as to why I had become paralysed from waist to toes over a matter of hours, covered in a deep purple rash and with a strange, flu-like illness that utterly depleted my strength and vigour.

Leaving the cocoon for a few minutes to discuss their findings, I could hear the group of doctors mumbling, a short distance away, on the other side of the curtains. Peeping in with a smile, Nurse Gower then squeezed through the curtain like it was made of heavy armour.

"I need to take some more blood, is that okay?"

Smiling to her, I nodded yes. "I think I'm getting a bit better," I whispered to the nurse who had just become my best friend within the confines of the cotton-curtained cocoon.

"Let's hope so," she said as her wrinkled mouth curled into a big smile.

Withdrawing the needle with its syringe full of blood, Nurse Gower collected the tray of equipment and went back through the curtains. Seconds later the doctors, Thomas and Shelley, returned without their colleagues in tow. As they delivered their encouraging words of improvement and detailed the next steps to aid my recovery, which would entail a vigorous course of physiotherapy to teach me how to walk again, I remained seated on the bed, staring in disbelief at the two highly qualified men. They still didn't know what was wrong with me! They were still perplexed by the whole course of events and the unusual pattern of symptoms. Well, if they didn't know, then I certainly would not have a clue what had been happening to me.

Late in the afternoon, in the déjà vu of another ambulance, I lay on the stretcher once again, trussed up like a Sunday roast joint of lamb. Peering through a small gap, I could just see out of a side window. The real world was out there basking in the sunshine, I thought sadly as we approached the motorway. Unlike the previous journey, there were no flashing lights or sirens and the paramedics were not like the couple who had memorably been the highlight of Grant and Emma's year, the previous night.

After we came off the motorway the journey seemed much longer than the one last night, and that was accounting for the fact that we were travelling at a normal speed, in the flow of the traffic. Peeping through the gap again, I tried to make out where we were but didn't have too much of a view to establish any known landmarks or road signs. From the small field of vision, I could just make out the cars rushing past on the other side of the road, an odd tree dotted along the pavement, and a few houses. Once my eyes had adjusted to the brightness of the sunlit roads, I actually started to recognise the area we were in.

"Are you taking me home?" I enquired to the paramedic seated on my left.

"We're taking you to the General, love." He spoke patronisingly, making me feel stupid.

A little annoyed, I asked, "Aren't we going in the wrong direction? I live down this way!"

"We've got someone else to drop off, love," he replied nonchalantly. Looking back through the window, I watched as glimpses of familiar roads and buildings showed the way to my home.

Continuing to watch intently as we approached my beautiful house, I filled with sadness when we passed the turning in to Pinewood Avenue. A strange feeling of deep anguish filled me entirely as I pined for my home, my children and my husband. Little did my family know that I had just travelled straight past them. Heartache and silent tears filled me as I realised that my son Jack was only seconds away from me, yet he could have been a million miles away. I'd longed to see him for the last six months.

After dropping off the elderly man (of whom I had been completely unaware), sitting right at the back of the ambulance, we turned back and headed for the General. I watched eagerly as we approached the area where I lived again, hoping irrationally for a brief glimpse of anyone I might know, or better still, a member of my family casually strolling along the road. Neither of these was forthcoming as we drove past. Maybe it was just as well, as I couldn't have guaranteed that I would not scream out *"STOP!"* possibly even causing an accident.

Unbelievable! Surely I wasn't going back in the very same dingy little room, I wondered, as the stretcher was skilfully parked just outside the door, by a young porter.

A familiar face peered down at me and said, "Hello Alex, back again? How are you?" The young nurse had remembered my name. Spinning in an emotional whirlpool, I found myself twirling downwards, deeper and deeper, as I looked to her and sighed.

"Hello." Tears pricked my eyes as she smiled warmly, but I didn't want to go back in that depressing, dull room.

Back in the same prison cell, I gazed at the familiar patterns on the wall, cast by the last rays of sunshine – another beautiful day was drawing to a close and it felt like the weekend was also ending, even though it was a long one with Easter Monday tomorrow, it felt like the end. The evening meal trolley clanked its way around the ward, outside the room. I had to take a meal that was left over as I'd not been here to order one earlier, but to my pleasant surprise, it was the most delicious meal I'd had in a long time, and considering it was a hospital offering, I was very impressed.

Resting back on the plump pillows, my full tummy gurgling away happily, I looked at the clock and wondered what time Grant would come to visit. Somewhat disappointed that he had not come sooner, I wished he had more of a desire to rush over to the hospital at every given opportunity to see his beloved wife. Perhaps he was too busy, but surely I was the most important thing in his life and nothing could match the need to be with me. There I go again; insecurity reigning as usual. Why was I so insecure sometimes, and then other times I felt like I had the world at my feet, and that included having Grant right where I wanted him? But today, he was not where I wanted him.

"Your husband called, he said he'll be here very soon," said the young nurse, as she almost danced into the room. "Is there anything I can get for you?"

"No thanks, has he just called?"

"Yes, he wasn't sure where you would be," she replied, plumping up the pillows behind me and straightening the bedspread, as if we had visitors coming round for tea. "Are you warm enough with this blanket?"

"Yes, it's fine." I smiled, wondering why it had taken Grant all day to call the hospital. Then the usual observations were performed, before the young nurse left the room.

Dozing and semi-aware that occasionally, a rippling gurgle of a snore resonated from deep inside my throat, I heard a familiar voice speak outside in the conscious world. It was Grant. He had arrived! Praying I hadn't been dreaming, I opened my heavy eyelids and looked up to see his smiling face peering down on me. Blinking the blurriness away from my eyes, I beamed at him and then noticed Emma stood by his side.

"Hello darling," he said softly, leaning over to kiss my lips. "How are you doing?"

"Hello Mum," whispered Emma as she shuffled past Grant and reached over to kiss me on the cheek. My two precious visitors took their usual seating positions, one each side of the bed.

"I thought you might have come sooner Grant." Cringing as I spoke, I knew it sounded terribly selfish and needy of me, when poor Grant had probably been running around doing all sorts of chores all day.

"I was waiting to find out if you would come back here or stay in Southampton," he replied guiltily.

"Oh, okay. I could have been here all day though, and you only phoned a little while ago didn't you?" I really didn't want to be asking this, but I couldn't stop myself showing my annoyance at his lack of care that I was stuck in this miserable little room. And for all he knew, I might have been lying here most of the day, staring at sunlit, patterned walls or reading a mini *Joy of Sex* handbook, as there was absolutely nothing else to do.

"Sorry babe, I've had a hell of a day. Your mum and dad have been over all afternoon." Looking pensive, Grant scratched his head and glanced over at Emma. Seated on a higher chair, Emma leant over the small washbasin, twiddling with the mixer tap and staring down the plughole.

"No, I'm sorry Grant. I'm just feeling sorry for myself because it's so boring here-I'm so fed up." Realising I was being over-emotional, I tried to lighten the mood, that I alone, was beginning to create, or so it seemed. "Emma, what was all that stuff you put in the bag for me?" I asked. Shrugging her shoulders, she pushed out her bottom lip and looked at me briefly before turning back to the sink. Surely she wasn't still sulking about the letter, I wondered, but decided not to mention it. Looking puzzled, Grant frowned, so I enlightened him as to the contents of the bag.

"I think we should take the bag home again and get you some more stuff!" laughed Grant, after I had carefully mouthed, whispered and played charades to demonstrate the particularly embarrassing book found in the bag. Grinning superciliously, Emma grabbed the bag from the floor at the side of the bed and tucked it under her chair.

"I'll take it home when we go. Dad can bring back some stuff," she mumbled. "I've got to go to Grandma's for dinner tomorrow, haven't I?" she said sarcastically. It was the same every single year: we all had to go to Mum's for dinner on Easter Monday, so she could share her homemade Simnel cake, topped with lemon icing and decorated with – yes, you guessed it – fluffy chicks and mini eggs.

"Oh yes, the weekend has gone quick, hasn't it?" I asked rhetorically, looking to Grant for any signals, as I sensed Emma's awkwardness. "How are Mum and Dad?" I asked jovially, in an attempt to lift spirits in the doom and gloom of the small room.

"Yeah, they're good. Your dad is really looking forward to Tuesday now. He was saying today that if you're not better by then, history will repeat itself so that you can benefit from it when you're better- hopefully by next Sunday." Grant smiled and rolled his eyes at the same time.

"Oh for goodness' sake! You know what that means don't you?" I proclaimed while rubbing my forehead with clammy fingertips.

"Umm," muttered Grant, screwing his face into a side-grin and raising his eyes to the ceiling.

Pop! We both looked to Emma, who had been sat quietly next to the sink, mobile in one hand and sink in the other. *POP!*

"Emma, will you stop that?" said Grant huffily.

"You can't let my dad do anything stupid like that Grant, just because I won't be there. It's a ridiculous thought."

"How can I stop him, Alex? You know what he's like once he's made his mind up about something!" Fidgeting in the chair, Grant watched Emma on the other side of the room. *Pop!*

"Emma, I've told you to stop that!" Grant's raised voice startled her and surprised me.

"It's a bit annoying Em, do as your dad says." Trying to bring peace and harmony back into the room, I felt uneasy again about my husband and daughter, just as I had the previous night. Perhaps my sudden illness and absence from home was preying on everyone's nerves. They both seemed to be somewhat peeved about something. Shuffling in her chair, Emma moved her hand away from the sink overflow hole that she had been using to create the irritating popping noise. Pushing her thumb in and out of the small hole, she had bent her knuckle to cause a suction effect, hence the 'pop'. Now, having been told off, she placed both hands on her mobile phone and proceeded to move her thumbs frantically as they alternated between the letters on the tiny keyboard, typing several sentences. Finally her right thumb paused heavily on the 'send' button and she looked up.

"Sorry," she mumbled sarcastically.

"What's wrong, Emma? You don't seem to be very happy again," I asked, not expecting a reply.

"Don't know." She shrugged and recommenced the rapid touch-typing on her phone.

"Anyway darling, I want to know how you have been today?" asked Grant, a little edgy. Verbally downloading the course of events over the period since last night, I also told him what I knew about the illness...which was not a lot.

"They said I would start physio today but I haven't done anything physio-ish yet," I chuckled. "The paralysis is moving with the rash, so I don't know what will happen next."

"Can you move your legs now?" asked Grant hopefully.

"No, just some of my toes." Wiggling the two biggest digits under the bed covers, I pointed down at them. "Look!" I could feel the tension lift in the room as both Grant and Emma peered in wondrous elation at the little lumps undulating under the bedspread.

"You're getting better!" exclaimed Grant desperately.

"I do feel a bit better today." I smiled at them both warmly.

A nurse I hadn't seen before knocked gently on the open door. "Hello, I'm afraid we need some more of your blood. Would that be all right?" she asked.

"Surely I have given enough blood to feed a crypt full of vampires, have I not?" I joked. Lacking a sense of humour, the nurse frowned and prepared her tray of tools.

"You are having a lot of tests," stated the nurse as she wrapped the band around my arm and pulled it tightly, "Therefore a lot of blood is needed for those tests, madam," she said with a straight face. "The doctor will come and see you soon."

Are all nurses trained to say that to patients all of the time to shut them up? I wondered as she pushed the sharp needle into my battered and bruised veins.

"We'll nip out and get a coffee," said Grant, standing up to move out of the way. Grinning at him, I waved my hand to gesture a goodbye and watched

Emma start to follow him out of the room. Approaching the door, she turned round, waved daintily and smiled as she left.

"I found this on the table down in the café - thought you might like to read it. Your mum brought some magazines for you but I've left them at home with two bunches of grapes. Sorry – I'll bring them in tomorrow." Grant smiled as he passed the tattered *OK!* magazine to me.

"Thanks." Slurping a hot cup of tea, I took the magazine and beckoned to Emma, who shook her head in disapproval. I knew she would not want to bother reading it. Her mobile phone had much more interesting material to offer. Stretching herself across the hand basin again, she continued the ardent mobile conversation she was obviously taking a leading role in.

"Who are you texting?" I asked.

"Friends." I could tell by the tone of her voice that she probably hadn't seen any, and I expected she'd been doing chores all day to earn the money back quickly.

Deep in thought, Grant reclined in the comfy chair and watched as I drank the sweet tea. A tormented look was cleverly masked behind his face. I could see through his blue eyes that something was on his mind.

"Are you all right Grant?" I queried.

"Yes, just thinking that I forgot to bring your phone back," he lied guiltily.

"I was going to ask about that. I really need it, Grant. I feel so cooped up in here. This horrible little room hasn't even got a TV. I hope I'm not staying in here for long."

"I know babe, I promise I'll get it all sorted out for tomorrow. I'm not going to your mum's for dinner. I told her I'd be visiting you."

"Was she okay about that?"

"Yeah, sort of."

"I would've thought you'd want to go. At least you'd get a decent meal. I bet you're living on takeaways, aren't you?

"Yes, but I've got a lot to sort out and do, Alex. You know what I'm like, I'd much prefer to stay at home and catch up with some paperwork."

"Hmm," snorted Emma, "don't see why I have to go then."

"Because I promised Grandma that you and Joe would definitely be there." It was Grant that was doing the scowling this time, and I thought to myself how childish he could be sometimes.

"What about Jack and Aaron, don't they have to go?" whined Emma.

"I don't bloody know, they didn't get home till this morning. I haven't had chance to talk to them, have I?" Grant sounded pretty stressed and angry.

"All right, calm down you two, for goodness' sake. What has got into the pair of you?" I asked in a low voice. The room went quiet and all I could hear was the click-clack footsteps of people outside in the corridor.

POP! Simultaneously, both Grant and I looked at Emma and said, "Stop it!"

"Argh Dad! Oh no – argh," she screeched from the left-hand side of the bed. Jumping from the sudden burst of noise, Grant leapt up from his chair and stared in panic at Emma. Turning and arching my body to see over Emma's shoulder I looked in horror at the hand basin. "Dad, I'm stuck. Mum, help me!" she cried as tears burst from her eyes. Edging himself quickly around the room to Emma's side, Grant grabbed her hand and pulled. "Dad!" she screamed, "You're hurting me."

"For Christ's sake, I bloody well told you not to do it," he uttered angrily, looking around to me for help.

"What can I do?" I exclaimed. The fact that Emma's thumb was wedged firmly in the overflow hole was a horrifying, humiliating hassle and I struggled to cope, seated helplessly on the bed. Crying profusely, she wiggled and wriggled her hand in the sink, desperately trying to loosen her thumb from the hole. Reaching for the liquid soap dispenser on the wall, Grant pumped the lever repeatedly and rapidly, filling his hands with copious amounts of slimy gel. A useless spectator, I tried to calm Emma with harmonious, reassuring words that everything would be okay and that her dad would sort it out. The gel seeped from his hands onto the floor as Grant attempted to carry it over, to cover Emma's thumb knuckle in the lubricant. Stepping closer, Grant moved his feet, which landed straight in a puddle of gel and twisted around as he lost his footing in the sliminess on the floor. A split second later he grabbed hold of the basin as his right leg departed and splayed out sideways. Gooey hands desperately holding onto the edge of the ceramic sink, Grant's grasp loosened and he slid uncontrollably downwards, doing the splits as he went down to the floor with a thump and a ripping sound.

"Oh no, Grant, are you okay?" I called out, peering over the edge of the bed. In a crumpled heap on the tiles, Grant looked up with moist eyes. Surely he wasn't going to start crying too, I worried as I lay completely motionless. The sight of her dad performing a rather perfect gymnastics split pose instantly stopped Emma from crying, as she sat on the chair holding her phone in one hand and the sink in the other, with her jaw hanging open in shock. Her thumb appeared to be swelling by the second under the pressure of the small hole it was wedged in. Gel lay everywhere as the tumultuous scene seemed to freeze momentarily.

At the very moment of Grant's artistic departure to the floor, the commotion and crying had alerted members of staff working on the main ward, who hurriedly came running into the room. The chaotic situation they found caused them to halt in the doorway, as they watched Grant's downfall materialise. Covering my face with my hands, I stared through fingers at the visitors frozen in the doorway, their jaws hanging open wide.

"Please can you help?" I pleaded, suppressing tears. Welling up again, Emma started to sob and placed her mobile onto the cabinet next to her. This was a serious situation, as she'd relinquished her prosthetic limb, as we often called her mobile phone.

Scrambling through the door, the male doctor and his assistant, a trainee doctor, attempted to lift Grant from the slippery floor. Calling for assistance, the trainee beckoned a nurse into the room to quickly scoop up as much of the gel as possible. Appearing extremely puzzled, the nurse briskly pulled paper towels from the dispenser and mopped the floor around Grant's contorted body, as the two men supported him in rising and hobbling around to the comfy chair. Looking ashen faced and shocked from his fall Grant limped and stumbled whilst holding onto his groin and moaning. He sat curled up in the chair and winced like a little boy that had fallen off his bike. Moving hastily back to Emma, the doctors stared disbelievingly at her swollen thumb protruding from the hole. Mumbling quickly and incoherently, the two doctors reacted to the situation with great professionalism and then the trainee left the room to collect supplies.

Sitting perfectly upright on the bed, I stared from one side to the other, not knowing what to say or what to do, although the 'what to do' was rather limited as I couldn't move. Deciding that Emma was far needier of my support, I stretched across and could just reach her other hand as the doctor began to twist and manipulate her thumb. Moaning and groaning in severe discomfort, Emma looked around the back of the doctor as we held hands. Her puffy brown eyes were full of sorrow and remorse as she flinched and twitched from her affliction.

After several attempts to free Emma's thumb from its captive state, a prescribed dose of anti-inflammatory medication and copious amounts of lubricating gels, the doctors decided their only option was to call in the maintenance staff to carefully chip away the ceramic bowl from the retaining ring which held Emma's thumb securely. Once this had been achieved, Emma would be left with a metal ring around her thumb which could be removed with a ring cutter. Still holding our sweaty hands together, I squeezed gently and smiled at her, sensing her fear and anxiety.

Ten minutes later, under the watchful eye of the trainee doctor, the senior maintenance man skilfully chipped away the ceramic around the hole, loosening the metal ring. Emma couldn't watch him and turned her head towards me as the sharp tool was precisely lined up and steadily knocked to eventually release her. Grant had hobbled from the room like a pregnant penguin five minutes earlier, in a desperate need to have a cigarette, and he hadn't cared who heard him as he said he was going for a smoke.

A few minutes later, Emma was free from the basin. The maintenance man looked in surprise at the tiny hole that Emma had managed to wedge her thumb into. The back of the sink was millimetres from the hole and somehow Emma's thumb had bent around the back, in between the two layers of ceramic. Her ballooned, purple thumb continued to pulsate as the doctor quickly organised a wheelchair to take her down to the accident and emergency department to have the metal ring removed.

"Where's Dad?" she cried in terror.

"He's just coming darling, don't worry, it's nearly all done now," I said softly as a wheelchair was pushed through the door by a nurse.

"I don't want to go on my own," cried Emma, looking to me with pleading eyes.

"Dad will be back in a minute, I'll send him straight down to you." As I said it, Grant limped back in and smiled with relief to see his daughter free.

A thin metal shield protector was pushed underneath the ring on Emma's thumb, and the cutting wheel was attached to its holder. Crying again, Emma held onto her dad's hand as he stroked the top of her head tenderly. The cutter sounded like a drill as it slowly went through the metal ring, stopping every few seconds, so the doctor could check that the ring hadn't got too hot on Emma's thumb. A nurse standing next to Grant held a syringe of cold water, ready to cool the ring should it heat up during the cutting. A few minutes later, Emma suddenly felt the pressure relieve as the doctor inserted a spreader under the ring and prised the metal apart. Further floods of tears followed as Emma looked at her distended thumb and the realisation of the trouble she had caused dawned on her.

"I'm so sorry, Dad," she sobbed as Grant put his arm around her and cuddled her tightly.

After many apologies and even more thank-you acknowledgements, Emma and Grant returned to my room. The hand basin had already been dismantled and the water pipes shut off, while the evening staff called around the hospital trying to locate a spare room for me. Due to the unknown nature of my illness I had to be segregated from the main wards, and unfortunately, unoccupied individual rooms were a rarity. Sporting her new giant-sized thumb, Emma came straight to the bed and leant over to hug me.

"I'm sorry Mum," she whispered and kissed me on the cheek.

"It wasn't too bad was it?"

"No, it was okay," she sighed, and moved back around to the chair where she'd sat previously. "Where's my phone?"

Emma soon learnt how to text speedily using only one thumb, while Grant and I filled in accident forms and discussed the situation with the hospital staff, who wrote down lots of notes. Feeling stressed and worried, Emma was quizzed as to how she actually got her thumb through the hole and then bent it around the back. "Don't know," was the only explanation she could come up with, which left the mystery open for debate by the clerical staff, Grant and myself.

News arrived that there would not be an available room until the following morning, but I would be going to the top level of the hospital tomorrow. Relieved to be moving, I knew I could put up with the dishevelled-looking room for one more night. Constantly complaining about his groin strain and moaning like a strangled hyena, as he clutched his manhood discreetly, Grant decided it was time for them to leave. He needed to go home and attempt to sew the small tear in his trousers, just below the zip. The accident paperwork had been completed to everyone's satisfaction and we had all sat in stunned silence for what seemed like forever once we were left alone in the room. None of us knew what to say to each other and we immersed ourselves deep in our own thoughts about the extraordinary events that had just taken place. Practically speechless, I agreed with Grant that they should go home and Emma could get some sleep after her traumatic experience. I too needed to evaluate what had occurred and try to get some sleep, in between the regular and annoying nightly interruptions and observations. It would then be decided the following morning as to whether Emma would go to Grandma's or have a day at home to recover.

As they left I felt sadness rise up again, but not because they were leaving; this time it was because I felt that we hadn't had any time together to talk about home and family. There were so many questions I hadn't asked and so many things I wanted to know. Although Grant took the bag of erroneous items that Emma had packed, I hadn't explained clearly just what I needed. Fearing a repeat of the last package, I could only hope and pray for the best. If only Grant had remembered my phone, I wouldn't feel quite so isolated and useless. I could have texted him a list of the things I needed and that way at least he would remember. I could have also sent a message to Jack, welcoming him home, and I could have called my parents quickly to assure them that I was all right. What a mess this evening had been. What a mess this whole mystery illness was. Maybe I should have been thanking my lucky stars that things weren't any worse than this. From this low point, surely everything could only get better.

Grant

"You didn't tell Mum about the fire," said Emma as they drove away from the hospital. The parking meter had been kind, bearing in mind that it was not as late as previous nights had been. The evening visit was relatively shorter due to the emotionally sapping, unbelievable catastrophe.

"I didn't get a chance to, did I? I'll tell her tomorrow, when I go back," replied Grant, feeling irritable and condemned. "The night was taken up with you and your irresponsible behaviour," he barked. Sliding down into the passenger seat, Emma wished she hadn't spoken as she recognised her dad's anger building. They drove the rest of the way home in silence while Grant mulled over his failings to tell Alex anything about the last 24 hours. Surely it should have been the first thing on his list. On the other hand, shouldn't he have found out how she was feeling first? Or should it wait until she was much better so she could cope with the bad news? He really didn't know what would be the best way to do it. Realising he was rubbish at these sorts of tricky decisions; he pushed them aside and tried to forget about the whole bloody mess.

The tranquillity on the outside of the house hid a menacing turmoil of chaos inside. As Grant and Emma entered, the burning smell clung to their nostrils; it had not gone away. The almost empty kitchen looked dismal and dirty although it had been scrubbed with bleach earlier in the day. Through the open patio doors, Grant could just make out the figure of Jack sitting in the darkness. Rushing out to the garden, Emma stood directly in front of him and proudly displayed her sausage-shaped thumb.

"What have you done, sis?" he asked quietly, sipping from a glass of Jack Daniels and Coke.

"Well—" She stopped suddenly as Grant clumped onto the patio.

"Well? Go on then, tell him exactly what you've done," said Grant, noticing the drink in Jack's hand and acquiring a strong urge to get one for himself.

Hours later, after Emma had gone to bed, Jack and Grant remained seated in the garden in the cold April air, drinking and talking about the weekend and Alex. Everyone had been putting on brave faces, for some unknown reason, about Alex's sudden illness, but just under the surface they all feared her rapid downfall. The bed sheets lay on the lawn where they had been left, and several pots and pans still rested upside down, having been washed thoroughly by Dot earlier. The boys had spent some of the evening collecting most of the kitchen equipment and returning it to its rightful place. However there were a lot of items stacked up on the dining table as the cupboards they lived in were of no use anymore. Five of the cupboards needed replacing and Grant had decided that it would be wiser to buy the new kitchen that Alex wanted now, rather than later. Drunk, weary and chilled out, Grant said goodnight to Jack, patted him on the shoulder and went indoors to the living room; his other favourite place. Flicking the television on, he settled down into his comfy recliner and skipped through the channels. Before he had even chosen a suitable programme to watch, he'd drifted into a heavy sleep. A short while later Jack stumbled through the living room, switched off the TV and turned out the lights, leaving his father snoring and dribbling, as he too went to get some much needed sleep.

With a thudding headache, Grant woke as dawn was breaking. Shuffling into the kitchen with bleary eyes and an aching groin, he halted abruptly as he saw and remembered what had happened. It hadn't been a terrible nightmare. It was all real, but on this bank holiday Monday morning it all seemed so surreal. He wished it was a normal day: he goes off to work, then the kids go to school and college and Alex leaves last after she has frantically whizzed around the house, tidying up and put the washing machine on. But this was unlike any Monday morning he had ever known, and to make it worse he felt ill and battered. Tea was the only cure, and in abundance, he thought as he switched on the new kettle. A plan of action was the only way he was going to get through the day; he had to do it Alex's way, he conceded. She would have known what to do today, how to do it, when to do it, which way to do it and who to do it with! Grant smiled inwardly and limped through to the office, an extension on the side of the house which he had built some years ago. Picking up a notepad and pencil from the drawer, he returned to the dining room and found a space on the table amongst the bleach-cleaned kitchen equipment.

Returning to the table, mug of tea in hand and two headache tablets swallowed, Grant decided to make a list of jobs to do as it was too early in the morning to do anything else yet. The first thing would be to text Jeff and tell him to cancel his appointments for the rest of the week. He wasn't due back until Wednesday anyway, but Jeff and his wife Ali should know about Alex. His business partner would understand, but he'd hardly believe the story of Grant's weekend of hell. It was very unlike Grant to take any more days off than was absolutely necessary. His work and the success he had achieved meant so much to him, and the accolades that came with it made all the long hours worthwhile, but this was a situation that truly warranted his absence.

Grant and Jeff, the directors of a quantity surveying company, were good friends as well as business partners. They had met a long time ago at university, but upon successfully completing the course, Jeff went his own way while Grant continued to qualify for professional accreditation and became a member of the Royal Institute of Chartered Surveyors. This gave him the highest rank of Chartered Surveyor. Ten years ago Jeff and Grant met up again and decided to start a business together, which had always worked very well.

His next job would be to check that Emma was all right to go to Grandma's for dinner, and possibly Joe too (at least that would keep Dot quiet, and off his back). Realising it was very thirsty work, thinking and writing lists, he made another mug of tea before continuing his list proudly. Thinking for a moment about his next plan, he suddenly realised he had to speak to Dot! He'd have to explain to her that he hadn't been able to tell Alex about the fire. If she heard it from her mum he'd be in big trouble. It would look like he was being efficient and responsible if he called Dot first, before she could get to him. Now that was a plan, he decided as he started to enjoy writing his list, while the world awoke outside and the sun shone in a cloudless sky.

Stopping suddenly, Grant thought he should call her right now. She got up before the sun at this time of the year, and knowing how Dot worked and what she thought, he realised she'd call very soon. Painfully walking into the living room he reached for the phone and grabbed it from the base, fearing that it would ring at any moment.

"Good morning Dot."

"Grant, is that you? Are you all right?" she asked in astonishment.

"Yes it is me," he laughed into the phone; too loudly, making his head hurt more.

"Are you drunk or having a nervous breakdown Grant? Do you need me to come over?"

"No I'm not drunk Dot, everything's fine, we're all okay here. I just called to let you know that I haven't actually told Alex about the fire yet—"

"Why?" Dot jumped in.

"Well, as I was just about to say, Emma had an accident at the hospital last night which took over everything else. She's okay...she trapped her thumb in a hole but she's fine."

"Trapped her thumb in a hole? What are you talking about? Do I need to come over and look after her while you're at the hospital? Where is Alex now, anyway?"

"Listen Dot, I'm not going to come for dinner today as you already know, because there is too much to sort out, but Emma is fine and she'll be there, with Joe hopefully." Pausing for a breath, Grant then continued calmly. "Alex is back at the General, she's feeling a bit better. They are moving her again today to another ward, but I'm not sure which one yet."

"I'll call the hospital and find out," said Dot, quite sternly. "Are Jack and Aaron coming for dinner?

"No, they want to go and see Alex today. They haven't even spoken to her yet. Well, neither has Joe but I'm not sure that he'd want to go to the hospital – he can't cope with it, you know what he's like."

"Yes I know he can't, poor beggar, but if she doesn't get better, he'll have to go and see his mum. How many visitors can she have?" she asked, sounding like she'd calmed down.

"She's in a small isolation room. I think it's only two at a time," Grant guessed.

189

"You know that I would love to see her Grant, but I don't want to interfere with any of your chances of seeing her."

"I know, maybe it would be better to leave it just for another day or two." Momentarily, Grant had forgotten about Tuesday's events, and then remembered as he continued. "If she's still there on Wednesday, why don't you go over then? Or I could take you?" Grant listened intently, as there was a pause at the other end of the phone.

"Umm, all right love. We're busy most of the day tomorrow, aren't we? I imagine Charlie won't feel up to going over there tomorrow night and I know you'll want to see her, so maybe it's best to leave it until Wednesday."

Sighing with relief, Grant relaxed. "That's great Dot, and I will break the news to her tonight about the fire. I know she'll be worried out of her mind but I suppose she needs to be told."

"I think she should be told, Grant. It wouldn't be nice if we all pretended nothing had happened and she came out of hospital to find her kitchen in cinders."

"You're right," Grant agreed. "What time shall I come over tomorrow morning?"

"The photographers will be ready at around nine o'clock, so you could come over then. Is that okay?"

"No problem, I'll see you then."

"All right love, bye for now." The phone went silent and Grant put the handset back onto the base. *Phew!* He'd done it. He'd actually beaten Dot to the phone for once. This called for a celebratory cigarette out on the sunny patio.

"Yeah, I'm fine. I want to go to Grandma's anyway," mumbled Emma as she lay in her warm bed examining her black and blue thumb. "It matches Jack's eye now," she said, holding it up in the air.

"Come on then, up you get," Grant called through the opened door. Crossing the landing, he knocked on Joe and Aaron's bedroom door. "Joe!"

A muffled '"Yeah!" came from within and Grant knew that Joe was awake. Once Joe was awake, everyone else could possibly be awake. Unable to keep down the volume control of his voice box, he was naturally very loud.

Having taken a shower, Grant felt slightly more alive than he had earlier. The carefully overwrapped bandage on his toes had slipped off, exposing the burns as he peeled off his sock, and he spent most of his time under the shower screaming silently as the warm water trickled to his feet. Upon close examination Grant could see that his toes were still glowing red like angry little devils. Dressing them more lightly than Emma had, he cringed as he pulled on a fresh pair of socks.

The phone call (instead of a text – Grant was feeling adventurous) to Jeff had been quite humorous, yet also not funny at all. Jeff listened in disbelief as Grant detailed the course of events and misfortunes, starting at Friday night and finishing his tale at Sunday night.

"Bloody hell Grant! I can't believe it," Jeff responded down the phone. A few more words between the two and Grant knew that everything would be taken care of and he wouldn't be expected in the office until next week.

The list-writing and planning strategy was actually working. He was feeling better by the minute as he solved one problem after another. Taking a moment to reflect on his morning of successes, Grant sat on the patio with a mug of tea and smoked his cigarette heavily. Joe and Emma went off happily with Charlie when he came to pick them up. Jack and Aaron were still in bed and the garden gnomes were busily posing and grinning around the edges of the lawn. Life was almost great, just for a very brief moment. Knowing there was so much more to accomplish today, Grant finished his tea, stubbed out the butt of his cigarette and went indoors to survey the kitchen once again and decide what he was going to do.

Stomping down the stairs like a Neanderthal man, Jack headed for the kitchen and hazily searched for a breakfast bowl amongst the charred remains of the cupboards. Rising from his bed at midday annoyed him as he felt he'd wasted half of the day and his precious holiday time. The mission today was to lie in wait for his brother Aaron to surface, and then go on the bus to visit Mum.

Trawling through countless kitchen websites, Grant concluded that it would be a much better idea to wait until Alex was home and feeling well enough before he ordered a new one. If he went ahead now, it would surely be the wrong one – he wasn't that accomplished as an Alex-clone yet. Switching off the computer, he collected a rucksack from the cupboard under the stairs and went up to their bedroom in search of items that Alex might need. Discovering that he didn't have a clue what she would want, he screwed up his eyes, opened her knicker drawer and delved in; grabbing the first pair he touched. Repeating the process, Grant presumed that she may need two pairs, depending on how long she had to stay in. Gathering up random items and the spare tube of toothpaste in the bathroom cabinet, he realised that he was probably no better at packing a bag for his wife than Emma was.

As soon as Aaron was awake enough to walk in a straight line (which could take hours), the two brothers left the house and set off to the hospital. Grant had offered to take them over there but Jack preferred the adventure of an English bank-holiday-nightmare bus ride, independence, and of course chance encounters of the female kind. The glorious summery weather was getting more unusual for April as the days rolled by and made the trip far more pleasurable for him. Sightseeing along the way, Jack pointed out every bit of bare, pink, female flesh he could spot, which bored Aaron to the point of despair.

"How's everything going there?" asked Grant, as Zoe politely answered the phone.

"Hi Grant, yeah everything is just fine. How's Alex?" The cheeriness of her voice echoed in the phone.

"She's getting better slowly. She's still in hospital. I think it could be a while before she's well enough to return," warned Grant.

"We'll manage, tell her not to worry. I sent her a text yesterday but haven't heard back so I guessed she might still be there."

"Oh, I've got her phone here, it's charging. You've just reminded me I need to take it in to her," he laughed.

"Okay, maybe I might hear from her then. But honestly Grant, if there are any problems I'll call you. I've sorted out everyone's hours and they're all happy to help out."

"Well done Zoe, we knew we could count on you to deal with it. Thank you."

"Anything I can do, just let me know and please give Alex our love and best wishes for a speedy recovery," she almost sang.

"I will, cheers. Bye Zoe."

"Byeeee!" she sang.

It was all going really well actually, surmised Grant, replacing the phone and flicking through the TV channels. Jack and Aaron would arrive home hungry as usual, but finding something to eat would be fun if they had to guess the contents of each of the tins, carefully scrubbed and peeled of labels by Dot and her evil counterpart Evelyn. A flash went through his mind: *Aaron had got up earlier than normal on a holiday.* The thought nipped and momentarily niggled at his brain.

Another flash whizzed by as Grant flicked absentmindedly through the TV offerings. *Jack came home yesterday. Jack and Aaron had gone out together* – again it picked at the dense matter inside his head, but not enough to spark any recognition. Settling for a wildlife documentary about otters, Grant slid down in the recliner to get more comfortable. Flash: *Jack and Aaron have gone to the hospital on the bus.*

Just time for a quick nap before Joe and Emma get home, thought Grant. Flash: *Jack and Aaron have gone to visit their mum.*

Heavy eyelids starting to droop, Grant drifted on the brink of unconsciousness as the broadcaster droned on.

"The Southern River otters inhabit both marine and fresh waters, from rocky coasts to rivers and canals. Medium in size, the otter ranges from—"

Flash! *Fuck!* Grant's heart skipped a beat as his eyes opened, wide and alert. Jack and Aaron were on their way to see their mum! Sickness caressed the back of his throat as he gulped and gasped. Heaving himself up and out of the chair, he reached for the phone. Heading for the garden, Grant grabbed his packet of cigarettes, flipped the top open and pulled one out with his teeth as he listened intently to the continuous ringing of Jack's phone. Shit, no one answered the call. Desperately, Grant fingered through the directory and called Aaron's mobile number instead. Again, a continuous ringing could be heard, but strangely echoing through the house this time. Typical – as usual, Aaron's phone was ringing upstairs in his bedroom. Angrily, Grant hung up, left his cigarette burning in the ashtray and went indoors, frantically searching for his own mobile. *That bloody Aaron never takes his damned phone anywhere. I don't know why he bothers having one*, he judged harshly, growing more uptight as he couldn't remember where he'd left his own phone. Dashing backwards and forwards with a strained groin and tender toes, Grant's temper rose as the elusive little mobile remained hidden and his desperate urge to send a text message multiplied.

"Bloody stupid thing!" he shouted, throwing Aaron's phone across the bedroom. Bouncing off the opposite wall, the casing split in half and the insides of the high-tech mobile disintegrated into several small pieces. Attempting to use someone else's phone to send a text message while in a rage was not a good idea. Grant's technological aptitude was non-existent and sending a text message on his own phone was difficult enough. He much preferred to simply call people. Hurting and aching from the last few days of injuries, he stomped out of the room, kicking the pieces and scattering them as he went. Fury raged within him and he knew he had to quell it. Sidestepping into the bathroom, he turned on the cold tap, cupped his hands and splashed water onto his flushed face. Opening his eyes, he glanced up at the windowsill in front of him, and there it was, his mobile phone.

If you get this, Jack, don't tell Mum about the fire or anything else. I'll tell her tonight. Pressing the 'send' button, Grant's heated disposition began to melt. A solitary tear smarted in his eye as he mellowed and softened. The weekend of consecutive calamities was catching up with him and taking a toll on his mental state. Short-tempered, overtired, aching and throbbing from head to toes, Grant's distress was beginning to show in many ways.

Returning to Aaron's bedroom, he picked up the pieces of metal and plastic and promised himself that he would buy a new phone for his son, whether Aaron used it or not. It wouldn't have been an issue in normal circumstances, as it had been today. Troubled with worry, Grant dared to imagine what was going on at the hospital. His wife could have discharged herself by now, he thought, visualising her racing through corridors and hopelessly attempting to manoeuvre a wheelchair in order to escape. Knowing her so well, he guessed what she would think once she discovered the truth. She'd determine that the family and their home really couldn't survive without her around. A ridiculous assumption, but one that Alex held close to her heart and believed in. The boys had more than likely told her everything. Although they weren't at home during some of the incidents, they certainly knew it all and could tell a jolly good story.

Struggling to compose a lighter, brighter attitude, Grant recalled the morning's lists and plans that he'd enjoyed working on. Somehow he needed to get back to that brief moment of serenity and hope. Perhaps another cigarette would do it. A 'breath of fresh air' would help to clear his mind and clarify what the hell he was going to say to Alex when he visited her later. He could feel it in his bones: she knew about everything. He'd had the chance to tell her last night and he'd blown it.

Alex

Most of the morning had been spent talking to several well-dressed, well-spoken members of the hospital's management about complaints, claims and litigation. *No! I will not be making a claim for my daughter's injuries. Stop panicking and go away!* A representative from facilities management and the Nursing Director's team of two gentlemen proudly displayed badges that I couldn't bother to read or even manage to decipher. As they left the room, looking somewhat perplexed by my lacklustre attitude, I sighed with relief. Memories of the previous evening filled me with contempt and embarrassment. Seeing my daughter attached to the plumbing and my exasperated husband sprawled out on the floor, doing the splits, while pink gel dripped off him, I desperately wanted to try and carry on as normally as I possibly could under the circumstances. I hoped I'd seen the last of the suited workforce.

Tottering through the door again, the cheery, fragile old man carried in a small box and carefully placed it under the pipes sticking out of the wall.

"You'll be going soon, love. I can fit the new sink then." He beamed a brown, toothy smile and proceeded to open the cardboard box excitedly, like he had just received a Christmas present.

"How do you know I'm going? Going where?" I asked excitedly. The dismal room had looked even more prison-like since the old washbasin had been removed. During the night I'd been sure that the walls were closing in around me, and in my condition I wasn't up for any *Indiana Jones* dramatics.

"Nurse said." Pointing an arthritic finger to the door, the wobbly little man continued. "She said you're going upstairs so I can get on with the job."

Feeling immensely relieved, I thanked him for letting me know and started to collect as many of my things as I could reach. I was moving soon, and elation propelled me to reach further than I should have to grab all my belongings. Gripping the opposite side of the bed with one hand, I just managed to collect everything without repeating Grant's performance and landing myself on the floor by the old man's feet. Plumping up the pillows behind me, I sat upright and looked smug as I waited patiently for my departure from the room of doom.

Straining my eyes to adjust to the sunlight pouring through two large windows, I blinked as the porter wheeled me into the new room. Another single room, offset from the main ward – nice, I thought as I surveyed my new home. Two storeys up, I took in the panoramic view of the bustling, bank holiday bargain-hunters in the town below, and the hazy, azure sea stretching out beyond the town's perimeter. A cloudless blue sky crowned the picturesque scene, and a strong desire to be outside and feeling the sunshine on my skin overwhelmed me. It almost felt like heaven here compared to the dingy isolation unit I'd come from. *Grant and Emma will like this*, I decided as I lifted the bags from the bed, reached across and placed them on the bedside table.

"Hello, you must be Alex?" asked a sprightly young nurse rhetorically, as she bounced into the room like Tigger at a birthday party. Smiling warmly, I nodded.

"Yes. This is a much nicer place than the assessment unit." I sighed with relief.

"Oh, we do try to look good up here." She laughed, as she took the notes from the end of the bed and left.

Above my head hung a television/phone unit, ready and waiting for me to give my credit card details. Annoyed that I wouldn't be able to watch the news for free, I set about filling in the onscreen form to set up an account. At least I'd be able to catch up with the world outside, if nothing else. Craving normality was torturous. I only prayed that the nightmare of being ill and hospitalised would soon be over, and then I could return to my life; the life I loved. Regaining a normal existence took precedence over the health issues I was suffering from, which was pretty ironic in the current circumstances and quite a ridiculous notion. Realising I had my priorities the wrong way round, I lay back on the pillows and willed myself to get well soon as I drifted into a peaceful snooze.

"It's my mother!" The instantly recognisable voice and familiar catchphrase filtered through my sleepy thoughts as I opened my eyes and smiled.

"Jack!" I squealed excitedly, rubbing the sleepiness away. Reaching with open arms, I embraced him as he towered over me. Standing at the bottom of the bed, Aaron grinned. "Hello darling, you're back from your UK tour then?" I laughed, proud of my quick wit, having just woken. I heaved myself up and turned to study Jack's muscular physique, "Bloody hell, what has happened to you?" I said, noticing his eye. Grabbing a chair and pulling it towards the bed, Jack began to explain how he'd acquired a brilliantly black and blue eye. Approaching the other side of the bed, Aaron leaned over to kiss me as Jack continued his story.

Roaring laughter echoed through the ward as I attempted to hush the boys at the same time as trying to shush myself. Giggling and crying, I waved my hands at them both to stop.

"I can't take any more, stop it both of you." The two comedians were on form and bouncing off each other as they told me about their journey home. Detailing the lives and horrors of the elderly couple on the plane who went to visit their dreadful daughter, Jack was the star of our private show. Almost topping the number one act, Aaron explained his unpleasant bowel dilemma in the train station toilets and how he managed to jump on the wrong train. This was what I had been missing. I'd hardly laughed all weekend. I had so desperately needed a cure and the boys were my tonic, my ticket to good health and the way home.

After the raucous, uncontrollable cachinnation, I glanced through the door to the adjoining ward, wondering and worrying what the patients and nurses would be thinking about our unsophisticated behaviour. Realising my visitors looked like two overgrown delinquent teenagers to those who did not know them, I was perturbed momentarily that the impression we were giving to my new neighbours was far from welcoming. Jack's black eye, cropped hair and tattooed arms only enhanced his already menacing, Herculean appearance, and as for dear Aaron, he was so shy, unassuming and profoundly pessimistic that he could be mistaken for a drug addict purely by his vacant expression. Why was I even worrying, for goodness' sake? I reminded myself that I was in a hospital; no one else would care what I or my guests were doing. Hopefully it was a refreshing change to hear a bunch of nutters laughing their heads off.

Caring too much what other people thought about anything and everything, I'd spent a lot of my life in quite a reserved fashion, and maybe it was time to change. Time to let the proverbial hair down that had always been kept tightly knotted on top of my head.

As quiet and calm was restored and we returned ourselves to well-adjusted dispositions, I sensed the atmosphere had changed and those heavy grey clouds were on the horizon again. Something wasn't right. I always managed to sense when things were amiss. Behind Jack and Aaron's façade was an underlying truth: none of my children or my husband were of any use in trying to cover up or hide something from me. Or was it that I had some sort of psychic ability and could weed out truth and discover lies?

"Is everything all right at home?" I quizzed. "How's Emma's thumb?"

"I couldn't believe what she'd done, Mum. Dad told me last night. I haven't seen her much today," said Jack, looking to Aaron for some backup which would never be forthcoming due to his lack of confidence. "What did Dad tell you last night when he was here?"

"Nothing. Why?" I asked curiously.

"Did he mention our little accident?"

"No, what little accident?" A sense of foreboding rose again. Glancing across to Aaron, who was perched on the end of the bed, I knew something was wrong as he stared at the floor with a vacuous expression.

"We've had a fire in the kitchen," proclaimed Jack as quickly as his tongue would allow.

"What?" I probed, searching for answers on the faces of my two sons. "How big a fire? How the hell did it happen?" Aaron wouldn't look up. He couldn't, he was too scared that he might give more away if I saw the fearful expression painted onto his cadaverous complexion.

"Mum, it's quite bad," drawled Jack as he too looked down to the floor.

"Why didn't your dad tell me last night then?"

"Don't know." Jack shrugged guiltily. "It was Joe's, Dad's and my fault. We were playing the tea towel game. The toaster caught fire."

Propped up straight with the pillows behind my back, I braced myself for the shocking details. I required every last minute detail, and Jack knew that I would. The laughter and banter of earlier had evaporated into ashen clouds of dubious mistrust.

"Are you telling me everything Jack?" My spiritual intellect was buzzing loudly. Aaron continued to sit tensely at the end of the bed with his head propped up in the palms of his hands, elbows resting on his legs. "Aaron, aren't you going to say anything?" My poor boys looked exasperated, and I tried not to vent my anger on them. Curbing the resentment that was building and directed towards Grant, I calmed down enough to reassure Jack and Aaron that I wouldn't explode with outrage.

"Dad got arrested two nights ago as well," squeaked Aaron nervously. Rolling his eyes, Jack sighed, realising by my expression that I knew nothing of this either.

"Oh my God," was all I could manage to say as thoughts raced through my mind. *Why? Where? How?* Burying my head in my hands, I suddenly became aware of my toes moving. It was as if they were cringing for me. Was I regaining movement? Could the paralysis be magically disappearing? Was I getting better? Or was it all my imagination working overtime as my desire to get home had just grown tenfold?

"Bloody hell, start at the beginning. I want to know what the hell is going on at home." Glaring from one to the other, I waited for someone brave enough to reveal all. Looking as if he wished he could shatter into a zillion pieces and disperse unnoticed into the atmosphere, Aaron remained silent as Jack took the brave steps to tell me exactly what was happening at number 23 Pinewood Avenue.

"I wish I could get out of here and get some fresh air. It looks so nice out there," I said, breaking the icy atmosphere I'd created by my sheer disappointment and resentment that I'd been so unaware of the goings-on at home. Gesturing to the expansive windows and the sunlit views, I looked pitifully at Jack and Aaron.

"Mum, you can. There are wheelchairs down at the entrance, I think they cost a pound to hire, just like shopping trolleys," answered Jack. "Shall I go and get one?"

"Yes please, I'm sure they wouldn't mind if I go out and get some fresh air. I've been cooped up inside since Friday night." Jumping up, Jack nudged Aaron on the shoulder and beckoned him to follow.

"Come on, we'll go and have a look if there are any left," he said, pushing Aaron in front of him. "We'll be back in a minute Mum," Jack called over his shoulder as they left.

"Jack," I shouted back, "will you ask one of the nurses if it's okay for me to be taken out?" Nodding his head, he raised his hand in acknowledgement and shunted Aaron along and out of sight. Within ten minutes they returned with a rickety old wheelchair.

"Jack just got told off, Mum," Aaron couldn't wait to tell me.

"Why?"

"He told me to get in it," he said, pointing to the chair. "Then he pushed me really fast along the corridor." Aaron attempted to cover up a giggle – badly. "We nearly crashed into an old man on a stretcher and the porters told Jack to walk through the hospital sensibly or leave." Holding on to the handlebars of his new toy, Jack pulled a sad face and blinked exaggeratedly with his big, brown, puppy-dog eyes.

"You idiots, what if you'd been thrown out? I would have been sat waiting here all night." Looking closely at the prehistoric artefact which was supposed to be a mobile chair, I said, "Oh dear. How am I supposed to get in it? It looks like something from the Victorian era."

"It'll be all right Mum. It was the last one there so I thought I'd grab it as you're desperate to get outside," replied Jack sincerely, "and it is nice outside, really warm."

"Did you ask the nurse?"

"No, we can do that on the way out. Don't worry. Come on, climb over." The boys supported and lifted me across to the hard, tattered leather seat of the wheelchair. "Do you want a blanket?" asked Jack.

"I'd better had, I don't want to get cold, or catch one either." Wrapping the blanket from the bed around my shoulders, Jack grabbed another one to cover my legs. Grinning silently, Aaron looked pleased that I was mobile and on my way out of the hospital. Two nurses hovered around the reception area chatting and gossiping as we approached the exit of the ward. They agreed that it was perfectly fine for me to go outside, in fact, they thoroughly recommended it.

"It's gorgeous out there, it'll do you good," said the plump nurse leaning over the countertop. "Can you let us know when you're back?" I nodded as Jack carefully steered the wobbly wheelchair through one side of the double doors which Aaron held open.

As we arrived at the main entrance, I smelt the muggy sunburnt air and instantly warmed as the sun's rays teased the blanket from my shoulders. A glorious appreciation for such a simplistic universal entity, I beheld the flaming star dazzling in the late afternoon sky. Balmy air caressed my face and the sultry sun washed over my tired, unwashed hair. It was positively wonderful to feel alive and be outdoors again, breathing fresh air deep into my lungs. Tears strained in my eyes but I blinked them away, not wanting to spoil the view or the spectacular sensations rushing through my veins. This was going to make me get better. I just knew it would.

The tree-lined pathway stretched further than I'd expected, but from a sitting position, everything looked bigger or further away. Dappled sunlight filtered through the ornamental trees and the light breeze served to create dancing patterns on the paved walkway. "Where do you want to go Mum?" Jack's voice penetrated through my euphoria as I watched people rushing in and out of the main entrance. Visitors, patients, outpatients, families, proud new fathers and many other types of people walked, dashed and limped past my chair in one direction or another.

"What?" I asked in a warm, dazed and lazy voice.

"Where do you want to go, or do you just want to stay here for a while?" asked Jack. Aaron's eyes searched for a vacant bench at the sides of the pathway.

"Down there Mum, look, there's a bench," said Aaron excitedly. "Quick, before someone sits there." Turning sharply, Jack manoeuvred the chair round and quickly marched towards the bench, following behind Aaron. The speed that the boys walked emphasised the light breeze blowing warm air through my hair as it kissed my already flushed cheeks. The wheels of the chair bowed outwards and I gripped onto the armrests tightly as I undulated to the bench like a clown riding a wobbly-wheeled circus bike.

A quarter of an hour drifted by, many people drifted by, last winter's withered leaves and litter drifted by in the breeze and my thoughts drifted by, undulating like the wheelchair from bad to good to bad again. How could Grant have got into such a mess at home? How could he have been so stupid? Why hadn't he said anything? Was he scared to? Was I so terrifying that he couldn't bring himself to tell me? Yes, probably I was chillingly intimidating when things didn't go my way. Perhaps I should re-evaluate my life, stop trying to be perfect in everything I do and stop expecting everyone else to be perfect too. Fury and pity battled in my mind while I watched Jack and Aaron having a quiet natter. The conversational atmosphere had become subdued since Jack had brought me up-to-date with the family's activities.

"Shall we go for a walk?" I asked, trying to inject some merriness into my voice. The boys stopped their idle chit-chat instantly.

"Yeah Mum, where would you like to go?" asked Jack, looking relieved at my refreshed, cheery disposition.

"How about down that way?" I pointed towards the car parks in the distance. Aaron stood up, rubbed his hands together and beamed a smile of appeasement.

"Come on then," chortled Aaron. "Who's pushing?"

"Let Jack do it up that hill, then you can push me back into the hospital." Fearing Aaron's slight frame wouldn't cope with pushing my extra weight up the small hill towards the car park, I preferred the robust figure of Jack.

"Madam, your wish is granted – we have lift-off, flight-wheelchair-wobble mission in progress," laughed Jack as we headed off past Aaron, waving as we went. The April afternoon was starting to chill so I wrapped the blanket tightly around my shoulders, and tucked the other one further under my legs. Then I held onto the armrests with a vice-like grip. "Compass bearings, Sarge? Which way? Enemies flanked to the left and right. Mission abort requested."

"Shut up, you bloody idiot," I laughed loudly.

"Which way, Sarge?" Jack asked again, picking up speed and leaving the tense atmosphere way behind us. Skipping along beside us, Aaron had left his worry demon behind too, exposing his childish side. "Target approaching, enemy borders in view. Permission to land, Sarge."

210

"Slow down Jack, where are we going?" I shrieked, gripping the arms as I laughed out loud again, watching Aaron trotting alongside me.

"Mission accomplished," shouted Jack as we conquered the small hill up to the car parks. Surveying the area I realised there was nothing of interest around, unless I was interested in opening a car showroom, which I certainly wasn't.

"Okay, shall we head back to the hospital? I've had quite enough fun for one day and it's getting colder." Turning around, we headed back down the slope as I recalled the odd looks we had from passers-by on the way up. Two adult men racing up a hill with a middle-aged woman in a wheelchair, wrapped in waffle blankets. It must have looked a very strange sight indeed.

It was inevitable: suddenly the wheelchair bumped awkwardly down a high curb. Jack lost control of the wobbly heap of metal and the chair twisted over, enough for me to lose my grip on the armrests. *Thump!*

My momentum carried the chair right over onto its side and straight down to the ground. Reaching out desperately to stop myself from splaying out across the paving slabs, my arm caught underneath the chair as I landed on top of it. The padding of my arm between the chair and the ground saved me from hitting my head hard on the pavement, but the side of my face skidded across the ground, burning and grazing my cheek and temple. Horrified, Aaron looked on like an Ice Age man frozen in time, as Jack

211

managed to pick up his lost footing and bring himself to a standstill as the twisting chair left his hands. Holding his arms outstretched like Jesus on the cross, Aaron desperately searched in the nanoseconds of disaster to catch someone – anyone – but he missed. Bringing his arms in towards his face, he covered it in repulsion as he saw me lying in a crumpled heap, half-buried under the rickety wheelchair. Blood oozing from my face.

"Oh my God, Mum, are you all right?" cried Jack, picking me up. "Grab the chair!" he shouted to Aaron, who was momentarily buried in his shell, wrestling with the worry demon that had caught up with him. Aaron grabbed the chair and hoisted it upright as Jack lowered me back onto the seat. Scurrying around, Aaron collected the blankets and hurriedly wrapped me up until I looked like I was wearing a burka.

"Cover your face Mum, it's cut and bleeding," he rambled in a panic as he quickly placed the gritty, dirty blanket across my face.

"Bloody hell Mum, I'm so sorry. I don't know how that happened. Are you okay?" Jack looked almost tearful.

"Yes, I think so," I muttered in a state of shock. My arm and the right side of my face throbbed and burned. No one had actually witnessed the catastrophic accident, luckily. "Don't take me straight back to the ward, let's find some toilets." I had to have a look at the damage before I went back to the ward. What the hell were the nurses going to say when they saw the state of me? I knew from the pain that I was probably going to look a mess. Treading extremely cautiously, Jack tentatively pushed me back into the hospital. Hiding under the blanket, I couldn't believe this was happening. Feeling (and probably looking) like a bunch of villains we searched the ground floor for some public toilets and eventually found them.

"How are you going to get in there Mum?" asked Aaron anxiously, looking up and down the corridor.

"Can you just push me in quickly? No one is around." I looked from Aaron to Jack.

"I'll take you in, I'm not bothered," said Jack, eyeing his younger brother.

Minutes later, Jack and I returned to the corridor where Aaron had stood guard. "I couldn't really see anything. Bloody mirrors were too high," I grumbled at Aaron. There was no way I would let Jack pick me up in the toilets, lean me over the sink and hold onto me from behind while I examined my face in the mirror. The situation would have looked dreadful if someone had walked in, and it could have been very difficult to explain. "Let's go back to the ward. You can leave me outside and go in and get a mirror from my handbag."

"We can't do that Mum they might think we're stealing something. You'll just have to go back and hope nobody sees you before you get to your room." Jack had his sensible head on again. "They'll see you later anyway. You will have to tell them Mum. What if you get an infection in it? I think you should let the nurses have a look at it. They can clean it up for you," he said guiltily.

"Yes, okay let's go." I was now at the point of not caring. I'd be out of this bloody hospital soon enough anyway. I felt so much better. The fresh air had done me some good and the fall had probably given me an adrenalin rush, and that was always good for you, wasn't it? Although I was battered, bruised and bleeding, the proverbial train that had morphed back to a bus had morphed again to a small car.

"I think we'll get those covered over, Alex," said the nurse as she cleaned the wounds on my face and arm. "I'll dress them for tonight until they stop weeping."

"Okay, thank you. Sorry that you've now got more work to do looking after me," I apologised rather sheepishly.

"Oh don't worry about it," she replied, busily covering me in patches of lint. "I bet your boys felt terrible about it."

"Umm, they did."

"A report has been made about the poor state of the wheelchair, so I'm sure immediate action will be taken."

"Oh that's good," I replied a little sheepishly, knowing it wasn't entirely the chair's fault as it had an accomplice in the form of Jack.

By the time Nurse Clair had finished wrapping me up I looked like a partly embalmed Egyptian mummy with a few missing patches. I lay on the comfortable bed, gazing out of the window, and wondered if Jack and Aaron had made it home safely on the bus. With the track record of the Frey family just recently it wouldn't surprise me if they got lost or were hit by a passing rhinoceros, or they might even have hijacked a carnival lorry loaded with Hawaiian dancers to get home. Surely the last three or four days were all a bad dream – or had it really happened?

Grant

"Stop panicking Dad, she'll be fine. She needs you there after what happened to her today," sighed Jack as he paced up and down the dining room. "I didn't know you wanted to tell her everything, did I? You should have told her last night."

"No, I know you didn't know. It just looks bad doesn't it?" huffed Grant as he sorted through the unlabelled tins, becoming more frustrated. "I don't know why we're bloody well keeping these stupid things anyway," he cursed as a tin and its secret contents went rolling along the worktop and stopped abruptly at the kettle.

"Dad, will you chill out? I'll sort out some tea for everyone. Stop getting so stressed. Go to the hospital," said Jack, growing more exasperated. "I'll go to the chippie again if I have to."

"I can't let you keep having chippie meals, what's in the freezer?" Searching through the iced trays, Grant decided that the better option was in fact to go to the chip shop. "Everything in here would take too long to cook. I haven't got time and I'm sure you don't want to bother with it all," he grumbled as he slammed the freezer door shut. The vibration sent the mystery tin on the last leg of its journey, away from the kettle and towards the edge of the worktop where it commenced a freefall just as Grant managed to catch it. "Huh, nearly had that on my toes too," he smirked.

"Go on Dad, we'll get tea sorted, stop fretting about it. Go!" said Jack in a slightly raised voice, as he pointed in the direction of the front door. "We'll have bloody sandwiches if we're desperate, don't worry about it. I found some stale bread in the cupboard earlier." He laughed. "And there's a small chunk of cheese in the fridge so I could make a round of cheese and salad cream sandwiches for everyone."

Grinning to himself, Grant imagined how surprised the kids would be to find they didn't have salmon paste on their bread. There were an awful lot of good points to Alex but she did have some failings. She could bake beautiful cakes but she couldn't cook a dinner to any culinary standard, and everyone in the house had to endure salmon paste on four days out of five each week for their packed lunches. On that respite fifth day, they'd all get a treat like crab pâté. Alex's lunchboxes were a standing joke in the household, and one she'd tried to change several times, but to no avail. Each time she replaced the contents of their sandwiches for something far less seaworthy, they gradually reverted back to familiar fishy delights after just a week or two. "It's quick and easy just to slap some paste on, get over it!" she would shout in her defence.

The evening had grown chilly after such a warm spring day. As the light faded, Grant drove through the bank holiday traffic in his automatic pilot gear. Thoughts

217

raced through his head about Alex and her illness and the whole weekend of calamities. He found it hard to comprehend that so many things could go wrong in just three and a half days. *Don't bad things happen in three days, or is it in threes?* He couldn't remember what the saying was but he was sure they had been given more than their fair share of bad luck. *Maybe it's that bad things come in multiples of three. Oh dear, that wouldn't be good. How many strokes of bad luck had there been? Does that count for a group of people collectively or is that per person?* Shaking his head at his ridiculous train of thought, Grant came to and pulled out of autopilot gear.

Nursing her blue thumb, Emma had decided to stay at home for the evening. She'd had a stressful day, her thumb was sore and her grandma hadn't let her ease up on peeling the potatoes for dinner. She was somewhat disappointed that she'd not gained a little more sympathy from her grandparents as she told her story to them. Guessing that they were more worried about her mum than they were about her bulbous thumb, Emma decided not to mention it again and instead spent the day frowning and sulking.

Fearing that he would have to see Alex on his own, Grant had pleaded with the boys for one of them to visit their mum with him. That way the wrath would be lessened by the presence of one of the children. Alex didn't believe in arguing in front of them.

"You haven't been to see your mum yet. You should come and see her tonight," beseeched Grant as Joe sulked guiltily.

"I can't, I don't like the hospital Dad. I don't want to see Mum in a hospital. I'll wait till she comes home. I was going to play football tonight at the pitches anyway," replied Joe, staring down at his footie-socked feet. Speckles of pity peppered Grant's mind – he knew Joe couldn't cope with the thought of his mum being in hospital (or anyone else for that matter), and what Joe couldn't see, didn't exist. It was probably better for him that he didn't go to visit her. The aftermath could be harder to deal with.

The heavy evening traffic slowed to a halt as Grant tried to bypass the town centre on the main road leading up to the General Hospital. Holiday caravans headed home after a sweltering Easter weekend and the bargain-hunters travelled along smugly with boots full of half-price, half-melted chocolate eggs. Switching the radio channel over, Grant listened to the local event listings for the centenary remembrance and memorial ceremonies. The momentous commemorative anniversary activities were in abundance across the entire country, it seemed. Switching back to the classical channel, he rolled his eyes and tutted at the hype. The continuous build-up over the last few weeks and the relentless advertising, reporting and promotional media had been a bugbear to his ears and to think that he was going to be immersed in the thick of it himself tomorrow, made him cringe. Shaking his head from side to side, Grant briefly held a slight, although guilty, grudge towards Alex, realising that she would escape the whole thing while resting in her refuge. It was a very selfish thought, but one he couldn't help but feel.

As the traffic started to disperse, Grant puzzled over the oddity that was traffic jams. People got caught up in them all over the country every minute of the day, yet when they came to the end of the jam, well, there wasn't one. He could never figure out how the flow of traffic could resume to a steady passage at some given point, without a trace of the reason behind the build-up in the first place. Heading out of the town, Grant made his way nervously towards the hospital.

Tucking the car park ticket into his jeans pocket, Grant stopped at the display board in the foyer and studied the lists detailing each level of the hospital. Hoping that Jack had given him the right information about Alex's whereabouts, Grant headed towards the lifts. The boys had to track down their mum after they arrived at the MAU and were told she'd been moved up to level E. As he ascended in the lift, Grant could hear Alex's voice in his head, telling him off for being so irresponsible and impulsive. At the first level an elderly lady hobbled in and smiled at him.

"Going down?" she cheeped.

"No, up – level E," Grant replied politely.

"Never mind," she chirped, flapping her arms up and heaving a sigh. Pressing the ground floor button, the frail woman stood back and crossed her arms across her small handbag, staring ahead into the middle distance. As the lift reached level E, an automated female voice announced the arrival and the doors smoothly parted. Stepping out, Grant looked along the corridor for a sign that would indicate the direction in which he needed to go.

"Yes, just through that door on the left," said the nurse, trying to point with her hands full of sheets of paper. Hesitantly Grant entered Alex's new room. Surprised by the pleasant surroundings, the large windows and the mod cons, he stepped towards his sleeping wife. Feeling guilty and melancholy, Grant sat down next to the bed and held her soft hand. Her partly bandaged face and arm reminded him of her dreadful misadventure during the day. Gently squeezing her small fingers, he comprehended that she was and had been in a much worse place than he. His irrational, overbearing fear and guilt had consumed him to the point of ignorance. The prickling sensation at the back of his eyes returned, but Grant blinked the pain away. *What a bloody mess this has all been,* he thought, just at the moment that his beautiful wife opened her eyes.

"Grant – oh." Pulling her hand from his, Alex raised it to the side of her face and touched the cloth covering her wounds. Stiffness had crept in to join the stinging grazes on her face and her arm.

"Babe, I'm so sorry I didn't tell you everything last night, but what with Emma and her thumb, there just didn't seem to be an appropriate moment."

Alex stared silently at him as she continued to hold her sore face.

"I know you're really mad at me for being so bloody stupid. I know I shouldn't have done the things I did. I'm truly sorry, you really don't need this," he pleaded wholeheartedly.

"I'm tired, come back tomorrow. Have you brought some things for me?"

Oh shit! "Oh no. I've left the bag at home. I'll go back now and get it," he stuttered.

"Don't bother, I'm really tired Grant. I just want to go to sleep and the visiting times here are only until eight o'clock. I can continue to live like a filthy tramp and I'm sure no one really has bothered texting me, so I don't need my phone just to feel alive and have a friendly chat with someone. Just bring the stuff tomorrow, I don't care," slurred Alex as she looked away and gazed out of the window, her deliberate sarcasm cutting Grant like a knife.

"I'm so sorry darling. I know you hate me..." Grant paused, hoping for some response, but none came. "Are you getting any better?"

"A bit." She shrugged, wincing from the burning sensation in her face.

"Sleep if you want to, I'll just stay here until they kick me out."

"Go home. The kids probably need you there. You must have things to sort out. I'd imagine the place must be a mess. I'll be fine. I'm not in the mood to have visitors," she continued coldly. Shocked by her cruel and calculated distance, Grant reached for her hand again. "Please go, I want to sleep." Turning her body sideways in the bed, Alex pulled her legs over and faced the window, giving an obvious signal that Grant should leave her alone. Motionless and speechless, he sat quietly, staring across the bed, unsure whether to sit it out or leave.

"I'll go and get a coffee. I'll be back soon," Grant whispered softly as he rose and left the room.

At the reception counter, a nurse sat behind the desk, filling in forms.

"Alex Frey, is she okay? I mean, how is she doing apart from the accident? She's nodded off so I just wanted to know how she is," Grant spluttered.

"She's doing great, considering her awful accident today," said the busy nurse with a beaming smile.

Draining the last dregs of sweet coffee from the cardboard cup, Grant stubbed out the cigarette under his sore foot, walked back through the foyer and returned to Alex's room with a slight limp. The lights had dimmed and she remained in the same position as she'd been in when he left her. Halting at the door, Grant hesitated – should he go or stay? Creeping inside, he approached the end of the bed and could clearly see that she was asleep. The clock on the wall was ticking away the visiting hours and Grant reluctantly decided to leave.

"Have you got a piece of paper and a pen I could use?" he asked, leaning on the reception desk. "My wife has fallen asleep so I'd like to leave her a message."

"Yes sure, I'll just find you a pen. Here, take some sticky notes," said the nurse, cheerfully.

Dear Alex, I returned to find you asleep. I'll come back tomorrow night after I've seen your mum and dad. Wish me luck for tomorrow, ha ha. Don't worry, we'll get everything sorted out at home and you'll be back there soon enough. Love you with all my heart, and I'm so sorry for being an idiot.

Grant xxx

The evening traffic had died down to a dribble of stragglers as Grant drifted along the bypass in another daydream. Surprised by Alex's reaction to his visit, he felt empty and lonely. He much preferred the other side of her character, the bossy, dominant, angry Alex. Detesting ignorance and silence, Grant wished there had been a war of words, rather than the aloofness he'd just received.

At the junction he turned right, absentmindedly, instead of going straight ahead and onwards to home. Deciding to go and have a drink in the pub, he realised he didn't want to go home early, get the third degree from the kids and have to explain that their mum had given him the cold-shoulder treatment. Just one drink in neutral surroundings would make him feel so much better and he needed something potent as he thought about tomorrow's schedule.

The King's Arms was a lively place even on this bank holiday Monday evening. Situated just outside the town's perimeter the quaint old public house had a long history. A well-established, family-run business, both the bar and the inbuilt restaurant managed a roaring trade. Many commuters used the restaurant facilities whilst staying in one of the bed and breakfast hotels further up the road, and among the local residents and general passers-by (such as Grant), the King's Arms was a well-known landmark.

Leaning on the bar and clinging onto a whiskey and lemonade, Grant surveyed the tables around the dimly lit room. Groups of people sat talking in twos, threes, and on some tables more. Some milled around waiting for a table in the busy restaurant while others leaned over the bar, seated or standing, drinking and talking. Dotted around sparingly were the people, like Grant, who sat or stood drinking quietly on their own, watching and listening.

As the last droplet was teased and sucked from the glass, the urge to have one more was overwhelming. Would he get away with another? Would he still be able to legally drive his car home? Unsure whether another whiskey would take him over the limit or not, he beckoned one of the barmaids over. The thought of tomorrow had made the decision for him. Maybe he should leave the car in the pub's large car park and get a taxi home to be on the safe side – he could always pick it up in the morning. Safe in the knowledge that he could have another drink and not worry about driving home, Grant ordered a second spirit and savoured every drop. Then a third...

As the blonde barmaid took the ten-pound note from his hand, Grant sipped his fourth tipple. Two ladies stood next to him in the queue at the bar, chatting and giggling as the pub heaved with activity and cachinnation. Woozy and dull, Grant listened to the women's conversation about work and their colleagues in the office, with a smirk on his face. As his alcohol-induced confidence grew he watched intently as the lady stood closest to him ordered two vodka and Cokes. The taller of the two, who was standing on the other side, noticed that Grant was lounging on the bar with his head propped up on his hand, listening to their conversation. Smiling at him, she nudged her friend's elbow and diverted her gaze quickly to the bar counter, coyly. Touched by her bashfulness, he smiled as she raised her head and glanced from the corner of her eye towards him. Laughing to himself, Grant shivered from the fuel of the alcohol and the thrill of excitement that sped through his stomach.

"Hi," mouthed the tall, slim and incredibly attractive woman in Grant's direction. Turning sharply, Grant looked over his shoulder to see who she was talking to. Realising that the 'hi' had been directed towards him, he nodded and smiled.

"Let me get these," said Grant softly as the barmaid brought the drinks to the counter.

"No, you don't have to do that," exclaimed the woman next to him.

"No, please let me, I don't often buy fine young ladies like you two, a drink. I would love to," he slurred, pulling the wallet from his pocket. "No strings. Please enjoy." The two women thanked him graciously and giggled bashfully. *Did I really just do that?* he thought as he began to swagger on the bar stool.

"Could you get me another please?" asked Grant, just before the barmaid went to walk away. Downing the fourth drink quickly, he smiled to his new acquaintances, winked at the taller girl and watched the barmaid pull his fifth whiskey and lemonade. His head felt fuzzy and his chin was numb, but it felt really good. Grant didn't have a care in the world and the flashing imagery in his mind's eye made him chortle inwardly. What a wacky weekend he'd just had. How funny it was. Visions of PC Oakes on her knees in the dining room sent Grant's head spinning in merriment. The thought of the bed sheets laid out on his lawn, full of kitchen equipment and washed tins, made him silently roar with laughter in his mind.

"Are you okay?" The husky voice of the tall beauty interrupted Grant's thoughts. Guessing she was of similar age to him, Grant looked up and noted that she'd moved closer by switching sides with her friend.

"Huh, you wouldn't believe me if I told you," he smirked, eyeing the woman's curvaceous figure. Her white blouse and knee-length skirt gave the impression of an office worker, or maybe a personal assistant to some top-notch bigwig. Perhaps she was a doctor or a receptionist, but whatever she was, it seemed the poor girl had been working on a bank holiday.

"Try me." She grinned seductively with parted lips.

A tingling sensation burst inside his mouth like a fizzy sweet, and his spinning head caused Grant to pull away. Their hot lips parted and he opened his eyes to gaze intently into hers.

"I can't do this. I'm sorry...I need to go." Reality dawned and Grant cringed, knowing he had been bewitched for the last couple of hours by this sexy, voluptuous woman. Guilt washed over him like a tsunami as he turned away from her and cupped his hands to his face. "I'm sorry Rachel, I'll call a taxi. I really shouldn't be here." Sobering with each word, Grant pulled the phone from his pocket and stared at the screen.

"It's okay, I understand. Here, use my phone," she whispered as she passed the handset to him. "I really appreciate you walking me home. Thank you," she said, with a strange glint in her eye. Grabbing the phone, Grant placed his mobile on the side table and dialled a number on the landline that he remembered from years ago, and hoped it was still an active taxi service.

A few moments later, Rachel ran her fingers through his hair as she moved to kiss him again.

"Are you sure you won't change your mind?" she breathed, as her hot lips pressed against his and her tongue began to probe at his lips. Grant succumbed to her advance once more and opened his mouth slowly. With no resistance, Rachel took his large, strong hand and placed it upon her breast. Slowly undoing her shirt buttons, she held his hand again and pushed it inside her bra. The soft, ample flesh swelled in his hand as she inhaled—

"I've got to go Rachel, I can't do this. It's wrong." Carefully removing his hand, Grant pulled her opened shirt together and adjusted his manhood to a more comfortable position.

"I know you want me," she whispered in his ear.

"Yes...no...I can't. I'm a married man, I am sorry Rachel." Jumping up from the sofa, Grant's head began to throb as his sobering mind screamed at him to leave.

"Please stay, we could have some fun. I won't say anything to anyone."

"I'm sorry, but no."

Luckily, within a few minutes the taxi arrived and Grant walked out of the front door backwards while grovelling, and uttering a thousand apologies.

The diesel engine chugged noisily outside the house as Grant paid the driver and tipped him the change. With a thumping, hung-over head he hauled himself out of the car and searched for his front door key as he shuffled up the driveway. At gone 4.30 in the morning, he was relieved to find that the house slept silently as he crept in. Tormented by his actions, Grant headed for the comfort of his new kettle as tidal waves of guilt resurfaced to try and drown him. *If Alex ever finds out what I've done, it'll be over, I'm sure.* Recalling his ludicrous reaction to the weekend, when he was standing at the bar, he realised how drunk and vulnerable he'd been and how the alcohol masked his true emotions, turning unshed tears into absurd mirth.

Grant, Charlie and Dot

Tuesday the 10th of April. Grant stared, bleary-eyed, at Alex's scribbles on the calendar, waiting for his faithful friend to boil. *Boat – Mum & Dad's house, 9am.* Today was the day – Alex should be at home, everything should be normal, the kids should go to school normally, Aaron should go to college normally, Jack should chill out indoors or go out as normal, the kitchen should look normal, Joe's bike should be in its normal place, the lawn should be normal and Grant's head should feel normal. But it was the Easter holidays and nothing was normal and worst of all, it was the 10th of April.

Grant dared not put the radio or the television on as they wouldn't even be normal today. The centenary remembrance for the *Titanic*'s fatal voyage, which departed from Southampton on the 10th of April 1912, was already beginning. How Grant had managed to be talked into taking part in today's local events, he really didn't know. It probably wouldn't have seemed so bad if Alex was here. She could always make light of any mundane situation that involved her parents and although today was not particularly banal, it was in fact, very unusual. It was most certainly Charlie's special day and he had waited four years for it. Dot, Grant and Alex were supposed to be there to make sure the day ran smoothly and to ensure the launch was successful.

At six o'clock in the morning, seated on the patio, Grant ticked off the weather on his mental tick list for the day. He was starting to like these lists, whether they were imagined ones or real ones. Studying the sky, looking for any cotton wool balls floating by, he noted that there wasn't a single one. A succession of cloudless sunny days was very out of the ordinary, and definitely fitting for the tasks that lay ahead today, the first one being to recover his car from the King's Arms car park. He prayed it was all right after being left overnight, and undamaged. He would then nip into the supermarket on his way back and pick up some bread and fillings for the kids' sandwiches, determined that they would remain salmon paste-free for as long as he was in charge.

Every year, the kids spent part of the Easter holidays visiting an outdoor activity centre which was linked to their local youth club, and Grant wished he was going with them today. Emma would enjoy showing off her thumb to friends and telling a tale or two, while Joe took up every challenge available on the course, from rock climbing to caving. As for Aaron, he was too old for it now and quite relieved about it, too, as the only activity he ever enjoyed was 'Badger Watch', as he didn't have to do anything apart from...well...watch badgers.

Pulling into the drive, Grant glanced into the rear view mirror and spotted the Black Widow approaching the back of the car. *Reverse, reverse – it could be an accident. The spider would be splattered under the tyres.* Reluctantly switching off the engine, Grant grabbed the carrier bag of items for the kids' lunches and hesitantly hobbled out of the car. His burnt toes were still sore, and more so since he'd started to neglect them.

"Morning lovely, is everything all right with your car? You had a late night at the hospital, how is Alex? Where has your car been all night?" quizzed the hairy black predator.

"Morning Evelyn." Grant mumbled. *Aren't people supposed to die when they get to your age?* "I'm really busy this morning. I've got to get the kids sorted out; then—"

"Oh I know, you're off to Charlie and Dorothy's aren't you?"

"Yeah, it's a big day for—"

"Charlie, I know. I spoke to him last night, he's quite nervous." She grinned cunningly.

Well why don't you just fuck off then if you already know everything? "Yes, I expect he is. Look, I've really got to go, Eve." Grant lifted the carrier bag up. "Got to do the kids' lunches ready for, 'Go For It'."

"Would you like me to give you a hand? You haven't told me how Alex is. Why did you have to stay at the hospital half the night?"

"Alex is getting better and she's started to move her toes." Cringing at the thought of inviting Evelyn into the house, Grant knew he didn't have any other option. If he said no he knew she'd go straight back

232

home and phone Dot. How was he going to explain his late night and the car's absence? *Maybe she's phoned the in-laws already. Maybe they're wondering where I've been for half the night. Or maybe I'm just overreacting. Maybe guilt is playing tricks with my mind. Maybe I'm becoming completely paranoid. I'm turning into a vulnerable bluebottle caught in the spider's web yet again. Or maybe there are just too many maybes.*

"Come on, I can see you're getting yourself in a fluster, Grant. Let me help you get those lunches done." Taking the bag, Evelyn let herself in the door, leaving Grant stood on the drive, dumbfounded and speechless.

To Joe's evident surprise and horror, Evelyn came crawling into the kitchen clutching a carrier bag as he munched and slurped his way through a large bowl of cereal.

"Morning Joe. Don't mind me love, I'm helping your dad. He's a bit muddled this morning." She gave him a wrinkled grin and proceeded to empty the contents of the bag onto the worktop.

"Evelyn, I think I can manage, especially as Joe's up now. You'll sort out the sandwiches won't you Joe?" Glaring intently, Grant's piercing blue eyes sent a desperate plea of 'rescue me' to Joe.

"Yeah sure, I'll do them Dad." Draining his bowl of excess milk, Joe put it on the draining board and took the bread and a tin of corned beef away from the spider's grasp. "Blimey – corned beef?" said Joe in disbelief.

"Well, if you're sure I can't help?"

"Thanks Eve, but we'll manage. I need to get going soon myself," muttered Grant, feeling completely stressed out. Unable to concentrate on any one thing, his mind darted around sporadically as he assisted Evelyn to the door. "We really appreciate your offer, thank you." Gently shoving her out and onto the drive, Grant was just about to shut the door when she turned.

"Grant, are you sure you can manage? Something's wrong, isn't it? You seem incredibly harassed."

"Yes, I can manage. I've got to go Evelyn, sorry. I'll catch up with you later." Gently closing the door, he slumped to the floor behind it and sat with his head in his hands. In his mind's eye, Grant watched her cross over the road, creep back inside her lair and pick up the phone.

Majestic and proud, the wooden replica of the White Star liner *RMS Titanic* stood in its holder. A beautiful model of intricacy, patience and perseverance, every minute detail of the original historical ship had been etched into Charlie's masterpiece. Four years of dedicated service to the design and building of his most ambitious project had finally paid off and the planning and preparation for this day had come to fruition. Obsessed with the tragic story of the *Titanic*, throughout his life Charlie had had a fascination with anything to do with the liner. His idea had surfaced five years ago, in the ninety-fifth commemorative year of the rise and fall of the White Star Line's most ambitious ship. Making his mind up then that he would sail his own scaled replica for the centenary. The last 12 months had seen Charlie's enthusiasm grow and widen as he introduced the media to his idea of launching *RMS Titanic 2* into the local lake for its maiden voyage on the same date as its mother ship, one hundred years ago.

Constructed from plywood and pine, the superstructure had several layers of metre-length pine strips meticulously glued to the ply formers to give shape to the ship. The promenade deck was made up of individual strips of plywood, each slat was just one millimetre wide and half a millimetre thick, and these had been laboriously stepped to create the effect of the decking and then glued together one by one. Deep within the hull, Charlie built the steam engines that would power the port and starboard wing propellers. Once the magnificent ship had been assembled he spent month after month rigorously painting and then varnishing the model. After four coats of each, the glossy replica was ready. Pristine and glorious it took centre stage in Charlie's workshop.

Standing with his hands resting on his hips, Charlie admired his work of art for the last time in his private room. Today would be the real test. The ship's buoyancy had been tested to some degree in his bath, but its sheer length had caused some problems with the bathroom taps, which had to be removed temporarily in order to determine, for sure, that there were no leaks in the hull. Utilising his expertise and craftsmanship, Charlie had made a toughened glass casing which attached to a wooden tray base. Then he fitted supporting struts to the base which would hold the ship securely throughout its transportation, and protect the delicate fine details of the upper decks and the rigging when it reached its final resting place. The new maritime museum was thrilled to accept his offer for them to house such a wonderful piece in its *Titanic* memorabilia and artefacts department.

The local newspaper and the *South Coast Television Company* had been informed about the launch of Charlie's ship into the nearby park's boating lake to coincide with the *Titanic's* first and last voyage from Southampton. Buzzing with enthusiasm, the media saw this event as an apt link to the activities, ceremonies and memorials taking part along the coast.

Coverage had already started on Saturday, when countless photographs of the great model shipbuilder Charlie Stern and his creation were snapped, ready for today's newspapers. A lengthy interview had been conducted to get some background information about Charlie for the half-page spread in their *The Titanic – One Hundred Years On* series of articles which would run for the five days leading up to the anniversary of the disaster.

During the photographs and interviews, Dot had opted for tea duty and presented herself as the doting wife. Her immaculate presence and lily of the valley fragrance filled the house with the overwhelming smell and feel of being in a brothel. As she hovered around the journalist, the photographer and the curator from the museum, her questions, opinions and irritating ability to dictate left everyone exasperated.

Itching to leave (including Charlie) and feeling consumed by the excessive flowery fumes emanating from her, the guests tried to complete their tasks speedily.

"Can I get you another cup of tea?" she asked for the umpteenth time.

"No, really. No more, thank you," John, the curator, replied desperately. Having spent just an hour with Charlie, he'd drunk two cups of tea and been offered two more.

"So what have we got planned then?" Dot leaned over the table and examined the paperwork closely.

"Well, I'm not sure when we'll be taking it over to the museum," said Charlie, rubbing his forehead. "I've said to John that our Alex is in hospital and we don't expect her to be out before Tuesday."

"What has that got to do with anything?" whined Dot, glaring at him with piercing eyes.

"I've told you. We'll get the camera crews back out on Sunday the 15th and sink it in memory of the disaster."

Mouth hung open in astonishment, John gawped from Charlie to Dot, then realising his appearance, he quickly snapped his mouth shut again.

"Oh for goodness' sake Charlie, don't be ridiculous. You can't do that!" shrieked Dot as she put a hand on John's shoulder. "The museum really wants this." Dot pointed at the model with a shaky finger. "You cannot sink it, Charlie, just because your daughter won't be there to see the launch. She can watch it on the bloody television."

Nodding in agreement, John remained quiet and unassuming.

"Umm, we'll see." Charlie pouted. "My little girl was supposed to be at the launch, I don't want her to miss it and now she's in hospital...very unwell."

John and Dot looked at each other, not knowing what to say. Charlie's eccentric behaviour was a trait that had earned him the title of the 'nutty professor' and now he seemed to be 'nuttier' than ever.

Pressing the doorbell, Grant waited patiently for an answer.

"How many times do I have to tell you, Grant? You don't need to ring the bell, just walk in." Dot was highly agitated. Stepping in, Grant struggled to make a snap decision as to whether or not to tell her that she had bright red lipstick heading off up towards her nose, as if she'd tripped whilst applying it. He determined that it was better to keep quiet, as she seemed very het up.

"Oh you know me Dot, I always ring the bell." *It's no good...I'll have to tell her, she looks bloody ludicrous.* Raising his finger and pointing to her lips, Grant mumbled incoherently and pointed back to his own lips, miming a lipstick with his finger.

"Are you okay, Grant? If you need a cup of tea, you know where the kettle is, love," she grunted as she turned to climb the stairs. "Make us one as well, would you?" Dot called after him.

Hopefully she'll look in the mirror and see what a mess she is. Daft cow! he thought as he went through to the kitchen, still hung over and increasingly weary of his aching muscles.

Grant's mind swam with lists again as he switched on the kettle: 1) go to the police station and make the statement, 2) see a nurse about infected toes, 3) get some shopping, 4) sort out the mess with Alex, 5) make sure he never got within kissing distance of Rachel ever again. It was simple. He'd definitely take the rest of the week off work and sort everything out once he'd got today out of the way.

Descending magnificently down the stairs, Charlie appeared in the doorway of the lounge. Tall and upright, he wore a dark grey suit, white shirt and blue tie. "Morning Grant, how are you?" he asked rhetorically. Charlie was nervous – to those who knew him well it would be apparent, but others would only see his eccentricity. The sound of Dot's hooves stomping down the stairs caused Charlie to move through the door and into the lounge as she charged past him and along the hallway.

"Is everyone nearly ready?" she shouted from the kitchen.

"We're waiting for you," Charlie bellowed back and rolled his eyes at Grant. Appearing at the lounge door, Dot stood proudly like a peacock displaying its feathers, in a blue paisley dress, navy Hush Puppies and a short navy cardigan.

"Well?" she beamed. Nodding enthusiastically, Charlie smiled and Grant cringed: the red lipstick streak had not been removed and from a distance she looked like she'd been smacked in the mouth. Subtlety would have to be the key, predicted Grant as he tried to avert his eyes from the high-gloss, ruby-red botch. It would be down to him to tell her as Charlie wouldn't even notice it...he never really looked at his wife. "Just enough time for a quick cup of tea then," said Dot as she popped the red lipstick into her navy bag.

Gilbert's Park was dotted with a few spectators who had heard a whisper of Charlie's special day. Photographers and cameramen from both the *South Coast Television* station and the museum's technical department were busy setting up equipment. Fortunately the Black Widow was nowhere to be seen and the innocent flies were safe as they skimmed the surface of Gilbert's Lake in pedal and rowing boats, enjoying the warm morning sun. Unsure whether Evelyn would catch the bus to come and watch or just stay at home and see the news later on TV, Grant prayed she would stay away. Her interfering mouth had caused enough problems for him.

The hired van driver rode carefully over the grass and along the pebbled pathways leading down to the glistening lake. Shooing a couple of ducks out of the way from his window, the driver manoeuvred the vehicle, pulled up alongside the bank of the lake and Charlie climbed out. *RMS Titanic 2* lay in wait inside the back compartment of the white Astra, encased in the glass cabinet and secured to all sides of the van with web strapping. The twenty-minute journey to the park had been a tentative one as Charlie clenched his teeth and watched his beloved ship wobble gently and tilt slightly as Jim, the van's owner, drove along the windy roads with care.

"Thanks Jim, we'll wait for Grant to get here before we get it out."

Nodding fervently, Jim opened the back doors and stood with one hand resting on the roof of the van as he pulled a cigarette from behind his ear and admired the ship inside its glass case. The photographer from *News Today* strolled over and shook Charlie's hand.

"Good to see you Charlie. Is your wife here today?" he asked, glancing all around for the weird, irritating woman he had met only a few days ago.

"They'll be here in a minute. We'll get it out then," said Charlie, nervously looking towards the pathway for any sign of Grant and Dot. He didn't want anyone else to touch his beloved boat, let alone remove it from the van.

"Mr Stern, good to meet you. I've heard a lot about you – oh my, it's an absolute beauty!" The cameraman from *South Coast News* shook Charlie's hand vigorously as he too admired the *Titanic*. Placing the large handheld video camera onto the grass verge, the plump man leaned in to take a closer look as the back of his trousers slipped past the cleft of his buttocks. Glancing up to the trees, Charlie pretended he hadn't noticed the hairy bottom cheeks staring him in the face. Turning away, smoking his cigarette down to the butt, Jim ignored the unsightly scene of a bristly, fat arse protruding from the back of his van.

The museum's technical team consisted of Steve and Dan 'the techno-man', justly named due to his expertise in practically everything technical, mechanical and scientific. The two young men sat on a wooden bench next to the boat rental kiosk, both kitted out in flat caps and canvas pumps and drinking cans of fizzy orange. Being knowledgeable about the latest trends and fashions, Dan 'the techno-man' displayed great all-round prowess and oozed a luminescent aura.

Turning round from his tree inspection, Charlie heard footsteps along the gravel footpath and glanced across to see Grant and John the curator striding along in awe of Dot, who was participating fully in a lengthy discussion with herself. The two men escorted her down to the lake in silence as she continued to twitter on and on and on. (About what, nobody seemed to know.)

Picking up the video recorder, Dan nudged Steve in the ribs with his elbow and pointed to the rest of the photographic equipment as he hauled the camera onto his shoulder and walked towards John and Grant. The time was approaching 10.30 and everyone had to be in place by eleven o'clock – the council had arranged for the boating lake to be closed for an hour in order for the filming to take place undisturbed.

A few early morning romantic couples were milling around aimlessly in their boats, growing more curious about the gathering of men, technical equipment and a glamorous elderly lady sporting what appeared to be a swollen red top lip. Aware of the effects of her lush new lipstick, Dot had noticed how everyone she talked to couldn't take their eyes off her pout. They almost seemed to be puzzled, she thought to herself, not realising that her admirers were actually mulling over the absurd idea of an old lady having collagen fillers so late in life.

The group gathered around, discussing the viewing and filming plans. The small jetty had been chosen as the launch site earlier. It was low enough to ensure a safe delivery of the ship to the lake, performed by Grant and his new accomplice, 'Senior Citizen-Collagen Chops'.

The museum trio set up their camera and sound equipment, as Charlie stood watching the man with the downy bottom. He would record Charlie's first interview, and had chosen to film from a left-hand perspective while the other three were on the right. Jim and Grant cautiously carried the glass cabinet from the van and down to the jetty, placing it onto a metal-framed stand that Jim had positioned earlier. The stand allowed the ship to be displayed at waist height while both cameramen filmed close-up shots before the launch. Dot looked on as everyone prepared for the first stage of filming, and Jim returned to his van for a short nap, knowing he would not be required for some time.

"The name's Alan by the way," said the tubby man from *South Coast News*, pulling his trousers up from behind and shaking a leg.

"Ah, Alan – will we be doing a rehearsal first?" asked Charlie, feeling the nerves pinching.

"Nah mate, we'll go straight into it. I'll be cutting and editing it when we get back to the studio, and Justin will be here any minute."

"Justin?"

"Justin Hope, our top reporter. Have you heard of him before?"

"Of course," replied Charlie sheepishly as Alan went over to the jetty and started recording, focusing and zooming in and out with his ultra-expensive camera lens.

"Ooh, make sure you capture all the little people on the deck – Charlie bought those from a model shop. He's even put Leonardo DiCaprio and Kate Winslet at the front. He snapped their little arms off and re-glued them in an outstretched position, just like in the film." Hovering over Alan like a rain cloud, Dot gave a running commentary on the finest of details, as if she was the one who had built the model. Alan stopped, looked towards her with contempt and forced a grin.

"Sorry love, I just need to get this close-up done. Could you move aside please?"

"Oh, I'm sorry," she replied, taking a step back, scanning the horizon all the time. Glancing across the lake, she kept a watchful eye on the rowers disembarking from their love boats. Obviously, if they wanted to know what was going on, she needed to be available to tell them, once she'd launched the ship, and also to be available to give any information required while her husband was interviewed.

Lapping up the imagined attention, Dot repeated her narration, much to the annoyance of Dan, as he too, slowly advanced along the length of the ship, with the camera lens twisting and turning in his expert hand.

A gleaming, deep red Grand Cherokee came to a halt just in front of Jim's van, and the suited driver stepped out, flicked the door closed behind him and nonchalantly glided over to where Charlie stood.

"Charlie Stern?" Holding out his manicured hand, Justin smiled as they shook. "I see you've met Alan already." Peering over to the jetty, Justin pretentiously raised a hand to his forehead and shielded his eyes from the sun's glare, although they were stood in the shade of a tree. "I would like to do the interview while the boat is being lowered into the lake in the background, then Alan can continue to film you controlling it around the lake once we've finished talking. Does that sound okay with you?"

"Yes, I'm happy to do it any which way. My wife and son-in-law will put it into the water."

"Great, great – Alan, are we ready to roll?" hollered Justin, still shielding his eyes. "I'll nip back to the car and get my shades first." Winking at Charlie, he sauntered off.

Leaning against the trunk of an old tree, Grant smoked his cigarette like it was his last rite. He watched and listened as Dot stole the limelight, completely unaware that the exposure she was receiving was pure wonderment at her incessant, rambunctious behaviour. The lake had emptied of the few morning floaters and the slight breeze barely caused a ripple across the expanse of water. Grant's mind wandered to the girl from last night and then instantly vaporised her into a million shards of glass as Alex appeared, walking into his imagination. The guilt still hung heavily over him as he tried to forget his troubles, just for now, until this show was over. He still had a job to do, although unfortunately it wasn't as planned and it would be done with Dot instead of Alex. At least he would have some good news to tell her when he saw her later, and whether she talked back to him or not, he could tell her about her dad's special day.

The plan to lower the ship into the water had been rehearsed at home many times. Charlie knew it was a delicate job as Grant and Dot would have to ease the boat carefully over the side of the jetty and then lower the supporting straps.

"Are you sure you can do this Dot?" asked Grant worriedly.

"Of course I can! I know Alex was going to do it with you, but I'm perfectly capable, Grant. I've lived with this thing in my house for four years *and* carried it up to the bathroom on several occasions," she replied huffily. There was no way that she was going to miss out on being in the thick of the action, not to mention on TV. "Can you picture Evelyn's face when she sees me on the television?" she chuckled.

"Er, yes I can just picture it," mumbled Grant, cringing at the thought of anyone seeing him on the TV – including that girl, Rachel!

"Is everyone ready?" called Justin, lifting the dark reflective sunglasses from his eyes and propping them on top of his styled hair. To the right, John, Steve and Dan nodded and waved. Down at the jetty, Grant and Dot smiled and grasped the straps tightly in their hands. The sizable model looked heavier than it actually was, but the length and height of the masts made its launch from the jetty cumbersome.

"Hang on, Charlie, can you hold this?" Passing a long, furry microphone to Justin, Alan gesticulated to him to hand it over. Gripping the fur-covered mike, Charlie looked like he had a grey chinchilla tucked under his chin. "You're gonna have to lower it Charlie, I can see it on camera." Dropping the oversized rat to his waist, Charlie straightened himself up and posed, ready to be interviewed. "Lower!" roared Alan. "And... action!"

Justin started the interview while Alan took on a professional filmmaker persona, zooming from foreground to background, panning slightly left and right, capturing the small crowd of onlookers and the temporarily redundant boat rental kiosk man. As Alan twisted and turned, with raised arms holding the heavy recording equipment on his shoulder, everyone was guaranteed an encore from his frighteningly woolly gluteus maximus as his trousers slipped lower. Steve and Dan waited in suspense for the moment of launch and the unwelcome glimmer of Alan's unsightly lime-green underpants. Camera poised, they were ready to start filming as soon as Justin's interview slot had finished.

Gripping the supporting straps tightly, Grant and Dot teetered at the water's edge, ready to lift and move the ship out to its birthplace. Upon hearing Alan shout 'Action', Grant nodded to Dot and they slowly and carefully lifted the surprisingly light model from its holdings. Glancing over, Dot could see that Alan's perfectly positioned camera had everyone in view, including her, she assumed.

In the foreground Justin introduced his interviewee to the camera, while Charlie posed in the middle distance, gripping the carefully placed mike to his trouser belt, and Dot and Grant held the fort in the background.

"You ready Dot?" whispered Grant anxiously. "Let's go." With a miniscule nod he discreetly tried to create a new sign language with staring eyes, directed at Dot, as the *Titanic* started to lift from the ground. Sensing the camera's lens watching and zooming in on him, Grant hoped the show would be over as quickly as possible, saving him from the embarrassment of starring on the local news television programme.

Periodically prodding, puffing and tweaking his almost perfectly placed hair, Justin began the prescribed set of questions, prepared with the help of Charlie at the request of the television company.

"So Charlie, how long did it take to build this magnificent scale model of the *Titanic*?" he asked, brushing a strand of fringe from his eye.

"Yes – ready," buzzed Dot as she took the slack from her end. Her eyes darted around constantly, evaluating the capacity of her audience.

"I've spent four years building it. I wanted it to be ready for the centenary year. I've always had a fascination with the *Titanic* and wanted to do it for many years." Charlie's nervousness was apparent as his voice trembled and he rambled on and on.

A small step sideways and the synchronised pair had the vessel hovering above the lake's edge. Leaning over on his blistered toes, Grant felt the pressure burning inside his shoe and also in his groin. "Ease it down Dot," he breathed as the liner began to swing slightly in its webbing straps. "Drop it down," Grant insisted as his foot twisted around and the ship started to hover diagonally in the air. "Dot!"

"I am! Shut up Grant, you're doing it too quickly," mouthed Dot, struggling to correct the slant of the model.

"An amazing accomplishment Charlie – could you tell us how you made it?" asked Justin, nonchalantly, "We can just see the model being lowered into the lake behind you—"

Splash.

"Argh!" The high-pitched scream cut through the park like a laser beam. The impact on the water's surface and frantic splashing caused frothing, foamy ripples to seep over the edge of the jetty.

Steve and John the curator leapt to their feet, open-mouthed and stood rooted to the spot. Scurrying towards the jetty, Dan 'the techno-man' froze at the edge of the lake and stared in amazement. The lens on Alan's camera zoomed in at full capacity and fixed onto its target as he quietly pulled his trousers back to his midriff. Raising his hands to the top of his head, Justin clasped his fingers together and cupped his elegant blonde mop as his lips stopped moving abruptly and held the formation of his last word. Hearing the commotion, Charlie turned around quicker than he had moved in the last 20 years, fearing his beloved *Titanic* had met an earlier-than-planned disaster. Still holding a webbing strap in his outstretched hand, Grant peered down into the lake in disbelief, scanning the ship for damage. As the nanoseconds slowed momentarily, almost to a freeze frame, Grant watched the nightmarish scene unfolding before his eyes.

"Help!" Splashing and screaming, Dot gulped and heaved as her arms paddled uncontrollably on the water's surface. "Save me!" she spluttered. The small crowd of onlookers gasped and edged closer to the fiasco as the redundant kiosk man ran towards the jetty.

"Calm down, I'm coming in." Before anyone else could move, the kiosk man had long-jumped into the lake and landed a few metres away from the flapping drowning victim. He had to be close to the world record for a sprint and jump, thought Grant, knowing that his random musings were slightly out of context. The force of the water ripples sent the *Titanic* on its maiden voyage without the need of a remote-controlled signal. Pacing the last few metres through the lake in slow motion like an astronaut on the moon, the kiosk man approached Dot from behind and wrapped his arm around her waist underneath the water. Desperately flailing arms reached out in all directions as Dot's panic-stricken state overcame her. *Thump!* The kiosk man received a heavy arm thrust to the side of his face as he lifted Dot from the water and into a standing position. Dishevelled, drenched and distraught, she stood waist-deep in the murky whirlpool, dazed and delirious.

"Blimey! Calling all lifeguards...man overboard," said Charlie turning back to the camera and smirking, having just watched his wife belly-flop into the cold lake. The sound of her screeching and wailing, and the spasmodic splashing, had brought the local dog walkers hurrying to join the onlookers who had inched closer and closer.

Realising that she was only waist-high in the water, Dot felt a little foolish as she was pulled back up onto the jetty. Cautiously, Grant extended a hand, but she shrugged off his gesture of help in favour of Dan, who really was 'the man' now as he wrapped his padded tartan jacket around her shoulders. Speechless, Grant stood open-mouthed as Dot's sorry, soggy shape was led away to Steve's transit van, which was parked up the bank in front of a clump of trees.

"We've got some blankets in the back, we'll soon get you warmed up," Grant overheard Dot's superhero saying as she burst into tears.

As the *Titanic* set off on its maiden voyage, unaided by any mechanical means but powered purely by the surge of water ripples from Dot, it floated away towards the middle of the lake, almost out of reach of any radio signals. Hauling the kiosk man out from the lake, Grant made sure he didn't lose his footing and end up in there himself.

"Thanks mate," said the man as they both stood and watched the ship sailing away. "Guess I'll have to go back in there and get that thing before it goes too far out."

"No, I've got it...turning around now." Charlie and Alan had joined the spectators on the jetty. The remote control unit in Charlie's hands gradually turned the bow to the left and the *Titanic* was brought under control, making a steady return back to its berthing place.

Mesmerised by the bright sunlight sparkling and bouncing off the miniature waves in Gilbert's Lake, John stood perfectly still, hands in pockets, and listened to the people around him as the hot sun warmed his back. A smug look on his face suggested he thought that Dot, the nagging old hag, had finally got her comeuppance.

"Can you strap it to the side of the jetty, Grant? I'd better go and see if Dot's okay," said Charlie as he started to step away backwards, still steering the liner back to land.

"We'll need to resume filming soon," called Alan as Charlie headed for the back of the Transit.

Shoeless feet dangled out of the van as Charlie walked round and spotted Dot sat under a tatty travel rug, shivering. Her sodden Hush Puppies glistened on the grass, seeping in the sunshine.

"Oh, glad you could bloody well make it round here, Charlie. I heard what you said and this was all Grant's fault, stupid man," said Dot grumpily. "If it wasn't for Dan and Steve here, I'd still bloody well be in there. Grant did nothing but stand and watch!" In her eyes, Dan, Steve and the kiosk man were her heroes and they would be superstars forever.

"Um, he's a bit shocked, my love. Are you all right though?"

"Oh yes, I'm just great. Shocked? He's bloody drunk! Didn't you smell the alcohol on his breath this morning?" Pulling herself up with one hand and gripping the blanket around her neck with the other, Dot stepped into her ruined shoes. "He can't handle Alex being in hospital, he's falling apart like before. I hope you hurry up with the filming, Charlie, I want to go home. I'm not going back round there. I'll be an object of ridicule."

Privately, Charlie agreed.

"AND THIS HAD BETTER NOT BE IN THE FILM!" she cried as her hair dripped and her smudged lips remained smudged.

The rest of the morning's filming was eventually a success. The onlookers gradually dispersed and went their own ways after enquiring about the old lady's wellbeing, as did the caring canine clique. Resuming the interview, Justin frantically adjusted his flattened hair first and then carefully placed his shades on the top. Alan continued the wrestling match between holding his trousers and balancing the camera on a hefty shoulder. Steve, Dan and John waited patiently for their turn to film the *Titanic* on the lake, and briefly interview Charlie.

The technical boys had plans for the grand opening of the museum, at seven o'clock that evening, which would be hosted by the Mayor and his good wife, John the curator and an ancestor of one of the passengers on the *Titanic*'s fatal journey. Their rolling video display in the museum's *Titanic* department would show a selection of local events and interviews with people who had connections to the historic ship in one way or another. An empty stand at the museum awaited Charlie's remarkable model. Once it had dried out thoroughly, it would be exhibited in a central position in front of the giant video display screen on the second floor of the new maritime museum.

If John had had his way, Charlie's model would have been in the museum for the evening's opening ceremony, but Charlie's stubbornness had prevailed and he would be releasing it into the lake on the centenary. He was adamant that they would not get it until after the launch, but now that Alex had missed everything, he wanted to do it all again for her benefit.

Keeping out of sight at the back of Steve's van, Dot was waiting impatiently for the filming and interviews to finish when Grant peered around the side of the door.

"I'm really sorry Dot. I don't know what happened there," he mumbled guiltily. Her smudged red mouth remained downturned in a sulk as she continued to shiver, resembling a drowned puppy wrapped in a survival blanket. "I'll take you home Dot, come on, you'll catch a cold here."

"Grant, I'm not getting in the car with you. I'm not silly you know." She stood up in her squelchy new shoes. "You've been drinking haven't you? You couldn't stand up straight on the jetty. I'm very disappointed in you, Grant. No, in fact I'm furious with you. Go away!"

"That was last night, and yeah I did go out for a couple."

"More than a couple, I think. Why did you have to collect your car this morning? Where did you go last night?" The annoyance in Dot's voice was becoming clearer and Grant felt the familiar bubbles of anger begin to balloon in his stomach.

"Look Dot, I'm not being funny but I don't have to answer to you or Evelyn for that matter. I'm sick of having to redeem myself to the two of you, for heaven's sake." Grant could hear himself blurting the words out, but couldn't stop it. "I think I'd better go. If you don't want a lift home Dot, again, I'm sorry."

"Yes go, we'll sort this mess out later."

Without any goodbyes, Grant slinked off up the path. His hangover had been miraculously cured within seconds of Dot's dramatic exit from the jetty earlier, but now a new one lurked in the depths of his mind.

Alex

Oh no, have I really just done that? What's wrong with me? Why have I overreacted so badly? He didn't deserve that...did he? Straining to hear the sound of Grant's footsteps disappearing down the corridor, I lay motionless, eyes closed tightly, and then I really did fall asleep.

Waking from the first undisturbed night since I'd been in the hospital, I sat up, rather surprised that the nurses had not woken me to do observations. As my sleepy eyes focused, I remembered the new room with its beautiful views, and the short, bittersweet visit from Grant. Why I'd been so ignorant and standoffish I really didn't know, after all it wasn't the end of the world. He'd forgotten to tell me what had happened and probably feared my reaction as well. I picked up the note he'd left on the side cabinet and read it as a tear fell and landed on the paper.

Today was going to be a big day for my dad, and I sensed that Grant would be dreading it without me there to lighten up the whole affair and turn it into a laugh. And to top it all, he would be feeling even worse knowing that we had not really spoken to each other properly in a few days. Thoughts raced through my mind, and I suddenly recalled the accident yesterday with Jack and Aaron and reached up to touch my face which was partially covered in wads of bandage. What a mess everything was. Well, it could only get better, couldn't it?

The tea trolley rattled around the ward and slowly made its merry way towards my room. "Morning. Tea, coffee, fruit juice?" called the surly middle-aged woman.

"Tea please." I smiled an exaggerated smile, hoping it might encourage the miserable lady to brighten up. At least she could walk on her own two feet, so what did she have to be unhappy about?

"Morning, how are you feeling today?" Jenny the day nurse hurried in, picked up the clipboard at the end of the bed and sifted through the papers. "Did you sleep better?"

"Yes, but nobody came to wake me up for obs," I replied. "What's happening with me today, do you know?"

"The doctor will be on the ward at about nine o'clock, you could talk to him then." Jenny smiled. "How is the physio going now?"

"Okay, I haven't really done very much of anything, but they did say they want me to stand up and weight-bear today," I said as a rush of excitement pulsed through my veins. If I could progress with the physiotherapist and my temperature and blood pressure improved, then surely there was nothing keeping me in the hospital. It would just be a matter of time, patience and perseverance before I was completely recovered from this unknown illness. "When do you think I can go home?"

"Oh, I don't know, ask the doctor when he comes," she said as she started to peel away the bandages from my cheek. "That's looking better. I'll take them off, let it get some air and dry out."

"Come on, you can do it, just one step." The two therapists held me upright in a standing position as my legs wobbled and buckled underneath me. Determined to make progress, I screwed up my crusty, scabby face in concentration and willed my right leg to move forwards, but it wouldn't go.

"Alex, I'm going to let you go. Are you ready to stand by yourself?" The ginger-haired man nodded to his female colleague. "Are you ready?" Bracing myself to take the weight on my jelly legs, I felt like a wooden push-up puppet waiting for the thumb press from beneath.

"Yes. Ready," I replied apprehensively as the pair gradually released their grip on my arms and began to move their hands away. Feeling the sensation of weight-bearing again, my knees buckled slightly but held and locked at a slightly bent position as my ankles too became rigid. I was standing on my own, albeit in an awkward stance. I'd done it!

"Try to straighten your back Alex," whispered the girl, as if she had just witnessed a miracle. Her supportive hands still hovered just under my opened arms. Another set of warm hands gently pushed from the top of my left shoulder and the small of my back as the red-headed man eased my back into a straightened position. "Well done, you're standing upright. We're going to support you while you try and move your right leg forward now."

Grinning like a toddler who had just received a Christmas present from Santa, I relaxed and calmed as the therapists supported my weight once again.

"Okay, are you ready?"

"Yes, ready," I replied, willing my leg to move as they began to tilt me forward. The natural instinct of stepping forward to prevent myself toppling to the ground kicked in. My right leg flicked out with a jolt and haphazardly flopped back to the floor. I had taken a step, albeit a sloppy, uncontrolled one.

Tears stung my eyes and fell on grazed cheeks as the two therapists lowered me onto a chair. Four uncoordinated steps had taken their toll and I was tired out, but elated at the same time. I'd made progress and could walk... sort of. After a discussion with the younger girl about self-help physiotherapy and how to use a walking frame effectively, they both left. Well, that was it then – I just needed to see the doctor, who was late as usual, and then I could probably go home at some point today. I could borrow a walking frame and practise in the comfort of my own home. At least that way I would be able to sort out the trail of mess that I imagined I would find upon my return.

To my great disappointment, it turned out that I was not going home today. A top neurological specialist from somewhere in the south would be coming to assess me either this evening or early tomorrow, and knowing what a doctor's timescale was like, I guessed it could be next week before the 'top doc' arrived. I felt miserable and hopeless again. The rest of the doctors still didn't really know what was wrong with me and couldn't understand the conflicting symptoms: the rash and the temporary disabling of my central nervous system. Basically I was a guinea pig for the top neuroscientists to try and work out, exchanging ideas and concocting elusive conclusions.

"We hope you will be able to go home tomorrow, after Mr Treese has assessed you," said the doctor when he finally visited. "You have a physio plan in place I believe."

"Yes I do." I could now see the light shining brightly at the end of what had been a very long tunnel, as long as the 'top man' turned up when expected. The doctor kindly answered some of my questions as best he could, and explained why I felt like I was supplying the local blood donor clinic with enough blood to feed a vault of vampires for a month.

"Your white blood cells are very low, that's why you've had so many tests. Some of them, like the HIV one, will take a few weeks to process but all the other related tests will be ready in a week to ten days." The glazed look of shock and horror on my face must have been enough for him to decide to move on to the next patient. As he started to walk out of the room, he turned and said, "Depending on the results, we may need to see you again, but if you don't hear from us then all of the results will be sent to your own doctor." He wished me well and left.

Stunned into a silent, dreamlike state, I stared intently through the window at the far-off sea. *Blimey, that's serious stuff – AIDS!* I couldn't have anything like that, could I? I tried to recall a time when I might have been vulnerable to any conditions that could have made me contract HIV, but couldn't think of any. What about Grant? Had he been exposed to any possible situations? There were none that I knew of. What about situations I may not know about? Had he been involved in any clandestine affairs? How ridiculous – I now doubted my wonderful, loving and dedicated husband. *Pull yourself together, Alex Frey. Everything will be fine. You can't possibly have AIDS.*

Stirring from an afternoon sleep, I opened one eye and peeped out from under the covers. A solitary, small white cloud slowly sailed past the window, useless in its endeavour to blot out the raging sun. Euphoria bubbled in the pit of my stomach as I remembered the doctor's words: I was going home tomorrow (if the doctor turned up on time). Soon I would sit in my garden again with the busy gnomes and a magazine, waiting for the summer to arrive.

The aftermath of the kitchen fire had to be dealt with, but I knew that it was probably a blessing in disguise, and actually the wake-up call we needed to ensure that all the batteries were replaced in the fire alarms – it was one of those jobs I had been meaning to do, on my 'to do' list but never got around to. Then the doctor's other words sprang to my mind: HIV! I couldn't possibly dwell on it. It would drive me insane. I would just have to wait for the results. The doctors were probably just being overcautious and testing me for every disease imaginable.

The clock on the far wall ticked around to 4.30. I had to get to the communal room to see the television. I'd given up trying to sign up for an account to the television console hanging above my head and the prices were ridiculous anyway. Nurse Jenny had informed that there was a communal room just down the corridor and hardly anyone used it. Determination and a renewed vigour assisted my departure from the bed and into the wheelchair by the side of it. Wheeling myself out of the room, I headed for the TV area at the end of the ward, hoping to catch the local news that would be on at five o'clock.

"Are you okay?" called Nurse Trisha as I whizzed past her.

"Yes, I want to see the news on TV," I replied, pushing the wheels as hard as I could. Reaching the circular layout of chairs, I manoeuvred through a gap and parked in the middle of the empty communal area. Luckily the correct channel was on and I absentmindedly watched the last half of *Inspector Morse*.

Twenty-seven minutes into the local news programme, I hadn't seen a flicker or a glimpse of anything pertaining to the *Titanic* or any historic local events. Deflated, I tapped my fingers on the armrest of the wheelchair.

"And finally, a host of events and centenary ceremonies took place today as the anniversary of the *Titanic*'s fatal maiden voyage was remembered throughout our region. Penny Scott has the full details."

Bolting upright, senses on full alert, I listened and studied the television intently, waiting for a glimpse of my dad, my mum and Grant.

Hobbling in through the door, Grant appeared gaunt, weary and anxious. "Hello babe." His quiet, husky voice barely broke the silence as I watched him approach. Smiling sweetly in atonement for the previous evening's incident, I welcomed him with outstretched arms. I needed a cuddle desperately.

"Hello. I'm sorry—"

"No, I'm sorry Alex. I should have told you about the fire, it was important. I was looking for the right moment but we had to deal with Emma." Grant sighed. "I had so much on my mind and ached from head to toe. I haven't been coping very well without you babe."

A rush of emotions – love, lust and tears – filled me as his big brown eyes stared into mine.

"I might be able to go home tomorrow, and then we can put all of this behind us."

"That's great news, we need you at home. Do you feel better?"

Pulling away from our embrace, I blinked away unshed tears. "Yes, I feel much better and I can stand on my own now." I smiled proudly. "How did it go today? I saw Dad and the boat on the TV but only saw you for about a second and I couldn't see Mum at all. I thought they were going to film you both putting the boat in."

"Ah, I need to tell you about that. It wasn't such a good day. Things didn't quite go to plan," replied Grant uneasily.

"Why, what happened?"

"Your mum ended up in the lake and she is blaming me for it, but I don't think it was my fault. She just slipped, but she won't talk to me now and says I was drunk and—"

"Grant - Grant, slow down. Tell me everything from the start." Holding onto his hand to reassure him that I wouldn't be acting like I had the previous night, I asked, "Is Mum okay? I mean, has she hurt herself?" As Grant's words sank in, I felt a looming sense of dread building again. "Oh my God, is she all right?"

"Yes, she's not hurt, just a bit shaken up and very angry."

"Why is she blaming you, how did it happen?" Visions of my mother floating around in the lake sent shivers through me. "When did it happen, before or after the filming?"

"During."

"Oh no, I can see why she's furious. Mum would have wanted to be the centre of attention, but not as the starring role in a David Attenborough *Planet Earth* documentary about the blue whale." Mixed feelings and disbelief paved the way for watery eyes, and I didn't know whether to laugh or cry.

"Don't get upset babe, she's okay. Your dad found it funny."

"Yeah, I bet he did. Mum won't ever see the funny side of it at all," I said, wiping a stray salty droplet from my dried-up, crunchy cheek. "What a shambles it's all been, Grant. Everything has gone wrong since I came into hospital." I sighed, "So why is Mum blaming you for it?"

"She thought I was drunk or had been drinking."

"And had you?"

"No...Well, not during the day anyway," he snapped back, avoiding eye contact with me.

"When then?" I snarled, unable to stop the frustration building inside me again. Getting up, Grant started to pace up and down at the foot of the bed. "Well?"

"I went out last night, had a few drinks, but I was not drunk this morning like your bloody mother thinks." The tone in his voice suggested that he too was frustrated as he stopped abruptly and leaned over, placing his broad, strong hands on the bedspread. "Alex, I don't want us to argue, can we just forget about it?"

"Yes, but I just want to know where you went last night and who with," I asked in a calm voice. Grant wasn't the type to go out on his own or sit in a pub for long periods without getting bored, whoever he was with. I found it very peculiar that he'd gone out at all and would have believed it more if he had sat indoors and got blind drunk.

"On my own. I left here and went straight to the pub on the way home." Grant looked pensive as he plopped down on the edge of the bed, despite the constant requests from nurses not to.

"How many did you have? What about driving the car?" I quizzed, scarily resembling my mother.

"I had too many, so I left the car there and got a taxi home. I picked it up this morning before I went to your parents'. Can we forget about this now?" Grant shuffled uncomfortably and examined his shoes intently, as if there was something really interesting about them.

"Okay Grant. Are you all right though, you seem a bit edgy?" I pushed for a reaction, not sure which one I might get.

"Yes I'm fine for goodness' sake, just tired and achy." Returning his attention to his captivating feet, Grant twisted the right one from left to right, inspecting the stitching of his shoe as he chewed his bottom lip.

After another half an hour of hesitant conversation, fleeting glances and awkward silences, I couldn't bear it anymore. "Okay, I know something is wrong Grant, I can tell by the way you are acting. What is it?"

He froze, staring wide-eyed like a deer in the headlight of a car. The last 'let's avoid the issue' evening, two nights ago, had been easily masked by Emma's thumb job, but tonight there was no escape and nothing to hide behind. I knew Grant too well, and I could read him like a book.

"Nothing, everything is all right. Well, apart from your mum," he huffed.

"No, there's something else, isn't there?" I clutched at straws, led by my intuition. "Come on, tell me. You're not happy Grant, I can see it. Have you burnt the whole bloody house down this time?"

"No of course not! I'm okay, it's just that I didn't get home until about two o'clock and I just know that the old hag over the road will have something to say about it and I just don't want you getting the wrong idea," he replied, looking somewhat relieved.

A flush of heat ripped through me – there was more to this. Under the pressure of interrogation, Grant was usually easily broken down and I always found out what he was thinking or doing. I dreaded the thought that I might be considered the top dog in the Frey federation, giving innocent victims the third degree. However, it had always worked fantastically with the kids too. I didn't want to be classed as the sergeant major of the household but I had to be on top of everything and in control. Rightly or wrongly, that is how I am. But Grant was adamant that there was nothing dodgy going on. He was adamant that the previous evening had been above board and he'd ended up joining a lock-in party with a few other guys when the pub closed. Adamantly he stretched to telling me that I was getting paranoid and it was probably because I was cooped up in the hospital, and adamantly, I knew it was bullshit!

As visiting hours came to an end, Grant leaned over to kiss my cheek goodbye. The air between us was like static electricity, not from a burning passion but rather more like a raging bull, charging and ready to obliterate the holding gate. Unspoken words hung in the atmosphere as he turned to leave. He knew that I knew something was amiss.

"I'll call in the morning to see whether you are coming home babe. I'm not working this week, decided to take the whole week off. I'll come and pick you up when you're freed." He smiled as he turned and headed for the door.

"I'll see you tomorrow then. I'm praying I'll be able to go home so I can sort out the mess." Shooting a sideways glance at him, I managed a half-smile from the corner of my mouth. "Bye Grant." A Mexican wave of my fingers, and he was gone.

The hours crept by slowly during the rest of the evening, and all through the night my mind played cruel tricks with me, flashing images of other women disturbing any chances of sleep. Deciding that I would have to confront Grant with accusations of infidelity tomorrow, however ridiculous it seemed, I turned over, closed my eyes and relived the day from an imaginary bird's eye point of view as I watched my mum fall into the lake at Gilbert's Park with an almighty splash and a horrific howl. Paranoia was always at the fore of every thought.

Grant

Turning into the drive, Grant pulled on the handbrake and wearily climbed out of his sleek, silver statement of pride. The last few days had stripped him of any egotism, which some would say wasn't a bad thing at all. Not the boastful or gloating type, Grant did however manage to annoy some people with his aura of success, pride and arrogant self-confidence. However, this was all very superficial and underneath the façade was a shy, insecure man.

Something had bothered him all day. Unable to pinpoint the exact cause of his worry, Grant had blundered his way through the day from hangover morning through accused afternoon and into convicted evening. There hadn't been a moment of clarity in the tight agenda of the day for him to unravel his subconscious mind and decipher the coded messages being sent to him via a series of dulled brainwaves. But something was amiss apart from all the mishap he already knew about.

Approaching the heavy front door, he froze on the step as the sound of cackling laughter resonated through the letterbox. He knew that laugh.

"What the hell are you doing here?" Stumbling through the door, Grant's eyes darted around the room, staring at the uninvited guest and her audience.

"You're not going to like this, Grant – Dot called me and asked me to get here as quickly as possible." Josie grinned. "I've been here about half an hour. The way she explained things, I expected to see you all living in the shed at the bottom of the garden, like homeless gnomes," she chortled nervously, knowing that her brother was not going to be pleased about any of this. "I tried to call your mobile and I sent several text messages, but it turns out you've lost your phone."

That's it – that's what has been bothering me all day. How does she know I've lost my phone? Anyway, I didn't lose it – I left it!

"How do you know I've lost my phone?" asked Grant as he began to pace the living room.

"A woman phoned up Dad. She found your phone and she's bringing it round tonight," Aaron hooted from his perch on the armchair next to Emma. Full of dread, Grant tried to hide his guilt and the fear of exposure.

"What woman?" he asked, attempting to sound innocent.

"Dunno, she said she found it at the pub last night," replied Aaron vaguely.

"You look so stressed out Grant. Shall I make you a cup of tea or do you want something a bit stronger?" asked Josie as she plodded out to the charred kitchen.

"Tea will be fine, thanks," Grant called after her. Turning back to Aaron, he spoke calmly. "What time did this woman say she was coming round? You obviously gave her our address."

"I don't know, Dad. She asked if you was in and said she'd call round with it later. That's all she said." Aaron was becoming anxious and it always made him feel angry too. "I bet it will be in a better state than mine was when I found it yesterday." A brave streak of sarcasm shot from Aaron's mouth before he could stop it. Deciding it was time to exit the living room, he stomped past Jack and Joe, who were trying to watch a film, and went up to his room. He too was feeling the pressure and sensing his Dad's erratic mood swings. He too was missing his mum being at home, sorting everything and everyone out. He too was missing his phone.

Tutting as Aaron left the room Grant felt flushed and attempted to pull himself together. Wandering through to the kitchen with hands in pockets, he found Josie busying herself in her usual jovial way. "So what did Dot say?"

"Oh, you made me jump," she giggled. "Grant, don't get upset about it. You know what she can be like. She exaggerated on the phone but I thought I'd better come and make sure you were all okay. I wouldn't have heard the last of it if I hadn't come over." She shrugged.

"Yeah I know," Grant sighed. "I wasn't surprised to see you. I wish she would get off my bloody case though." Wiping a trail of sooty water off the swing bin, he continued. "As for that bloody Evelyn, she needs to drop dead!"

"Grant! That's a bit mean."

"You don't know them like I do, Jose. I can't do anything right in their glaring, grey eyes. They put me on edge, and then I make stupid mistakes which make me look even worse. I know they watch me like a pair of stalking, walkie-talkie prunes."

"Calm down, you'll give yourself a hernia. Here's your tea. Let's sit down and you can tell me what has been going on and how Alex is doing and then you can decide whether you want me to stay or go." Josie's soothing voice mellowed Grant's frazzled nerves. "I can see that you haven't burnt the whole house down. You don't look like you've turned in to a heavy drinker. It's not your fault that Em hurt her thumb and I can see it wasn't almost amputated as you slipped up and grabbed her in order to selfishly rescue yourself. It's not your fault that Alex is so poorly. She is a law unto herself and 'delegation' is not a word in her vocabulary so it's not your fault that she works too hard. I can see that the 'poor young children' are *not* at risk of neglect, starvation and even possible death if you get so drunk that you do actually burn down the whole house, while selfishly making toast. I'm afraid it's just your mother-in-law overreacting as usual, although it probably didn't help when you deliberately threw her in the lake today and tried to drown her – and on local TV too!" Josie had done it again. Her booming voice filtered through to the living room where everyone (apart from Aaron who had gone to sulk in his room) overheard her imitation of their grandmother and the whole household (apart from Aaron) roared with laughter (but not loud enough for the Black Widow across the road to hear).

"Dad, there's a lady at the door," Emma screeched. Almost spurting tea from his mouth, Grant put down the cup and hurried through to the front door, pushing Emma aside as he met with the chilly night air seeping into the porch. Clandestinely closing the inner door behind him, Grant stepped out onto the drive and pulled the front door to.

"Hi, I'm so sorry... er, thank you for bringing my phone back," he whispered shyly, avoiding eye contact with Rachel. Her outstretched hand beckoned for him to take his mobile from her, and the warm, heady scent of her perfume teased his senses as Grant tried to fight the compelling urge to feast his eyes on her and recall the steamy embrace of last night.

"You're welcome. I've put my number in there," she replied in a low, husky voice. "Give me a call sometime, Grant." Turning around on her stiletto heels and flicking her long hair from her neck, Rachel sauntered away down the drive. Glancing back over her shoulder, knowing her admirer was transfixed, she smiled at Grant and winked a false-lashed eye at him before climbing into her twilight blue Mazda MX-5.

Feeling like Roger Rabbit, Grant was sure he had little bluebirds flying around his head, tweeting annoyingly as his Jessica Rabbit drove away. He knew he had to forget her and forget the primitive desire of lust that burnt deep inside him, before he became the victim and leading-role of the sequel, *Who Framed Grant Frey Rabbit*?

"Ah, you got your phone back." Josie smiled at Grant as she plonked herself down on the floor next to Joe. "Do you know that woman?"

"No, no. I think I saw her in the pub last night. Can't be sure," replied Grant weakly, gripping his phone tightly and refusing to buckle under the niggling drops of culpability dampening his brow.

"Oh, very kind of her to bring it round then," mumbled Josie.

"I think you'll have to talk to Dot and get this mess sorted out before Alex gets home," said Josie wisely.

"Yeah, I know. Alex may well come home tomorrow if the doctors okay it. She knows about the accident at the lake."

"And it was an accident Grant, so I don't know why you should be so worried about it. Dot's always the same, isn't she? She likes to make everything a crisis and sensationalise the facts. I shouldn't worry too much about her." She yawned.

"No, I'm not worried Jose, I'll sort it out with her in the morning—" Grant stopped abruptly, a cold sweat seeping through his palms as his mobile phone alerted him to a new text message.

"Who's that at this time of night?" Josie stretched and yawned again. "Hope it's not Dot accusing you of any further crimes?"

Opening his inbox, Grant noted that it was from Rachel, and his eyes almost jumped out of their sockets as he remembered that she'd put her number in his directory. Gulping silently, he dared not open the message in case Josie saw it. "Oh, it's just Jeff. He wants to know how Alex is," he lied.

"Grant, I'm going to bed. I've made up the spare in the study. Let me know in the morning if you want me to stay or go. However I would like to see Alex before I go back." She smiled, stood up and hobbled off to bed. Nodding, he beamed back and mouthed a goodnight, gripping his phone tightly.

As soon as Josie was out of sight and the kids had gone to their rooms to watch their own television programmes, Grant looked through his inbox and pressed open on the unread message. *Hi Sexy, can't get you out of my head. Let's get together again and have some real hot fun. xxx* His heart skipped a beat. His mouth watered. Blood pulsated through the beginnings of an erection. His head screamed – no, no, no! Licking his lips spontaneously, Grant snapped his phone shut like an alligator's jaws.

Pacing the empty living room, he tossed thoughts and images around like tennis balls on a court. The pros and the cons bounced around as two batting opponents named 'Yes' (in the suspended stockings and black frilly underwear) and 'No' (in the conservative, smart, grey, calf-length skirt suit) who battled it out on court number one. Reaching into the drinks cabinet, Grant grabbed the Jack Daniels and a small can of Coke. Surely a stiff drink would help clarify the winner of this sordid Wimbledon final? And after just two JDs, the winner had been declared...

No matter how quickly he blinked, the frozen image remained imprinted on his eyelids. What had he done? Dragging himself out of bed, Grant dozily headed to the bathroom to check that the pornographic image could not be seen on the outside of his eyeballs. By the time he had splashed his numb face with cold water, the images were fading and the thump in his head was brightening. Too much JD and too much talking and too much—

Oh my God. Oh no! Storming downstairs and out to the garden, Grant grabbed the cigarette packet from the sideboard and hastily fumbled to release one from the silver foiled sleeve. *Bloody hell.* The cigarettes scattered across the patio and he grappled around on the floor to reach one, like a demented, starved dog. Moments later, the calming suppressant lingered long enough to dull the multi-directional pains. Pain in his head. Pain in his heart. Pain in his groin. Pain in his toes. Pain in his neck. Pain in his – everywhere. Pain, pain and extra pain.

Phone sex...

Somehow he had been led astray and sucked into the bizarre concept of self-indulgent masturbation with one hand, a roll of kitchen towel in the other, and all whilst balancing his mobile phone on his shoulder and holding it in place with his cheek. What a ridiculous, abstract, modern-day notion. The crick in his neck had far outweighed the pleasure of manual ejaculation. Burying his face into the palm of his hand, Grant shuddered, realising that he'd really got himself into a terrible mess now.

"Morning," chirped Josie merrily. "Tea?" He'd forgotten that his younger sister had arrived last night, upon request from the new Social Services department, D.O.T. & Co., namely Flipper, the local lake's splashing dolphin, and her accomplice Incy-wincy Black Widow spider, who spied from the top of any spout, come rain, snow, tornadoes or hurricanes. A smirk momentarily touched his face as he nodded a yes to Josie. He needed to get serious though, and sort all his mess out as quickly as possible. The pleasurable experience in his bedroom, very late last night, had not been worth the tormented guilt he now felt.

A buzzing excitement filled the house as everyone woke, had their laugh quota and breakfast (which consisted of a couple of jokes on buttered toast - there was nothing else left in the house to eat) expertly prepared and crafted by Josie. Then they all set about tidying each room under her strict orders...except Grant. He was showering, shaving and trimming all trimmable areas. He had one or two complications to deal with before he went to pick up Alex, and he prayed that she would come home today, he needed her more than ever.

"Grandma's here!" Emma's usual screech from the front door sent daggers shooting straight through Grant's gut. Composing himself, he went indoors and thanked God. It could have been much worse. It could have been Rachel and grandma.

"Dot, I'm glad you've come round. I want to apologise sincerely for yesterday. It was a complete accident." Grant grovelled, eyeing Charlie who stood close behind her.

"You need to stop that drinking Grant, I can smell it on your breath again. It's no good for you. It won't help you to cope any better. Pull yourself together, for goodness' sake." Her attempt to whisper spared the 'poor young children' from hearing her opinionated advice. There was no point in arguing with her. If Alex had been around then Grant would have stood a fighting chance of standing up for himself, but without her, Dot would make short work of him.

"Dot, please – there has been a total misunderstanding. Yes, I have had a couple of drinks over the last few days but that doesn't mean I'm turning to drink again. I haven't been sleeping well since Alex went in and the drink has just helped me to relax. You know what's been going on here and it's all just been a little crazy. You really have nothing to worry about with me." Impressed with his sorrowful plea, Grant continued. "I'm genuinely sorry about your fall. I almost went in myself," he lied. Charlie sat down on the sofa and nodded his head in agreement at Grant's every word.

"Hmm," huffed Dot, before walking through to the kitchen with Josie. Luckily, Grant's in-laws were only stopping for a short visit, firstly, to find out if and when Alex was coming home and secondly, to catch up with Josie.

When the phone call came, Grant was relieved to hear that Alex could come home and more relieved that he could get rid of his mother-in-law even if it was just for a short while. At least when Alex returned and the in-laws came back to visit, he would hopefully, not be the centre of Dot's attention anymore.

"We'll be back later on then, if you're going to pick Alex up in an hour," shouted Dot as they went out the front door and slammed it shut.

I want to tease you with my tongue and play—
God, this has to stop. How can I stop her? It's got to stop NOW. Clutching his suddenly-more-precious-than-life mobile, Grant paced constantly, smoked continuously and drank copious amounts of tea, provided by Josie. She was like Mother Teresa in a crisis, knowing what, how and when to do just the right thing. Noticing that her brother was acting quite unusual and that his neurotic behaviour was increasing hour by hour, she agreed with Dot that it had been a good idea for her to come over, and she was more than happy to have travelled the four hours to get here. Grant appeared to be losing the plot.

I'm sorry Rachel, this has to stop now. My wife comes home today. I love her dearly and should have never spoken to you. I'm very sorry. Grant. Pressing the 'send' button, Grant sensed the slight reluctance in his thumb. Reaffirming his love for Alex, the importance of his family and thoughts of a happy future once Alex had recovered helped him to make the right and only decision to end this farce.

I do understand but your desire for me makes your rod stir and the thought of penetrating me deeply makes you hot. Rach xx Her insatiable appetite tormented and worried Grant to the point of sickness. He had seen the 'bunny-boiler' film, *Fatal Attraction*, and didn't fancy explaining rabbit stew being on the menu, to Alex or the kids. But strangely, too, he was drawn to the messages and an overwhelming urge to read each and every one which aggravated his failing cool composure.

Alex

"Morning," hollered the habitual operator of the tea trolley as she pushed and pulled the cranky metal carrier, manoeuvring it around every obstacle with ease. She was an expert in her field.

Startled, I awoke, deliriously plagued by memories of Grant's last evening visit. The recollection of my incredulous words, which had teetered on the very edge of another altercation, sent shivers through me. Attempting a smile, I nodded my head at the sweet-natured lady waiting dutifully for the 'yes please' gesture from yet another dopey, sleep-deprived patient.

The comings and goings on the ward, just outside the door of my room, were like watching a television programme with the volume turned down. I lay motionless and stared into the middle distance as the business of doctors' morning rounds began. A cloud of hopelessness hung above my head as I turned thoughts over and over in my mind. *Is Grant really hitting the drink hard? Has he lost it again? Did he really try to push my mum into the lake? No, he wouldn't do anything like that, he's driven to distraction by Mum but he wouldn't see any harm come to her... would he?*

The doctors came, reviewed, decided and then left. I was going home, but I wasn't as excited at the thought as perhaps I should have been. I dreaded hobbling through the front door to find that mayhem had rampaged through my house. I wasn't capable of restoring order and taking over at the moment, as I had to learn to walk properly again. The doctor and physiotherapist said it would take a few weeks for my muscles and nerves to heal and correct themselves. I was an enigma, and they were still pondering over ideas and reasons for the strange assortment of symptoms. The one thing they were sure of was that my immune system had tried to kill me off, but they didn't know why. I supposed that I should feel lucky that I hadn't succeeded in killing myself, however bizarre it seemed. So that was it, I was going home this afternoon.

Nurse Jenny came into the room carrying a set of clean sheets and pillowcases, wearing a big grin on her face. "Morning Alex, how are you feeling today?"

"I'm going home." I smiled as the sudden and unexpected rush of euphoria hit me like the shock of walking into a lamppost.

"Yes, we'll get you all sorted out. You'll be leaving after lunch. They want some more blood before you go, I'm afraid to say."

"They can have as much as they like as long as I have enough left to get out of here," I laughed, suddenly realising just how pleased I was to be leaving, to go home, to see the kids, to be with Grant, to be in my own bed, to get my life back. "Jenny, would you be able to call my husband and tell him to come and collect me?"

"Yes, of course I can do that." Marching out of the room, her short legs moving rapidly, Jenny headed for the reception area as I watched through the door.

This was it. It was over. The life-changing experience of my illness had made me realise just how important my health was and how precious my family were to me. It had also made me realise that I had to change my ways a little – well, a lot. Re-evaluating my obsessive, controlling traits would be a good start to the new me, and probably a happier, more relaxed me, and possibly a calmer, more independent family.

There wasn't exactly much to pack when Grant turned up looking, once again, haggard and somewhat preoccupied. I'd managed to dress myself in the clothing I wore upon arrival (excluding any underwear) and was astonished to find that I had lost quite a lot of weight. My work clothes hung from me like the skin of a Shar Pei dog. Great start to a new diet, I thought as I smiled at my unusually anxious husband.

"Are you okay, Grant?"

"Umm," he barely mumbled as he stood with his hands in his pockets, staring out of the window at the expansive, summer-like view.

"The porter is bringing a wheelchair to take me down. Do you want to wait here or go back down and I'll meet you at the entrance?"

"I'll wait." A forced smile etched on his face, Grant turned to look at me with dark, secretive eyes. For a moment I wasn't sure if I knew him at all.

Struggling into the passenger side of the car, I lifted my heavy legs inside and sniffed the comforting scents from home. Blinking back burning tears, I would not allow Grant to see my weakness as we pulled away from the hospital. The bright, warm sunshine filtered through the windscreen, gently heating my hands and face. It was so good to be alive, and to be out.

"What's wrong, Grant? You've hardly said two words since you arrived." I spoke quietly and calmly, feeling upset by his lack of excitement about my return home. Staring thoughtfully at the busy traffic we were merging into, I waited for what seemed like an age for him to reply.

"Josie's at home," he snapped abruptly. Instantly averting my gaze from the slow-moving queues, I looked directly at him, startled by his words.

"Why? When?"

"Your mother called her to come and look after the kids – and me!" he blurted without taking his eyes off the cars in front.

"Bloody hell, what on earth for?" Confusion, doubt and annoyance surged through my mind. The fact that Grant called my mum 'your mother' suggested he was furious about the situation, and although I loved Josie dearly and enjoyed her company, I didn't want her to be there when I arrived home after being away for what seemed like a very long time.

"Because your mother thinks I'm a drunkard, I expect. She thinks I can't cope with anything and I've turned to drink again like I did in the past." Reaching into his jacket pocket, Grant took out his cigarettes and lit one while steering with his knees. "She also thinks I'm a child-beater, a cruel sadistic arsonist and a potential murderer." The traffic moved along slowly as he opened the window, inhaled a deep breath of smoke and aimed the exhaled blue remains of his fix outside. He was clearly *very* annoyed; he never smoked in his precious car. I wondered for a moment if he really was losing the plot again. How much had he been drinking while I was in hospital?

"We'll sort it out, don't get all stressed out about it. You know what my stupid mother is like; she always goes over the top. It'll be nice to see Josie again though," I lied. I'd been so happy and excited to be going home to see the kids, get the house back into some sort of order, survey the damage to the kitchen and deal with it and generally get back to a normal way of living. Normality for me was like standing in the kitchen buttering slices of bread and slapping salmon paste all over them and I couldn't wait to do it again.

The low, humming vibration of Grant's mobile phone told me he had it on silent mode. "Your phone is ringing."

"It's just a message."

"Do you want me to see who it is?" Usually Grant asked me to read his messages when his phone went off in the car.

"No, it's probably Jeff asking how you are," said Grant, shifting in his seat uncomfortably. "I'll look when we get home." The road was clearing slightly as we pulled onto the dual carriageway out of the city and he put his foot down on the accelerator, pulling out into the faster lane.

Pinewood Avenue was just as I had left it on the previous Friday night, an idyllic part of the suburbs, picturesque and peaceful in the afternoon sun. Jumping out of the car, Grant briskly walked around to my side and helped me out. I knew that he feared getting caught up by Evelyn across the road. Her hawk eyes didn't miss anything in the street and she would be here faster than a swooping bird of prey, which was a surprising feat on her spindly legs. Staggering awkwardly to the front porch under Grant's strong arm of support, I managed to hold myself up against the wall as he opened the door. The smell of home came pouring out, along with a shower of familiar noises, music and voices. Everyone was home. Any moment soon, I knew I would be cuddled and crushed to within an inch of my life, but this was what I'd been waiting for.

Buzzing with euphoria, I relaxed back in the soft, black leather recliner and sipped the sweet, milky coffee. It was wonderful to be home with my family, and actually it was fabulous to see Josie too. Her constant buffoonery lit the whole house and lifted everyone's somewhat dampened spirits. Even Grant's from time to time. Jack moped around, wishing he'd taken the offer of a last minute one-week holiday with his old friends to Spain, which he had turned down because I was in hospital. His black eye had spread further around his cheek and down the side of his nose, but he did now see the funny side to the accident at the hospital with the wheelchair. So did Josie. In fact Josie set the scene in a way that we had not seen before and turned the whole affair into a hysterical farce. This was her forte, turning bad situations into humorous ones, and even the kitchen fire had been a victim of her ridicule, but it was just what the doctor ordered.

I'd seen the devastation in the kitchen but felt more concerned and aggrieved by the lack of washing up and cleanliness, and worse still, the lack of edible food in the house. The fridge contained a number of festering items which had turned into miniature evergreen gardens, with touches of blue to add colour. Unable to move around easily or hold myself upright for long periods, I left the kitchen worries and decided to deal with them tomorrow.

Apparently everyone had been living on takeaway food or a snack from the local corner shop, and Josie wasn't the best of people to clean or sort out other people's mess, and why should she? Her job as the family comedian kept her more than busy. Knowing that I should delegate the cleaning and sorting out to everyone else, I cringed at my old habits resurfacing. I had to do it all myself.

Aaron and Joe's apathy was more than apparent as they sat in the living room with me, aloof and haughty, with the only brief respite being when Josie came out with a quirky, comical comment. Their silent protest was an act to gain my attention, to get their 'old Mum' back. Both boys had grievances they wanted to discuss but they were biding their time, knowing that I was relishing the notion of being home.

Joe wanted a good old moan about his bike being stolen but knew it would raise other issues, like why he never locked his bikes up (although to be fair to him, he had locked this one up) and why he and Grant had gone out searching for the culprits in the early hours of the morning.

Aaron was annoyed about his smashed phone, and whether he used it much or not, it was his phone and now it was in pieces. He also still wore a cloak of guilt for several reasons: it was his fault that Jack had a black eye, it was his fault that I had a bruised and scabby face, it was his fault that his dad had to pay Jack 70 pounds for his ticket home from Wales...in fact everything was probably his fault.

As for Emma, she sulked with a passion. She was an expert at it. She huffed and puffed about the letter and the jobs she had to do to pay for the school locker. She bemoaned her sore thumb and the embarrassment she had gone through - not her fault of course! And she scowled generally, just because she could.

Grant was something else. He was on edge. I could sense the unsettled, jittery tones in his voice and his manner. Something else was going on that he hadn't told me about – yet. I would get it out of him eventually, after all I was an expert interrogation officer.

"Grandma and Grandad are coming round in a minute," shouted Aaron from the living room. I'd managed to get up the stairs unaided, although somewhat undignified, by bumping up the stairs one by one, backwards, on my bottom. The physiotherapist had advised me to avoid stairs if I could or go up them sitting down, as the control of my legs was still erratic. The last thing I wanted was to fall and end up back in the hospital.

"I'll be down in a minute." A hot bath had been just what the doctor ordered and I felt more normal than I had in the last few days. Some clean underwear and my old pyjamas was another prescription I had required, and I didn't care who might turn up to see me wearing them.

Bumping back down the stairs, feeling rather foolish but stubborn as ever and refusing any help from anyone, I arrived eventually in the sorry kitchen. Josie and Grant were filling the dishwasher with disgusting, four-day-old plates and clearing away the rubbish of countless takeaway containers and chip wrappers. The swing bin was overflowing with rubbish and the smell of rotting food lingered along with the new sooty fragrance. Pallor covered Grant's face, he was obviously anxious about the arrival of his in-laws.

"Oh my goodness Alex, look at you." My mum squeezed me tightly while I peered over her shoulder at Dad. "Where have you disappeared to? You've lost a lot of weight in such a short time. You look gaunt, Alex. Are you feeling any better?"

"Yes I am Mum. It'll just take time to get back to normal completely." Pulling away, I looked towards Grant, who appeared to be cowering in the corner. Mum glared at him as she sat on the sofa next to me.

"I've tried to ring your mobile a couple of times Grant, have you switched it off? I wanted to know if you were still at the hospital, and whether it was definite that Alex would be home." Her eyes bore into his menacingly.

"Yeah, sorry Dot, I haven't had it turned on."

"Well it was on in the car because Jeff texted you, didn't he?" I asked suspiciously. "Or was it Mum's text?"

"Yeah, I'd just turned it on then and it was Jeff" said Grant as he rolled his eyes in annoyance at the constant interrogations.

"You didn't mention that mum had texted."

"No I forgot," replied Grant looking decidedly uncomfortable.

Catching up with Mum and Dad was a tetchy affair for both Grant and my mother. There were a few sarcastic remarks from Mum, which Grant didn't bite back at, surprisingly. In fact he was unusually quiet and acquiescent. Dad sat quietly, gazing at the television, nodding in agreement or shaking his head in disagreement (which was very rarely) at appropriate moments during Mum's verbal onslaught. Wisely, Josie had decided to keep out of the way while I chatted with my parents and retired to the spare room for an early night – she was going home in the morning. The boys had left, after their embarrassing kisses, cuddles and 'cheeky-chops' pinches, to see a film at the cinema. Emma sat in her room, sulking. Peeved that she hadn't been able to go to the cinema with the boys, she chose to stay out of the way of Grandma's cheek-pinching for a second time today.

"Have you recovered from your late night out – or should I say early morning, Grant?" Mum's radar was still stalking Grant and his unresponsive demeanour. "Evelyn said your taxi home woke her up." Darting her eyes from him to me, Mum tried to goad a response from Grant, but to no avail.

"Just forget about it now Mum, Grant told me what happened."

"Well, what did happen then? Where was he till the early hours? Nothing is open at half past four in the morning," she snapped. It suddenly occurred to me that my mother was suspicious of his actions that night as well, and my own doubts were now growing again.

"Half past four?" I sat upright with a knot in my tummy. "I thought you said you got home at two, Grant." Fear steadily rose from the twisting knot deep inside my stomach. Something was amiss. Grant's behaviour was amiss.

"Oh for goodness' sake, this is all getting out of hand." Heading out to the kitchen, and more precisely the kettle, he continued. "I don't keep a timed diary of my comings and goings, you know!"

Cringing through the embarrassingly heavy atmosphere, I tried hinting to Mum that it might be time to go. She didn't take hints very well and continued to sit on the sofa, asking me a hundred questions about the hospital, the doctors, what they said, what they did and what was the final diagnosis.

"I still don't know, Mum." Feeling agitated, I called through to Grant who was still making a cup of tea, but I feared he'd rushed off to China to pick the leaves himself. "Where's that tea, Grant?"

Teetering on the edge of my seat, I watched Mum drain the last drop from her mug. Conversation had been awkward for the last 30 minutes and I was itching for them to go. I could see that both Dad and Grant were desperately waiting too. A burning desire to be alone with Grant consumed me, but not in a sexual sense. I had to find out what was making him so shifty and shaky.

"Right, we're going now love, let me know if there's anything I can do or get for you. I'll give you a call tomorrow to see how you are."

Trying to hide the relief that must have been written all over my crusty face, I smiled sweetly. "Thanks for coming over." I looked directly at Dad, who had hardly said a word, even when the topic was about his boat and his special day. "Are you all right Dad? You've hardly said anything."

"Just been thinking, that's all."

"About what? When are you taking the *Titanic* over to the museum?"

"Umm, not sure. I think I will re-enact the ship's demise so that you can see it sail, Alex. I can get the press out again."

"No! Dad, you can't do that. I don't want you to sink your beautiful work of art."

"It's history, Alex. It's history." Pulling himself up from the chair, he winked at me and stood by the door waiting for Mum. Unsure of the meaning of Dad's expression, I pleaded with him, in fear of the bizarre things he had been known to do in the past.

"Please don't do anything silly, Dad. You should feel so honoured to have your model in a museum."

"It would be big news though, wouldn't it? Imagine what the papers would say." He grinned.

"Just ignore him, he's teasing you," said Mum as she grabbed hold of his jacket by the shoulder and shunted him through the doorway. Managing to raise his eyebrows at me, Dad stepped out and headed towards their car. "Bye for now, Grant," said Mum with a huffy tone to her voice as she flung her arms around me and squeezed. I was thankful that I hadn't been in hospital for broken ribs or a fractured collarbone as her anaconda grip enveloped me. Then they were gone – thankfully.

Returning to the living room, I sat down and waited for Grant to join me. He knew we had things to discuss, it was the only way to clear the air.

"I'm going to get a quick shower and then I'll be down babe," he called as he leapt up the stairs two at a time, before I could answer him. Hobbling into the kitchen, I searched for Grant's phone. Intuition told me to look for it, but it was nowhere to be seen. Guessing he'd probably taken it upstairs, I dialled his number with the intention of telling him to hurry up back down, but his phone was turned off. This was unusual, he was obsessed with having his phone charged fully and always available. Recalling Mum's words, I pondered over why it was turned off. I knew I had grown a bit paranoid in the hospital, but now my insecurity was working overtime. Or was it?

It cut like a knife, deeply and sharply. I sat rigid as the pain surged through my body, causing stinging tears to well, and my jaw dropped from its holding. The words echoed and repeated in my mind as I stared through Grant like a dazed rabbit confused by a preying fox. How could he?

Burying my head in my hands, I toiled with the whizzing, erratic thoughts, questions and crazy assumptions whirling around in my mind. Temporarily speechless, I fought back the tears and tried to compose myself – it was going to be a long night and I worried that the kids would be home soon and we would have to continue our confrontation in a whisper. There was no way I was going to let the kids get a sniff of this, unless it couldn't be rectified. Belief is a powerful tool, when it works, I wasn't sure it was working now. *I have made a really terrible mistake –* the words dug deeper into the wound again and again.

Visions of our own lovemaking filtered through my thoughts and briefly satisfied me with their passion and longing, but then to my sheer horror the image changed into that of another woman who I did not recognise, and Grant lustfully mounting her. Gripping my head tightly, I tried to make the image go away when he spoke again. This time his voice was trembling.

"I know what you're thinking babe. Please believe me when I say nothing really happened," he whimpered. Looking up, I saw unshed tears balancing on the rims of his pitiful eyes.

"Let's go to the bedroom." I stated harshly as he gave me a puzzled look. "The kids will be home soon, I don't want them hearing this," I added, just in case he thought I'd gone mad and was going to take him to the boudoir and shag him senseless.

The long bottom-hop up the stairs had exhausted me once again as I perched pensively on the edge of the bed. Kneeling on the floor by my feet, Grant tried to take my hands in his but I pulled away like a spoilt child scorned.

"What do you mean, nothing *really* happened?" I whispered viciously. Lowering his head, Grant attempted to explain what had happened at Rachel's house. Cringing with building anger and disgust, I listened to the sordid details, which were very sketchy. When he wasn't being clear or detailed enough I interrogated him further. I had to know every last bit.

"So you kissed her and that was all?"

"She made me touch her." Bowing his head in shame, Grant continued. "I'm so sorry, Alex – I love you and would never intentionally hurt you. It was a terrible mistake."

"Did she have you at knifepoint then?" I asked sarcastically. "What do you mean, she *made* you, Grant? How could she make you?" The cold sweat leaking from my palms irritated me to the point of wanting to wipe them on Grant's face via a hard slap. "Where?" I whisper-shouted.

"Where what?" he snivelled.

"Where the fuck did you touch her, you imbecile?"

Sensing my rage, he rose from his knees and moved to the end of the bed and hovered on the very edge as if he wasn't worthy of sitting on our sacred mattress.

"She put my hand on her breast." Burying his face in his hands, Grant leaned over. At that moment I knew he was crying. A torrent of mixed emotions cascaded over me, from pity to murderous rage.

"You make me sick." Fighting back tears, I whisper-screeched, "So what would you have got up to if I'd stayed in hospital longer? Perhaps if I'd been there long enough you could have settled down and had children." Knowing this was a ridiculous thing to say, I said it all the same. "Get out!" I really didn't mean it as soon as I spoke, but it was too late. The words spat from my lips like magma. "You filthy old man – get out. I can't bear to look at you."

The bathroom door lock clicked and I knew he'd gone to clean himself up, probably fearing being seen by the kids or Josie. Bursting silent tears, I wept for what felt like hours before falling asleep in my pyjamas and slippers on top of the quilt.

Grant and Alex

Sunlight filtered through the vertical blinds, casting warm, apricot-coloured stripes on the wall above my head as my heavy eyelids peeled themselves apart. The embedded knife of infidelity began to twist in the pit of my stomach as soon as I was fully conscious. Morning sickness rushed over me like I'd returned to my childbearing years. I was heartbroken. Lying still, I dared not breathe as I worried where Grant was. Had he left home?

A gentle tapping brought me back into reality as the bedroom door slowly opened. "Do you want a cup of tea Mum?" Emma's sweet voice almost brought tears to my eyes as she tiptoed over to the bed.

"Yes please darling." I smiled genuinely. It was just what I needed to start my manic mission day. In an instant I'd concluded that no other woman was going to destroy my family and take my husband away from me. The queasiness and the lump in my throat remained, but I was going to do my very best to sort everything out. Mission number one was to say goodbye to Josie.

"Sorry I was miserable when you came home. I went to bed early but feel okay now. I'm glad you're home, Mum."

"Me too darling," I gulped.

"Why is Dad on the sofa snoring?" she whispered with a mischievous glint in her eye.

"I think I took up all the room when I came to bed last night." Laughing falsely, I winked and ushered her to go and make the tea. "I'll be down in a minute."

"I heard you two whispering and giggling last night." Josie entered the dining room with her large dressing gown flowing behind her and I froze.

"Really? We were just—"

"You two never change, you're still like a pair of kids." She laughed as she wafted past me to the kettle.

"Yes, I suppose we are," I replied vaguely. For a dreadful moment I thought she had overheard us, and I had no intention of letting anyone in the family know of this awful situation I'd come to find myself in. Grant and I had to sort this out...somehow. The thought of a rekindled love affair with my husband kept me from wanting to tear his eyes out and remove his testicles with a blunt bread knife. My whole life had been turned upside down in just a matter of days, and I was now on automatic pilot to put things right and return my life to some sort of normality. I desperately needed to feed my dear family some salmon paste sandwiches. That would be normal.

"I'll be off about ten."

"Ah, do you have to go Aunt Josie?" whined Emma.

"Thanks for coming Josie, I do appreciate what you've done. Maybe we could all get together in the summer."

"Yeah sure, it's really no problem Al." She beamed. "I'll see you again soon Em. It's not long until the summer, you know."

"Umm," she harrumphed and walked off.

Waking to the sound of scuffled feet attempting an awkward tiptoe, Grant opened his eyes and remembered where he was as he caught a glimpse of Alex disappearing into the dining room. Knowing her well enough to know that he should leave her alone this morning, he skulked upstairs and climbed into their warm bed. The smell of his wife peppered the pillow as Grant embraced it in his arms and breathed in deeply. Then the thudding pain began between his eyes as he tried to go back to sleep. Remorse accentuated his thumping headache and Grant realised that there was little or no chance of him drifting off again. So he lay there, puzzling over what he should do. He had no idea.

Luckily the boys were completely unaware of the brooding bleakness bleeding from their parents. Noticing that Grant was doing as good a job as I in covering things up until we could be alone to fight it out, I gave him credit for that at least. Our time would come, and when it did, I had a plan. The day trickled by dimly under a cloud of deceit and despair and the kids came and went, doing their own thing but ever-present in numbers or singularly. Josie left later than expected with an inkling of doubt about her brother's and my state of mind. Her last desperate attempts to raise the curtain on her departure were dampened by a dark atmosphere, which she just couldn't put her finger on. Resigning herself to the possibility that it was her leaving that had created the sadness, she went on her merry way back to Wales and I breathed a guilty sigh of relief.

Spending most of the day in his shed, Grant kept out of the way, only appearing at intervals to take more headache tablets. I was sure he'd taken too many during the day but didn't care to mention it or worry about it, hoping he would throw up and be violently ill or even end up in hospital having his stomach pumped after an overdose. I didn't much care either way and could guarantee that I would not have been one of his visitors. The illicit mobile phone had remained untouched and switched off throughout the day and sat deserted upon the dining room sideboard.

My list was growing: phone calls, shopping, cleaning, paperwork, visitors and Grant. I had no inclination to do any of it, except the Grant one, which had been written cryptically (**ant**s **r** not **G**ood, *I like to crush them under my feet*) so no one would question why my husband's name was on my list. If it all got out of hand and I murdered him, the evidence would have been there in black and white on my 'To do' notepad.

Deep down in my heart, I knew he had made a terrible mistake. I knew he regretted his poor behaviour and I knew he would never do it again. I understood his vulnerability and weakness when I wasn't around to pick up the pieces, but just because I knew it all already, I still needed to hear it from him. I had to make him feel worse than he already did. I was not going to forgive him easily.

The staff at my shop were self-sufficient and I made another note to reward them for their expert capabilities as soon as I was able to do so. I'd taught them too well, and wasn't really needed at all. It had thrown me somewhat and jolted me into re-evaluating my current workload – perhaps I did take on too much after all, consequently putting me in the position I'd been in for the last five days. Putting people off wasn't my thing but I could not face anyone, least of all Evelyn when she rapped on the door mid-afternoon. I had just settled down to have a snooze when Aaron looked from behind the curtain.

"Oh God, it's Evelyn, Mum."

"Answer it or she'll be over every five minutes," I whispered. "Tell her I'm asleep." As I listened to the mumble of Aaron's voice and the squeaky sound of Evelyn's, I just about heard Aaron say that his dad was in the shed. Giggling to myself, I waited for Aaron to come back in and then said, "Give me a hand up the stairs, I'm going to bed for a while." Normally I would never have asked but I did not want the old witch to come in through the back door and catch me. I slept rather peacefully for the rest of the afternoon, knowing that Grant was under the watchful eye of Evelyn. He was trapped in his shed-haven, like a buzzing fly in a web.

Oh, fucking great, thought Grant as he watched her creep through the side gate. This was all he needed.

The arachnid had returned with her venomous fangs dripping with questions.

"Yoo-hoo, Grant!" She whistled through her teeth as she tapped the Perspex window.

"Evelyn, how are you?" he replied falsely.

"Good. How is Alex?"

"She's getting better all the time," he replied, looking over his shoulder for a glimmer of any hope in the shape of a child that may be in need.

"I popped over to see if there was anything I could do or get for you."

Yeah: get lost! "No, everything's in order now but thanks Eve." Edging towards the door and out of the shed, Grant sidestepped past the black mini-beast in a vain attempt to get away.

"You're not looking so well yourself Grant. Are you okay?"

"I've got a bad head, Evelyn. I was just going to lie down when you came through." *Instant fucking mistake!*

"Oh dear, have you been drinking heavily again? It won't solve any of your problems you know. You need help Grant." Her downturned mouth stopped for a breath. "I've been so worried Grant, you haven't coped at all well with this, have you?"

Fuuuuck off! You won't be coping well when I stand on your neck. "Just leave it please Evelyn, I've had enough. I'm going in for a sleep. Goodbye," bellowed Grant

"Well, I never," she harrumphed, storming off as quickly as a two-legged spider could.

The haven of the felt-roofed shed absorbing the warmth of the sunshine had been discarded immediately once Grant's cover had been blown. He had been sat inside, dozing at times and at others contemplating his next move in the battle to win his wife over. Now his only option was his bed. Sneaking through the house, he tiptoed upstairs and opened the bedroom door to discover Alex asleep under the quilt. Sliding in on the opposite side, he hardly dared to breathe for fear of waking her up and getting kicked out. At this present time sleep was his only escape from a world of torture and turmoil.

The warmth emanating from his body calmed me. He could stay. I lay by his side, crying silently, craving his touch, a cuddle, a kiss. The flip side was that I hated him. I never wanted to be anywhere near him again. I would never make love to him ever again. Hate...love...hate.

Two more days drifted by in a blur of confusion, emotional turmoil, vicious words (on my part) and constant avoidance of visitors and phone calls. Grant continued to sleep on the sofa at night, and when questioned about it, his excuse was that I needed some space until my legs were working better.

The glorious weather was on our side and ensured that the kids were mostly out, doing their own things or enjoying the outdoor activity centre. Emma had been given back some freedom, more for our sake than hers. The only person who didn't go out was Aaron. Only in a virtual world did he travel anywhere.

There had been many opportunities to talk, whisper-scream, curse and quiz Grant, but none of it had got us anywhere. My stubborn streak would not budge and his actions of that night would never go away, only pale into insignificance over time, or so I hoped and prayed. The mobile had remained untouched. Grant had not dared to turn it on or move it from its place of routine inspection, until now. Shakily I picked it up and walked through to the living room where he sat staring into space.

"Turn it on," I said abruptly as I threw it across the room to land in his lap.

"No Alex, I don't want this to get any worse. I'd rather go and buy a new one with a new number."

"Oh, don't be so ridiculous," I snorted back. "The text messages can't get any worse, can they?" Doubt raised its ugly head again. Reluctantly he turned the phone on and we sat together for the first time in days and waited.

Hi sexy, call me when you get this. xxx The first text message came through. *I'm hot and horny, wanna chat? Love R xxx* Then more and more: *Would love to meet up with you at the weekend if you're not busy* ☺ *R xxx*

"See what I mean? She's crazy."

"Right, let's go and see her. I'll tell her to back off." Feeling brave, I felt I had to go and see her and tell her myself. That way I felt more secure about it being finished.

"Bloody hell Alex, no way." Grant's eyes widened to the size of golf balls.

"It's the only way we'll get over this Grant."

"Oh my God, seriously Alex?"

"Yes, seriously." I gulped.

To be fair to Grant, I checked his sent messages and could see that he had not in any way encouraged her. In fact he'd discouraged her from calling or texting him in his own 'cute' way. Her persistence was at fault here and I needed to deal with it for myself if there was any chance of us getting back to normal. Finally agreeing to me texting a message to her from my phone, Grant hesitantly gave me the number.

My name is Alex, I'm Grant's wife. Please leave him alone and DO NOT contact him anymore. Thank you.

The phone stayed silent for a couple of hours before the familiar 'beep beep' announced a text message. Nervously I opened up the message from an unknown caller. *No worries, you can have him. Didn't fancy him anyway, LOL.* Furiously I replied, *BITCH.*

"Was that her?" whispered Grant as we sat in the living room watching TV and eating a takeaway, lovingly brought by Jack.

"Umm," I nodded with a mouthful. "She just said 'fine'."

Relief replaced the days of dread etched on Grant's face. I then understood that he had made the biggest mistake of his life and that he would never again risk losing me for a cheap drunken thrill. As the evening drew to a close a feeling of love and warmth drifted over me. I would never have given him up that easily anyway. I'm a fighter and my husband and family mean everything. Picturing the obsessive tart with huge tits sitting in a lonely bedsit plotting her next victim, I smiled as I surveyed the beautiful room I was sitting in, surrounded by beautiful people. Bedtime came and my husband and I were reunited as one, as his love making expressed a thousand apologies.

Staring at the ceiling in the darkness, Grant remained motionless as the euphoria subsided and his clammy body began to chill. His lovemaking had been gentle and erotic. Alex was his lifelong love and would continue to be forever. They now both understood this and realised the extent of the potential damage caused by a single person. No one would come between them ever again. Although he hadn't told her everything, he hoped he could forget the whole sorry affair and that it would never rear its ugly head to bite him again.

The phone sex session had been rather unusual, he thought – didn't most men fantasise about the woman they were talking to? Rachel had led him into a state of frenzy with her sexually sordid words and explicitly detailed description of her own actions as she coerced him into a state of heightened pleasure. The unusual part of it was that the image Grant held in his mind throughout the whole experience was that of his beloved wife.

The mysterious illness was the only pressing issue left to deal with, apart from Alex's mother and the nosey neighbour Evelyn. Grant knew he could deal with anything as long as he had Alex by his side. Admitting he had totally fallen apart when she became ill, he thought of the children and the strength he should have drawn from them. It was too late for that now, but maybe a lesson learned, he thought as he smiled to himself and fell asleep.

Another Sunday morning arrived. Mum had been on the phone constantly since I'd arrived home and I'd practically switched off my listening ear every time I was trapped into taking the calls.

"Evelyn's so upset, you know. I can't believe he spoke to her like that."

"Mum, he's been really stressed out. He hasn't coped well with me being in hospital," I huffed. "I'll get him to apologise to her. She'll be okay."

"Well he ought to learn how to cope in these types of situations Alex. For goodness' sake, he's not a child." Raising my eyebrows at the handset, I tutted. "Yes, I know Mum."

Having counted the calls and the repeated conversations, I concluded that we had gone through the same dialogue no less than fourteen times, over the course of three days. Oh, and the other one was—

"Will you have a word with your dad about this blasted boat? The museum has called twice now to arrange a convenient time to collect it but your father is adamant that he wants you to see it afloat."

"Oh for heaven's sake, put him on the phone."

Dad was a joker and I didn't take him seriously when he said the museum was not getting it. I reminded him that they had a special place reserved for the magnificent ship, a prime spot at the very front of their *Titanic* display.

"It's an honour, Dad. Stop messing about, you're doing Mum's head in." Dad was a quiet old chap but he did enjoy pulling Mum's leg – constantly.

Other calls had been taken by Grant and the kids, and each time I waved my hands rapidly to denote, 'I'm not here' and 'I'm busy'. The 'I'm asleep' gesture was the easiest one to convey as I clasped my hands together in a sideways prayer and tucked them under my chin. I hadn't been in any stable state of mind to talk to anyone other than Mum and Dad, and even that was very forced.

My renewed, gorgeous husband had been to the shop midweek to collect the mail and send my gratitude to the staff, and then came home with a carrier bag full of 'Get well soon' cards which brought a lump to my already lumpy throat. The mantelpiece ornaments were fighting for their rightful place amongst the countless cards I received. Not realising I had so many friends and acquaintances, I felt humbled to have been given so many gifts and flowers too.

As for the children, life had returned to normal, except for the fact that their mum was a bit slower off the mark, and their dad had been grumpier than usual and spent far more time in his shed in one week than he had done in the previous year. The house was more flower-scented and less sooty, and the shopping arrived on Friday night to fill the empty cupboards and fridge.

A smiling face suggested that Aaron was pleased with his new phone, and Grant too had a new mobile and number. My decision to text the other woman had taken the situation out of his hands and given him some relief. He could now start to lead a near normal existence again. Grant and Aaron's Saturday shopping experience had been heart-warming but haphazard as they both hated shopping on any day of the week, and weekends were even worse. But they had done it. They'd survived and they were happy as they could be. However, as they dashed through the precinct like two tearaway thieves, the local policeman gave them a decidedly suspicious stare as they ran from the shop with boxes tucked under their arms.

"You should have taken the carrier bags you were offered," I scoffed. "It wouldn't have looked good if you'd been arrested Grant, would it? Not after the things that you've been up to lately." I eyed him with contempt.

The police report had still not been completed, due to Grant's lack of responsibility and inept capabilities when situations arose. His motto of the week was "I'll do it ASAP."

Having resigned himself to the fact that yet another bike had disappeared into the underworld of bike thieves, Joe ranted on and on to anyone who would care to listen about the killer cows in Brookling Field, trying to gain an ounce of sympathy. Sadly he received the same response from every one of his listeners as he retold his story while everyone just rolled around laughing.

It was a momentous day for Emma when she decided one morning that she would train to be a nurse when she left school. Tending to her thumb and several of her Dad's ailments had gone extremely well, she said, although she wasn't sure whether to take up the embalming course as well.

In the knowledge that I was healing in body, mind and facial features, Jack decided to get a last-minute flight to the Costa del Sol, joining his mates on an extended holiday. He would be leaving in the early hours to catch the Monday morning flight from London. Whistling around the house and most annoyingly humming *Rule Britannia*, he packed Bermuda shorts and tight fitting t-shirts into his army-issue holdall. A real break, sun-kissed girls and copious amounts of alcohol were just what he needed before he returned to Germany and work.

Already back with the twins in Wales, Josie expected that the boys would be excited about a summer trip to the Frey household for one last time before they grew up and preferred to do the same thing as Jack, and they were pleased. However, accompanied or alone in the future, Josie would always venture east to spend some holidays in England, and more specifically, with the only family she had.

The walking was getting easier and easier by the day as my strength returned. The hospital discharge letter described my condition as a systemic viral illness, which I presumed left it open to many possibilities. Next week I would venture to the doctor's and pick up the test results, but for now I had no worries, certain that I was returning to full health, as before.

It was inevitable that the phone would start its usual trill on a Sunday morning. *Mum*, I thought as I hobbled over to get it.

"Alex, is that you?" she shrieked.

"Yes Mum, are you—"

"Can you get over here quick? Your father – oh," she sobbed.

"Mum, what's wrong?" I asked. Muffled sniffles and slurping noises came through the earpiece. "Mum?" I paused and listened. "Are you okay?"

"Oh dear, Alex, what can I do?" A sudden burst of howling and Mum was inarticulate.

"What is going on?" I shouted. "Mother, talk to me." Sniffing and shaky-voiced, she managed to pull herself together.

"I knew it Alex, I bloody knew it."

"Knew what?" I was getting anxious now. "Come on, spit it out."

"It's the garage, I've seen it." She started bawling again with more fervency.

"Seen what, for heaven's sake? What the hell is going on?"

"The garage. I wondered why he'd left the car..."

"Left it where?" *I bet it's been stolen. She's so over the top.*

"Left *what* where? What are you talking about?" she replied with a shirty tone.

"You just said he's left the car!" I yelled obnoxiously.

"Oh no, I can't take anymore. Can you come over?" The phone almost vibrated as she roared down it.

"Mum, tell me what has happened, will you?" Losing my patience, I held the phone away and shook it vigorously whilst growling at it. "Calm down please."

"Who's that?" whispered Grant as he strolled in from the garden.

"It's Mum," I mouthed with raised eyebrows as he tutted and walked past, pinching my bottom as he went. "Oh!"

"What did you say?" Mum asked frantically.

"Oh, it's nothing." Trying to contain a giggle, I said more seriously, "Right Mum, what's wrong with the car?"

"There's nothing wrong with the bloody car Alex. It's your father. He's gone completely insane."

I was now totally confused. Smiling at Grant, I rolled my eyes and shrugged my shoulders in despair.

"Are you still there?"

"Yes, but I don't know what you're talking about, Ma."

"Your father – you know, the man you call Dad?" she replied sarcastically.

"Yes, I know, what's he done?"

"What has he done? I've just told you for Christ's sake. Weren't you listening?" The crying had ceased, capped by sarcastic anger.

Struggling to take her obvious despair seriously, I winked at Grant. We'd been here many times before. Mum was so melodramatic. The problem was (and

Grant had highlighted the issue) that when the time came for a real emergency, no one would believe in her wailing and gibberish phone calls. She could cry for the country, at the most ridiculous things. The stupid thing was that when there was something to cry about, she didn't cry.

Only last year one of her manic phone calls rang alarm bells and Grant and I thought she was either going to divorce my dad or shoot him with his own pellet gun, and all because some pigeons had crapped on her head on three separate occasions. She'd had some sticky poo problems with the birds over the previous few months and complained to dad incessantly.

"I'll go and bloody well shoot them all then, shall I?"

"Oh my goodness, don't do that Charlie, no." Distraught at the mere suggestion of harming the little feathery things, Mum asked if they could get a scarecrow in the garden. You can imagine Dad's reply to that. On the day that she called me in tears, she had just discovered that Dad had actually been encouraging the birds by feeding them in the corner of the garden and throwing birdseed onto the flat roof of their conservatory. This explained the gloopy downpour onto Mum's head whenever she went into the garden to hang out the washing. Dad was given strict instructions to stop his form of pest control (controlling the birds so they defecated on his wife's head for fun), although he found the whole situation very funny. So did we. Mum did not.

"Can we start this conversation again? I'm lost." I spoke calmly although I wanted to scream at her. *Get a grip on yourself, Mum!* Over by the window, Grant watched me with his deep brown eyes and shook his head in disapproval. Shrugging again, I listened intently, trying to avoid Grant's gaze. I knew he wanted me again, and I wanted him too.

"Start at the beginning, Mum." Again I spoke calmly and quietly as the sniffles in the phone lowered to a barely audible puff.

"Your dad has been in the garage for days. I wondered why the car wasn't in there." She paused.

"Yes, go on."

"Then I saw him take it out this morning." Her voice trembled and I held my breath, waiting for the next deluge of bawling, but thankfully it never came.

"What?"

"He's tied it to the roof rack, Alex." Mum paused and presumably blew her nose as I heard a snorting noise like an elephant blowing water from its trunk. Images rose in my mind of what he could have possibly tied to the roof rack: a dead body? Evelyn's dead body? Or maybe it was just an unwelcome scarecrow.

"What has he tied to the roo—"

"He's going in a minute, you've got to stop him!" she squealed.

"Going where, Mum?" I screamed down the phone. Grant jumped up, sensing my anger building. It wasn't funny anymore.

"Shall I talk to her?" he whispered, reaching for the handset. Shaking my head, I asked her again.

"Where is he going?"

"To the park of course. Where else would he be going with it?"

"With what Mum?" I paused, waiting for a reply as Mum huffed and puffed down the phone and I desperately tried not to sound irritated. "Why is he going to the park and what is on the car?" I asked slowly as the realisation began to dawn on me. "What exactly is on the roof rack, Mum?" I asked again, more abruptly.

"It's a bloody three-foot-high, papier-mâché iceberg!"

Epilogue

Picking Mum up in the car, we drove down to Gilbert's Park, not knowing quite what to expect when we arrived. It was still fairly early on Sunday morning and the boating lake didn't open until twelve o'clock, so apart from the occasional dog walker, there weren't many people around. Driving down the path towards the lake, we could just see Dad's car in the distance, but there was no sign of any other vehicles or cameramen, which was what Mum was dreading.

"There – he's down there. I can see him standing by the edge. What is he doing?" Mum squealed. Her bulbous, red, tearful eyes glistened in the strong sunlight pouring through the windscreen. Turning the bend, we came to a halt in front of a large oak tree, and there it was, floating majestically on the water's surface, right in the middle of the lake. Looking menacingly real, the giant replica iceberg gently bobbed up and down on the breeze, blowing across Dad's Atlantic Ocean.

The *Titanic* had left the dock and was being carefully manoeuvred across the water with radio signals, under the expert hand of Dad.

"Dad!" I shouted as Grant helped me out of the car and down to the water's edge.

"Charlie, have you gone completely crazy?" Mum yelled as she cautiously made her way down to the familiar diving board.

"Don't worry I'm not going to sink it really. Just thought I would get some good photographs and film to give to the museum. They'll like it," said Dad, coolly and calmly. We all breathed a sigh of relief as the reality set in. Dad only wanted to replicate the sinking of the *Titanic* visually for the benefit of the museum, and probably for mine too.

"But you'll have to dry it out again now Charlie," moaned Mum as she stood well away from the edge.

"Umm," he replied nonchalantly, as he continued to move the ship ever closer to its demise. The park remained still and quiet as we all stood and waited in anticipation for the moment of impact.

It came. It was non-eventful – and Dad missed it on the camera. Reversing his propelled creation, Dad attempted to film the ship passing by the glittering white papier-mâché iceberg again. This time Grant was in control of the camera and managed to capture some epic shots with the zoom lens stretched to full capacity.

"Can we go home now?" asked Mum, shivering on the edge of the jetty as Dad steered the liner back to shore.

"All done." He smiled. "We can go home."

"What about the iceberg?" I asked as Dad and Grant lifted the boat from the water and placed it firmly back onto its base.

"It can stay there." Dad winked. "That'll be one for the newspaper reporters." Smiling warmly, I nodded in agreement and put my arms around his waist.

"You are crazy Dad, but I love you."

Parting company, Grant and I climbed back into his car and paused for a moment as we watched Mum follow Dad around like a shadow as he finished fastening the web straps to the inside of the car and gathered his belongings. Dad had become immune to her incessant moaning and ignored her ramblings.

"Get in the car, Dot. It's all over now."

"Well, don't you scare me like that again, Charlie Stern," she said angrily, knowing full well that he hadn't taken any notice of what she'd been saying.

Then they left. I felt content in the knowledge that my dad had lived his dream through to the end.

The lake had a different feel about it now. Somehow it looked colder just because there was an iceberg floating around in the middle. A few dog walkers stopped and stared at the unusual sight, and their dogs stood at the water's edge, barking at it. When the boat rental kiosk man arrived for duty, he was gobsmacked to find a large white object in the water. Not the usual man, this chap only worked at the weekends and had no idea how such a large, unusually shaped object could have got into the lake. More worryingly, how was he going to get it out before the pedal and row boats were hired out?

"Think it's got sumin to do wiv that *Titanic* ship, mate," said an elderly man, walking his poodle.

"Oh I see," said the part-time kiosk attendant as he stood staring out across the water, cupping his chin in his hand and thinking of ways to pull the object out. We remained silent and sat by the water's edge for a long time, reminiscing.

One week later, Grant and I drove to the outskirts of the park and strolled down to the lake for three reasons. The first and most obvious was to see what had happened to the iceberg, which was now a large, crumpled heap of soggy paper and paint sat on its ply base next to the kiosk.

Secondly, my legs were getting stronger and I wanted to start exercising them properly, so a good walk through the park was ideal.

Thirdly, Grant and I had only just straightened things out between us for the second time and a Sunday afternoon stroll through a beautiful, sunny park was just what we needed to refresh our relationship. It was far more serious the second time around and I did throw my wedding ring back in his face at one point. I slapped him, pushed him, threw a Twix bar at him (which caught him right in the eye and gave him a small black eye for a couple of days) and I tossed all his clothes into the boot of his car and told him to go and live with Rachel.

Luckily, Evelyn never found out about Grant's new wardrobe facility in his car boot and between the two of us, we discreetly carted Grant's clothes back in through the side gate after dark, once we'd sorted out the latest problem in our recently over-stretched relationship.

Rachel had texted me back a couple of days after she received my 'Bitch' message. It said, *You wanna give your hubby some phone sex – he loves it!* Of course, Grant couldn't deny it and told me everything there was to know, including his sad little secret about the image he used in his mind, and I truly believed him. He was such a 'saddo'.

Life slowly returned to normal in the Frey household. I took a few weeks off work but continued to run the business from home (when I felt like it), checking through the paperwork that Zoe dropped off and making and returning numerous phone calls. The results from the doctors were inconclusive and thankfully the 'big one', the HIV test, was negative too, so I began to live my life under the notion that I had been given a second chance.

Jack came back from Spain, tanned and happy, and spent his last two weeks at home with me before returning to Germany and the population of mangy cats.

Emma returned to school, somewhat disappointed that she could no longer use her thumb injury to gain sympathy, or as an excuse to skip writing lessons, or indeed any lessons at all.

Aaron went back to college and continued to carry his worry-demon around with him wherever he went, although he had already planned his next big rail adventure to Wales for the summer.

Joe managed to get an extra paper round at the local newsagent and he borrowed a friend's old spare bike to do them. He religiously saved nearly every penny he earned towards the purchase of his next bike and a failsafe booby-trap (just in case).

As for Grant, he was a changed man after everything that had happened in just a week or so. Somehow he was stronger, more decisive and far less lazy. The brief 'Rachel affair' had only strengthened our already strong relationship and it became almost perfect. After a short course of antibiotics, his infected toes healed, leaving a few barely visible scars. The only scars that would linger for longer were the mental ones, but we had the healing cream well in place for that.

Mum and Dad remained the same: Mum and Dad. The *Titanic* did indeed finally meet its resting place in the museum, much to the relief of the curator and his team.

And Evelyn shed her skin, ready for new beginnings.

Calling the Services

The firemen who put out our fires
and rescue us from terror
will also save the silly cat
that climbs the tree in error.

The ambulance whose siren sounds
to let us know it's coming
will dash along the busy road
and send the motorists running.

The policemen who drive around
catching thieves and robbers
will help you too, across the road
to join the busy shoppers.

The coastguards who watch our seas
to save unwary seamen
will rescue them from sinking ships
and take them to safe haven.

Joan Stevens